Now I Know My ABC's

Now I Know My ABC's

BRANDON HAIRSTON

authorHOUSE®

AuthorHouse™
1663 Liberty Drive
Bloomington, IN 47403
www.authorhouse.com
Phone: 1-800-839-8640

Published by AuthorHouse   04/04/2013

ISBN: 978-1-4634-3069-6 (sc)
ISBN: 978-1-4634-3070-2 (e)

Library of Congress Control Number: 2011911972

Acknowledgements

This is my first book, so I'm new to the "Thank You" speeches. First off, I'd like to thank my parents for supporting this new venture.

Thank you to everyone that was there to read through the stories and test out new ideas as I came up with them: Mike, Aunt Les, Ronal, Bianca, Charleese "editor-in-chief", Leah, DaSheia, Deven, Miatta, Lakaiya, Josiland, Zakia, and Mrs. V.

Professionally, I'd like to thank Angela Young for her great editing. I appreciate all the things you caught that I skipped over. I'd also like to thank Lonnie Woods, III for an amazing book cover. You both helped make this project what it is today. I'm grateful to have worked with the both of you!

Last, but not least, I would like to thank my family, friends, coworkers, and anyone else that supported this project. Checking in on my progress always motivated me to push more and stick with it. This is the first, but it definitely won't be the last!

Happy Reading!

A is for Andre

December 31st, 11:30pm. Just minutes before the big day. At midnight, I'm asking Karen to spend the rest of her life as Mrs. Andre Tyler. Her parents had connections, so for the big night, they rented one of those laid out penthouse suites for our friends. Her parents agreed to only invite close family so that the surprise wouldn't be ruined. The party room was beyond extravagant: maple hardwood floors with a 72-inch flat panel TV that was mounted between two Greek columns. The channel was preset to this year's Rockin' New Year's Party. Lighting the room were two gold chandeliers and flashing concert stage lights. It was like a famous New York A-Lister's party. I knew this was the best gift for such a memorable night.

Five minutes had passed and January 1st was rapidly approaching. Whitney, Karen's maid of honor, was behind the granite counter bar pouring champagne into flute glasses for the toast. "I can't believe you two are getting married," she said. She smiled, trying to hold back her tears.

"We're not getting married tomorrow," I joked. "Come on, Whit. You told me you weren't gonna cry."

"I know, I know," she said, wiping an eye. "Just help me pass out these flutes before I get all emotional in here." We both laughed, and then handed the glasses out to everyone.

In the corner was Greg, my best man. He looked more nervous than me. I took a champagne glass to him, shook his hand, followed with a nigga hug, then asked, "You aight?"

"Yeah man," he started, "just tryna picture you married. Shit's crazy."

"Whatever, man," I said jokingly. "You gonna be next." I tried to get Greg to come join the rest of the party, but he just wasn't his normal self. I've known him since seventh grade and he was always the life of the party. I made one more attempt to see what this nigga's problem was. "You sure you good, man?"

He looked down at his shoes, looked up at the party, then finally looked me back in the eyes. "Aight man," he said, "can we talk?" I nodded yes. We went over to another corner of the room that was away from the party and out of range for any ear hustlers. "Karen's been trying to tell you something for a long time man, but she wasn't sure how to say it." My stomach suddenly became uneasy. I felt like I was on a talk show where "shocking secrets" were about to be revealed.

"What is it man?" I asked nervously. Greg looked down and rubbed the back of his head. "Greg, you've been my boy since middle school," I began, "so keep it real. What has Karen been trying to tell me?"

3

He looked down once again, shook the tension out of his hands, and finally blurted out, "She's two months pregnant."

My heart dropped into my stomach, but this time for a good reason. I was overwhelmed with happiness. Of course I would have wanted the kid after the wedding, but this was still a blessing. "She's pregnant!" I exclaimed. "Nigga, you had me stressin'. I'm gonna be someone's daddy." The sound of fatherhood was frightening, but I was up for it. I looked at my watch: 11:45. "Forget New Year's. I gotta go back and tell everyone now!"

"Dre, wait!" yelled Greg, but I was too excited to turn back. I ran to the DJ and asked him to cut the music. He handed me the microphone so the big announcement could be made.

"Good evening, everyone," I started. "For those of you who don't know me, I'm Karen's boyfriend, Andre. I would like to say thank you to Mr. and Mrs. James for this great party." The guests clapped to show their gratitude. "I also have one more thing to say. Karen, can you come up here?" As she walked up, I could see she was still oblivious to what would come next.

"Baby, I had this planned before Greg told me the news." Karen's expression flipped from smile to grimace in that instance.

"Greg!" she shouted into the crowd.

"No, baby. It's ok. I know you thought I would be mad, but it's ok. I love you more than I love myself. I know this isn't the best time for kids but we'll work through it." I got down on one knee, in front of the entire party. Karen's mother wiped her tears of joy as she clenched her husband's arm. "Karen James, will you marry me?" The guests gasped, applauded, and anxiously waited for her answer.

"Dre, you want to marry me?" she asked with a tearful smile. "You never stop amazing me: this great party, a baby on the way, and now the fact that you're willing to work through the possibility of it being Greg's. Of course, I will marry you!" A dark silence fell over the room. My smile dropped to a frown.

"The possibility of what?!?!" I asked in shock, trying to hide my anger from the rest of the guests.

"I thought you said he told you?"

"He told me you were pregnant. Why wouldn't I assume it's mine?" I scanned the unnerved faces that looked upon me and found Greg looking apologetic.

"Oh my God, baby. I'm so sorry. I thought when you said he told you, he told you everything. I know I made a mistake, but I know with counseling and prayer we can work it out. Maybe a trip somewhere . . ." I went completely deaf as she continued her bullshit apology. I could see her lips moving, but nothing of substance sprung forth. I was in shock. Deep down, I knew the crowd sympathized for me, but through the eyes of my disgruntled mind, those surprised faces morphed into smirks, taunting me with the infamous quote, "They're all going to laugh at you!"

I went from denial, to humiliated, to heartbroken, and finally, to fury. I was pissed! The woman I had loved for over five years had stomped over my heart in a moment's time. My hearing tuned in just in time to hear her utter, "So, it's ok?" I closed the ring box, stood to my feet, smiled without revealing a single tooth, and slapped that bitch into the DJ's turntables. Her father ran up on stage, like I was scared of his old ass. I was in full frenzy, adrenaline steadily pumping. Her father caught me with a couple blows, but I had summoned crack-like strength that gave me the resilience I needed.

I laid him out as fast as Karen. Women were screaming at the events, as more and more men stepped up to subdue me. "Don't be a hero," I threatened. "All I want is that nigga Greg." I spotted Greg out on the balcony, unbuttoning his collar shirt. He was gearing up for the fight.

"I'm not tryna fight you," he pleaded, "but I'm not going out like the rest of these niggas."

"You were supposed to be a brother," I said, tearing up. "My best man. My nigga for life." We grappled hands and the main event was on. I flung him off balance, giving me time to throw the first punch. There was no end to the melee and wrath I brought, better yet, that he brought upon himself. I was so numb to the pain that his punches rolled off like drizzling rain. I, however, was on a warpath. The fight was over when I choked him out with his own shirt. He slowly collapsed on the ground.

"Dre, stop," begged Karen. She was holding a wet kitchen rag to her bruised face. "Please! If you don't want me I understand, but that's your boy. Just stop." She began to cry simultaneously to the beat of the forming thunderstorm.

"You don't give a fuck about me," I said painfully. "You just want me to leave your 'baby daddy' alone." I broke down into a hysterical cry. "Why did you do it, Karen? Did I do something wrong? Couldn't you just talk to me?" I almost fell to the ground, but refused to show any sign of weakness.

"Dre, baby," she began, "I'm so sorry. I don't know what I can do, but you have got to calm down." She walked towards me.

"Back the fuck up," I warned. She continued to slowly approach me. "Karen, does it look like I'm playing?"

"I do love you," she said while drawing nearer, "and I know you still love me." She was right. I was so angry and confused, but even so, that was my heart. She lifted her arms to hug me, but I jerked back. "It's OK," she said, extending her arms again. Without hesitation, I pulled her in and hugged her. As we stood on the balcony, she cried on my chest while the rain poured. "I'm so sorry Dre."

"We'll get through this," I said while embracing her. We turned to walk back to our ruined party. I know her family, especially her parents, would never forgive me for the display I had put on. I mean, I did fuck her father up.

Before stepping through the balcony corridor, Greg pulled me back outside. "Greg, it's cool now," I said, but he was obviously ticked from losing earlier. There was no getting through to him. Greg landed a hook to my jaw, then a jab, then dealt an uppercut, which placed me on the wrong side of the balcony.

"Dre!!!" yelled Karen, but it was over. A night of happiness ended with me losing my girl, my best friend, and my life. I was falling from the roof of a 30-floor building. The result could be nothing but fatal. I took one final look at my watch: 11:59:45. At this point, the only thing I wanted was to make it to New Year's. I stared into the sky, watching the city's clock countdown: 10, 9, 8, 7, 6, 5, 4, 3, 2, 1, Happy New . . .

B is for Bridget

Mama always told me, "Show me a woman that's beautiful, and I'll show you a man that's tired of fucking her." It's Monday, February 11th, and he left me. Three days before Valentine's Day and Keith's bitch ass left me. I knew we had problems here and there, but I never thought it would amount to this. I mean, just this Saturday we were cuddled up, and I listened to him telling me how he couldn't see me with anyone else. Yeah, that might have come after he slapped me for checking his cell, and I cut him for slapping me and blah, blah, blah, but is it worth losing all of this? Now I'm sitting in the car, teary-eyed wondering how I'm going to make it through the workday. I put my lil' '04 Altima in drive and started my dismal day.

It was a beautiful sunny day, but to me it felt like the darkest night. The flowers were blooming, yet all I saw was death. I needed to lift my spirits and the normal morning shows wouldn't do it today. Some rapper got shot or some singer bitch got beat, the usual shit, so I switched the radio to the gospel hour for an inspirational word. If I couldn't hold myself together, I could at least try some of this churchy shit. "We are so blessed," the radio host said, "and when you truly think of the things the Lord has brought you through, you have no reason to be upset." It felt like she was speaking to me and my situation. "This is a day that the Lord has made. We SHALL rejoice and be glad in it!"

The radio host was right. Keith was not going to keep me from being happy today because I know I am the last thing on his mind. I pulled out my cell phone, practiced my sick voice a few times, and let the boss know I wouldn't be coming in today. I was going to take a day to treat myself like the queen I am. Damn, I wish I didn't waste this outfit though. And if I knew I wasn't going in I could've saved these panties for tomorrow. This was the last pair before I needed to wash clothes. *Sigh*

Anyway, you know what the fucked up part is? I had already-

"Welcome to McDonald's can I take your order?"

"Yeah let me get a sausage biscuit meal with a medium orange juice. And can you put some grape jelly in the bag."

"Anything else ma'am?"

"No."

"$4.53 drive around please."

Yeah so the thing that makes me mad is I already knew it was coming. Keith had been hanging out with some ho, Eileen or some shit like that, from high school that just moved back in the area. She played the "I'm back in town so let's hook up" card and he fell for it. I guess she wasn't the geeky, plain girl he remembered cus

6

I seen the bitch. She was Brazilian, tall, golden complexion with dark brown hair and blonde highlights (all hers). She was slender or small, but she had thighs. I mean she was ok, but why take that when my thick, chocolaty ass was here at his beck and call?

I'm every nigga's dream—5'5", hazel eyes (they grey today though), bronze skin, and thick (not fat, but I prolly do weigh a lot). And let's face it, nobody could find a sweeter, prettier, more pink pussy than mine. Keith had it made!

"Thank you ma'am. Have a great day."

So about a month ago I noticed that hanging with the boys had been more than just a Friday night bar or a Saturday NBA game. I should've known when I saw the receipts for two dinners, but he hang with them broke niggas so I took it as helping out a friend. I mean, it is a recession right? What really tipped me off was a few nights ago when he came home. I guess after he got some from her, he wanted me to put him to sleep. He could've at least scraped the cum crust off his boxers before he pushed my head down. That's what caused the looking through his phone, which led to the slap, which caused the chasing around the house with a knife, and here we are now.

"Weeping may endure for a night, but joy comes in the morning." Damn that's deep. It was like God, not the radio host this time, but G-O-D just sent me a word. Yeah this Keith shit fucked me up, but I'm better than that. If he's willing to miss out on someone as good as Bridget, let him. I'm a gem and clearly all he wants is rocks. I mean that was my heart, but I was living without him before I met him, and I'll be fine without him now. I feel the joy already. Unspeakable joy! And nothing would bring me more joy than kicking the shit out of her bitch ass. Speak to me Jesus!

At the next light I'm making a U-turn to get this ho like only I can. The gospel hour gave me my Word, but now it's time for some headbussa music. I pulled out my disc changer remote, switched to CD number 3, track 4: Crime Mob "I'll Beat Yo Ass." Perfect!

Sigh So you know I'm pissed right? Not at Keith, not the ho, but they ain't put the hash brown in the gotdamn bag! I knew I should've checked before I pulled out the lot. This is just going to make her ass-kicking worse. I almost feel sorry for her. I mean this bitch got an ass-kicking sent from Heaven on the way and she don't even know it's coming. I'm passing Keith's street now. I got half a mind to make a quick stop and slash his tires. On second thought, it's broad daylight, and old Ms. Saunders is probably keeping an eye on his house, along with everyone else's on that street whether they asked for it or not. Plus, the matter at hand can't wait and she needs to get got NOW!

She lives in an older development not too far from Keith's townhouse. How con-fucking-venient. These were some nice places though. I almost envied Eileen; she was living comfortably paying a mortgage while I was scraping up dollars just to make rent.

Finding her place was a breeze. That nigga left me her address and phone number, saying it was so I could "trust him" when they hung out. I took it as call and hang up to see if she would answer breathing heavily from sex, and drive past a couple times to know exactly where she lives just in case. I pulled up behind her Corolla (Spanish girl with a Corolla: big fuckin' surprise, right?) and plotted out exactly how I was going to do this. I wanted the whole neighborhood to see this shit. I took a quick look in the mirror, fixed myself up, you know, just in case Keith was in there, and opened the car door.

I got to her door and knocked. Immediately, I felt a warming sensation; the type of warmth that comes from anger, sad flashbacks, rage, confusion, and pissedoffication. I could hear footsteps approaching the foyer.

"Who is it?" she asked with an accent. Bitch didn't even have a peephole in her door. She must not be as well off as I thought. I switched up my voice to throw her off.

"UPS package for Eileen."

"Ileana?" she asked with a correcting tone. I should've known she would have a more exotic name. When's the last time you seen a Spanish girl named Eileen?

"Yes ma'am. Will you sign for it?" I could hear the keys jingling in the door as she turned the locks. First, the top lock. I was getting anxious. Next, the bottom lock. I had it all planned: I was gonna slap the shit out of her all up and through her own house, then drag her outside so the neighbors could catch Round 2. The door opened, and there she was, looking like a true ho wearing a t-shirt, boy shorts, and slippers. Wait, that t-shirt smells like Keith's cologne. I caught a whiff, and it was on!

"Special delivery, bitch!" I said, just like I had practiced in my mind while I slapped that stank look off her face. I must have given her too much time to get herself together because my perfect day went downhill from this point.

Ileana wasted no time with petty slapping and went straight for the jugular. No literally, the bitch chopped me in my damn throat. Now that's some hurtful shit! While I'm coughing and gasping for air, she took it to the hair. She was smart, too. She skipped right past Sasha, the name of my quick weave, and grabbed a hold of my two jumbo, nappy braids underneath. I could feel her nails digging into my scalp, taking pieces of hair and squirts of blood as she pulled. I knew if I had any chance left at coming out victorious like God had promised me, I needed to think fast. In a state of panic, I hit a full-speed windmill with closed fists.

"OW BITCH!" she yelled. With these fists of fury coming at her, she had no choice but to let me go. I threw Sasha in the corner and readjusted myself. This wasn't the place nor the time to be worried about fighting cute. She wanted me to work for this win and I willingly accepted the challenge.

I tried to steal her, which is a punch for those who don't know, but she ducked and pushed me out the door onto her yard. Ileana came out running, ready to do more damage. She gave me just enough time to unloose my heel, and launch it directly at her forehead. POW! It landed smack in the middle and she went down. I climbed on top of her, grabbed her collar, and began to bang her head against the driveway yelling, "This is for Keith, bitch!"

Suddenly, her sprinklers hissed on, soaking us as the ordeal took place. We looked like two bitches in a beer commercial. One of Ileana's mud-covered fists caught me in my right eye. I rolled off of her in a blind daze, struggling to wipe the mud out my eye. Just when I thought things were looking up, shit hit the fan.

Ileana picked the shoe up that nicely danced across her face moments ago, and returned the favor to mine. She slapped me with the heel's sole so many times; I could understand how the pavement at the Million Man March must have felt. Once she grew bored of hearing me shriek from the pain, that skinny bitch dragged my fat ass to the curb like it was trash day. I was actually thankful. After the ass-whippin' I was just served there was no way I'd make it to the car. She laid me beside my Altima and said, "You should have gone into work today." She staggered back to her house, but she was clearly the winner.

I used the hood of the car to pull myself up, got in, and put the key in the ignition. This was by far the worst idea I had had in a long time. I was sore, my welts were burning, I lost Sasha (R.I.P.), and now I would have to decide to take another day off, or explain how these heel prints got on my cheeks. I'm just going to cut my losses, go home, and enjoy some Italian cuisine, fine wine, and a hot salt bath (which is pizza, Arbor Mist, and some dirt from the ring Keith left in the tub from his last shower). God, I thought you were really speaking to me this morning. I thought you had my back. See, this is why I don't go to church now. *Sigh* . . .

C is for Carlos

It's Thursday night, otherwise known as club night for college kids. Of course me and my boys are headin' out to the club, right? Wrong. While the ladies are gettin' ready to get bodied, and the fellas are meetin' up to put on for their city, I'm in the Carroll Hall biology lab at Greenhill University, studyin' for tomorrow's lab practicum. I got dressed for the club before I headed over, you know, just in case I finished up early. Who was I kiddin'? Studyin' is never over for a pre-med student.

People say that college years are the best years of your life, but I can't even count how many times I've missed club night, weekend hangouts, movie nights, and most importantly, dating. This was the time to smash any girl willin' to give it up to a future doctor. Yeah, the short-term looked bleak, but in the long run being a physician would help folks, and help me support my family. If it wasn't for that full scholarship, I wouldn't even be here. Since my Pops passed, I was the last hope for the family.

It was approachin' 9:30pm. I was tired, hungry, and still hadn't mastered all the anatomical structures and processes that would be on this exam. Let's see: the carpals are connected to the radius and ulna by the uh, um, the uh . . . shit! This was not lookin' good. I would need to be here until at least 1a.m. if I was gonna be prepped enough to get a C.

"Not going out?" a woman asked. I jumped. "I am sorry I didn't mean to disturb you." I swiveled my chair to face the door. She looked like one of the professors, but I had never seen her before. "I was just surprised you weren't out with the other students."

"I wish," I responded, "but the anatomy lab practicum is tomorrow."

"So I hear," she said. "What's your name?" This old broad was wastin' valuable study time I desperately needed. I kept my answers short and respectful, hopin' she would get the hint.

"Carlos," I answered, "but everyone calls me CT." She looked as if her next question was how do you get CT out of Carlos. I beat her to the punch, informin' her that, "My last name is Cruz-Thomas." I thought to myself, *Now that you know, please get the hell out.*

"I've heard a lot of good things about you, Mr. Cruz-Thomas," she started. "It's a pleasure to finally meet you. My name is Dr. Vivian Pearce, the biology department chairperson." I was in awe. It was rare that any students caught a glimpse of Dr. Pearce, let alone, hold a conversation with her. The "old broad" I was dissin' awhile ago was head of the department and actually knew who I was.

"Oh, nice to meet you," I said while shakin' her hand.

"The pleasure is all mine. I'm honored to meet one of the few students who has earned a 3.9 GPA in a rigorous pre-med program like ours."

"Thank you," I said with a smile. At that moment, my stomach decided to introduce itself as well. *Grrrr.*

"Sounds like all that studying has gotten you hungry," she said jokingly. "How about we grab something to eat before you call it a night?" I reluctantly declined her offer.

"I appreciate it ma'am, but I really should stay a little longer."

"Baby, you're being invited to dinner with the head of the department," she said with a hand on her hip. "Don't miss out on your medical school letter of recommendation." She raised an eyebrow as if to say, "I've got mine, now you need to get yours."

"Well, I could eat," I said while packin' my book bag. If I didn't know that shit by now, I just wouldn't know. This was an opportunity to eat with someone who could increase my chances of gettin' into the medical school of my choice. My future lay in the hands of one dinner. Plus, it didn't hurt that Dr. Pearce was fine! She was a middle-aged woman with dark brown eyes that were accentuated with designer eyeglasses, and caramel complexion topped off with a perfect smile. She wore a gray pantsuit to cover her best assets, but my trained eye could see her blouse buttons barely contained those 34 C's.

We made our way through the halls of Carroll. The floors were mad shiny, as if the janitors had just buffed them. Dr. Pearce began to search her purse for her car keys as we approached the door. She pulled them out, exposin' her Benz keychain. "You'll have a car like this someday, Dr. CT," she said. We hopped in the car, and headed off campus.

"So where are you from?" she asked, then jokingly added, "You don't get spiky, black hair and tan skin from being born here."

"My parents are from Puerto Rico," I answered.

"Ah, Puerto Rican. You must be a little heartbreaker." I couldn't tell if she was just makin' conversation, or tryna game me. If she was, I wasn't sure why. Nah, I figured I was readin' too much into it, and switched the subject back onto dinner.

"So where are we eatin'?" I asked.

"Nothing fancy," she nonchalantly replied. "Just a little place I know." It seemed like we were drivin' forever. We finally pulled up around 10:30 to some place called Renown that was way more than "nothing fancy". Good thing I had my club shit on, otherwise they probably wouldn't have let me in. Dr. Pearce pulled up to the door for valet parkin', handed over her keys, and we walked in.

The inside of the restaurant resembled the banquet hall on the Titanic. The charcoal walls were decorated with paintings by foreign artists. Crystal chandeliers and candles provided ambient lighting. "Good evening, Vivian," one hostess said. "Will you be dining at your usual table?"

"Yes, Dianne," she confirmed. Dianne guided us to a table draped with a white tablecloth, illuminated by candlelight. She seated us, filled our glasses with water, and handed us menus. Shit, no prices. This place must be mad expensive.

"Would you like anything else to drink?" Dianne asked.

"I'll take your Pinot white wine," said Dr. Pearce.

"And for you sir?"

I needed somethin' strong to calm me down, but figured it best to play it safe. "Just water."

Dr. Pearce chimed in, "If you were hanging with your boys tonight would you be drinking water?" She and Dianne laughed lightly at the thought of me in the club sippin' on water.

"Long Island iced tea, Dianne, with more Long Island than tea."

"That's a big step up from water," Dianne sarcastically said. "Have you two had time to look at our menu?" I still couldn't find anything that looked cheap enough for me to afford. I took another quick skim over the menu. There's gotta be something on here. A-ha!

"I'll have the buffalo chicken breast with steamed broccoli," I said. Dr. Pearce looked puzzled. She lowered her head, chuckled, and ate a piece of bread to refrain from laughin' any harder. She then lifted her head to explain where I went wrong.

"When someone is treating you to dinner, you never order chicken." Treated to dinner? "I'll have the blackened salmon with steamed vegetables, and he'll have your 10-ounce filet mignon with a baked potato. And when you bring out the meal, I'll be ready for a second glass of wine." After capturin' the order, Dianne collected our menus, and turned for the kitchen. I was still stunned by Dr. Pearce's generosity. My trance was suddenly interrupted when I heard her final request. "Dianne, make that Long Island top-shelf."

"Thank you," I said in appreciation. What the hell was Dr. Pearce up to? What I thought was a simple letter of recommendation dinner seemed like it was borderin' the lines of a date.

"Oh, it's nothing," she said modestly, "just a simple token for one of our best and brightest. So, CT, tell me what made you want to become a doctor?" Finally, some normalness in the evening. I had rehearsed the answer to this question a thousand times.

"I've always wanted to help people. And see that something I found, diagnosed and treated was the reason someone's life was saved." Dr. Pearce looked as if she could see right through that hospital soap opera shit.

"CT, pre-med students come a dime a dozen. Everybody wants to help people, or make the money that comes with being a doctor, but the money alone isn't enough to keep you going. To be a doctor, you need heart, a story that keeps you passionate about this job. The pay is good, but the long hours and sacrifices hardly make it worth it. What I need from you is something real. I need something that makes your application and letter of recommendation unique. A letter from the Dean will almost guarantee admission to your school of choice, but I can't write a letter built on, excuse my language, bullshit."

"Well, Dr. Pearce-"

"Vivian," she interjected.

"Ok, Vivian," I said with uncertainty. I took a deep breath before beginnin' my story. "I haven't had things handed to me in life. Growin' up in Jersey wasn't easy. You either ran with a crew, or you were a target. I wasn't a punk, but I wasn't bangin' either. One day I was approached by some dudes who wanted me to join their crew. They told me if I wasn't with 'em, I was against 'em, and they'd fuck me up from that day on 'til I got down." She stared in amazement as I let my childhood memories flow. "I got my ass kicked plenty of times, but I never joined them, which pissed them off even more.

"One day, I missed the bus and my father was gonna drop me off on his way to work. I went to get my book bag and he said he would meet me at the truck." I could feel my eyes tearin', but I damn sure wasn't sheddin' any tears in front of Vivian. "They must have thought it was me, because . . ." I banged my fist on the table, and wiped my eyes. "I heard gunshots. They sped off before I got outside. That was the last time I saw my father alive." A single tear from each eye was rolling down Vivian's face.

"It doesn't get any realer than that," she said.

"Vivian," I continued, "I promised myself, and Papa, that if I got the chance to go to college, I would show my little brother and sister that there are better things than the streets of Jersey." I wanted to lighten the mood now that Vivian and I were "friends". "Enough of that sad shit, is this place any good?"

She smiled, then confirmed, "You're going to love it CT."

Vivian was right, Renown was on point. This was my first time havin' filet mignon and it was hot! Over dinner, we got to know each other more. She told me how she grew up in North Carolina, was married for five years, divorced, and had a daughter named Stephanie about my age. We bounced after she paid the check. "Whoo, I'm feeling that Pinot," she said. "You ever drove a Benz?" I helped Vivian into her full-length black leather coat while we waited for the valet.

I was drivin' towards the exit ramp to campus when I heard Vivian say, "Keep straight. It's a shortcut. I'll tell you where to go." Seein' how it was close to 1 o'clock in the morning, I was in the mood for a shortcut. Then, she asked somethin' random. "CT, are you familiar with the term, 'cougar'?" She began to tickle the hairs on my arm with her fingers. The dinners, the flirtin', the whip-pushin' privileges . . . it all made sense. I couldn't play it off anymore. I knew what was up at this point.

"I've heard it before," I said tryin' to play it chill. "Why, wassup?"

"Make a left here," she directed. It was a single family home community. "My house is the one on the right corner." We stumbled up the driveway, still bent off the drinks. While unlockin' the door, I placed my hand around her waist to show I was cool bein' cougar bait.

We wasted no time. Vivian led me to the couch and began unbuttonin' my polo. I ripped the buttons off her blouse, releasin' her held-hostage bust. I kicked off my shoes while unbucklin' my slacks. "Fuck me," she pleaded, and I did, over and over again.

I woke up later that mornin' to the smell of French toast, sausage and eggs. I took a glance at my watch and saw that it was 10:15am. *Shit, my lab's in 15 minutes!* I thought. I got dressed crazy fast and was on my way out the door.

"No time for breakfast?" Vivian asked, wearin' my undershirt.

"Sorry, Viv," I began to explain, "but I gotta make that test." She grinned.

"You still don't get it, do you?" I watched with uncertainty as she made her way to the telephone. "Your test is with Professor Williams, right?" I nodded. She began to dial. There was a long pause, long enough for me to use to get back to campus.

"Hi Melanie, this is Vivian. How are you? Good, I can't complain. (laughs) Anyway, I was calling because one of your students is taking your mid-term today, but I was gonna ask if you can leave a copy on my desk so he can take it later? Uh huh. Carlos Cruz-Thomas. Girl, he's been interning at County Hospital. He's the best thing to happen to these terminally ill children." What!?!? "Uh huh. Yeah, we do need more good doctors like that. Ok, so just stick it in the top drawer and he'll hand it in Monday. Yeah I'll be in later. Ok? Appreciate it. Bye."

"So," she said, "how do you take your eggs?" Hmmm, this might be aight.

* * *

It's been a lil' over two months now, and me and V still goin' strong. I should've been hopped on the older woman train. V ain't give a shit if I chilled with my boys, or even hung out with some other girls. She knew that I knew there wasn't a college girl around that compared to a woman that owned her home, made six figures, could take me to Puerto Rico over spring break, and fuck me with skills you could only learn from years of experience. The sex was bananas, son! It took me a month just to figure out how to not bust off in five minutes. She was the truth.

It was about 5:30pm on a Tuesday evening. I threw on a plain black t-shirt, gray Greenhill U. sweats, a gold necklace with a cross, and left out to meet V. We made the traffic light two blocks from campus: my pick-up spot to keep nosy ass people out our relationship. I saw her car mergin' over, but somethin' was off. V's Benz came boomin' down the street to some dirty south music. When the window rolled down, it was some young girl in the driver's seat. She pulled a lollipop out of her mouth, looked me up and down, rolled her eyes, then sucked her teeth before finally sayin', "Hola. So you my new daddy, huh?" It was Stephanie. "Undelé, muhfucka! Get yo' ass in the car!" After tossin' my book bag in the backseat, she floored the gas, the tires screeched, and we sped off.

The car ride home was awkward. I tried to break the ice with some type of conversation. "So what are you doin' home?" I asked.

"Duh Papí. It's spring break, nigga," she said as if she were irritated.

"So, why didn't your mom come get me?"

"She's staying late for a faculty meeting. Damn, I thought couples were supposed to conversate?" Lucky for Stephanie, she was cute, cus her ass was buggin'. She was a couple inches taller than me maybe, maybe 5'10, dark-skinned with long hair that covered her right eye. I couldn't really tell what she was workin' with, but her phatness was spillin' over slightly from the driver's seat to the cupholders, but in a good way.

We got to V's like fifteen after 6 o'clock. Stephanie opened the door and shot upstairs. "She'll be here in a few," she yelled from the top steps. I went to the refrigerator to make a sandwich, then headed to the TV in the family room for some sports updates.

Stephanie returned downstairs a few minutes later, dressed in pajamas and a tank top. Her hair was pulled back into a ponytail. "My bad about earlier," she said. "I just don't get why you can't find any other girls your own age."

"Honestly shorty," I started, "I dunno how it happened either. Your moms is cool though. Just be happy she's happy."

"Yeah," she agreed, "but I bet you miss that young, tight shit too." Stephanie began undoin' the string on her pajamas.

"Ay Steph, come on, shorty," I said. "This ain't cool. This is your moms."

"She won't be here for at least another hour." She walked over to me, and rubbed my spiky hair, while pushin' my face in between her thighs. I caught a whiff of her fresh, spring chicken pussy, and couldn't help but massage her legs. She brought her face down to kiss me, but I pulled back. I had too much respect for V to kiss her. "What you want me to do?" she asked. I pointed to the lump in my sweat pants, and guided her ponytail down.

"I bet my mother doesn't do it like this," she said boastfully. I folded my hands behind my head and enjoyed her gift.

"I don't do it 'like that' because I don't give head to every dick I come across!" My eyes shot open to the sight of V standin' in the family room. I jumped up to try and explain how "this isn't what it looked like". I was trippin' over my sweats, rushin' to pull my boxers up, and pushin' Stephanie's hand off of me.

"Sit your high yellow ass down CT," she said. "My own daughter," she said with disgust. I can't believe you would do something so wrong."

"I'm sorry, Mama," Stephanie said, still shakin' with fear.

"Sorry? What are you sorry for?" V asked. "You gotta learn how to do this right. You're not going to bring the Pearce name down with those weak jaws."

Once again, V stunned me. My heart was still beatin' heavily from the whole situation, but seein' V as calm as she was added even more confusion. She took off her suit jacket and joined Stephanie on the ground.

"Remember, Steph," she instructed, "you always suck, but the key is to twist your wrist." She turned towards me with a disappointed, yet seductive look. "Lay back, Papí." If it was anything better than sex, it was a woman with mad head game. She demonstrated her skill to her novice daughter, while I chilled and let my eyes roll back.

Stephanie looked on, playin' wit herself. I hated them flicks where one girl was gettin' hers while the other one waits her turn. So, I motioned for Steph's attention, then ordered her to, "Venga aquí." She straddled my face while V continued. This was weird, but it was every man's dream.

* * *

I went to class the next day, still in disbelief about what happened last night. When I got to the door, Professor Williams told me that Dr. Pearce had requested to see me. I wondered what it could be as I walked down to her office. I stood outside her door for a few seconds to chill and get myself together.

Knock, knock, knock. "It's open," she yelled from inside. She had her readin' glasses on with a beaded strap on the earpiece. "Oh, Mr. Cruz-Thomas, come on in." I walked in and closed the door, hopin' maybe to get some more of last night. "You can leave it open," she said without even lookin' up over her papers.

"Ok," I said with a puzzled look. "You wanted to see me V?"

"V?" she asked sarcastically. "It's Dr. Pearce. I've worked too long to not have that doctor in front of my name." V was seriously buggin'. I guessed it was because the door was open, so I played along. "Sorry, Dr. Pearce. You wanted to see me?"

"Oh yes, that internship," she said with quote fingers, "to Puerto Rico? Won't be happening."

"What? Why? I thought everything was cool?"

"Perhaps you should have thought about that before you slept with my daughter, Mr. Cruz-Thomas," she said in a calm voice.

"But I mean . . . But you showed her . . . I mean, I thought . . ." It seemed like no matter what I said, it wouldn't be the right thing. "So are you still gonna write that letter for me?" I humbly asked.

"I'm not a petty woman," Dr. Pearce said. "You can pick it up from Jason, the student aide, tomorrow morning." I got my books and was headin' for the door, when I heard her soft laugh. "It was fun, Papí." That was the last of Dr. Pearce.

I stopped past Jason's desk on my way out to let him know I'd be there after class. "Man, I heard you won't get to get the Puerto Rico internship 'cus you'll be working at County with the sick kids." I ain't know what the fuck he was talkin' about.

"Oh yeah, the internship," I quickly remembered. "But yeah son, the kids need me."

He smirked. "Yeah whatever, nigga! You fucked Stephanie, didn't you?" He stuck out his hand for a handshake. This shit just kept gettin' crazier. "Join the club, man. Once Viv is tired of you, she brings Stephanie in so she can move on to the next."

"Son, stop playin'," I said with doubt. "So you was at Renown?"

"Wit' Dianne?" he questioned. We both started clownin'. I thought I was missin' out on somethin', but turns out this was just part of the Greenhill experience! Whoever said pre-med students miss out on their college years anyway?

D is for Daphne

"So who were you referred by?"

"Jasmine. We grew up together."

"I see you checked off available for day shift and night shift. Did Jasmine tell you that the night shift is a different crowd?"

"Yes ma'am."

"Do you have any waitress experience?"

"I used to wait tables part-time when I was in school."

She looked at me with one raised brow. "One last question: If you could be any drink, what would your name be?"

". . . Well, I don't drink that often, but I would have to say something that is dark and sweet at first glance, but has a kick once you get a taste."

She smiled. "Congratulations Daphne, I mean Chocotini, welcome to Secrets."

It's been 18 years since my interview with Ms. Eugenia Gray. I was 25, had just gotten out of college, and wasn't having any luck in the job department. On top of that, I had two little mouths to feed and clothe all on my own. Daddy wasn't there . . . what else is new? I hated taking a step back to serving, but pride didn't pay the bills. Eventually, I took my girl Jasmine's advice, and applied to join her at Eugenia's Secrets.

Eugenia's was a hole-in-the-wall soul food restaurant right off Route 301 in Crofton, Maryland. The outside resembled a southern style plantation. Indoors, the walls were wooden with wooden booths that looked as if they were growing out of the stained wood flooring. It didn't look like much, but you'd be amazed at what Eugenia's kitchen staff could whip up back there: homemade gravy-smothered pork chops, greens with bacon, stringy mac n' cheese, and finish it off with a piece of her 3-layer yellow cake with chocolate icing. And of course, no meal would be complete without a glass of Eugenia's famous iced tea lemonade.

Jasmine, along with the rest of the girls helped get me acclimated to the job during the day shift. Rule #1: Within two minutes of being sat, guests were to be greeted with a warm smile, and an even warmer basket of fresh cornbread and baked rolls with honey butter. Rule #2: Card everyone who looks 25 and under. And Rule #3: Law enforcement eats free ALL day.

Being a waitress again was good, but I still wasn't making enough in case of a rainy day situation. "Daphne," Eugenia began, "I need someone to cover for night shift. You ready?" Jasmine had told me that the night hours were a lot more fast-paced, but so was the money. I nodded, and called my mother to ask if she could keep my boys a few extra hours. That night, I learned that smothered pork chops weren't the only thing Eugenia was known for. The bulbs illuminating Eugenia's turned off so that a red-lit Secrets was the only moniker displayed. At ten o'clock, I became Chocotini, Jasmine became *Jell-O* Shots, and Marie, Camille, and Wanda became Screaming Orgasm, Sexy Alligator, and Top Shelf, respectively.

You could see nervous written all over my face. "Hey, you ok?" Jasmine asked. "When you get nervous, think of those two little boys who could use this money, ok?"

I let out an exhale, and pulled it together. After all, this was for my family's well-being, and it was bitches doing a lot more for a lot less. I tied my white shirt up in the back, made a mini-skirt out of a tube top, and went to my first night shift table. "Welcome to Secret's," I said with a smile. "Would you care to start off with something wet?"

"I'll have a chocotini," one of the dirty old men said with a laugh. He reached out to run his hands up my leg.

"Keep your fuckin' hands to yourself!" I warned as I reached for a glass of water from a nearby table to chuck in his face.

"Hey, hey, hey what's going on over here," Jell-O Shots said playfully. "Chocotinis are a punk drink, baby. What you could use is a shot." She placed a basket of rolls on her head, sat a scoop of butter between her breasts, and dropped into a split without knocking one roll out of place. The restaurant began to whistle and cat-call while the men at the table dunked their rolls. She grabbed one of the men's hands and took him to a door marked Freezer.

It was 2am, and I had just finished serving the last party. I was curious as to why so many of the girls were going in and out of the freezer all night.

"So, how much did you make on your first night?" asked Jasmine.

"$125. If only I could make that every night . . ."

"Not bad for starting out." Jasmine pulled a stack of cash from her bra. Hundreds, fifties, twenties, tens: there must have been over three thousand dollars.

"Not bad? You make my tips look pitiful," I said. "How . . . ? What did . . . ? What exactly goes on in that freezer?"

"Daphne, I need to see you in the back," said Eugenia with a sour face and harsh tone. She was so hard to read. One minute she was laughing and joking with the girls, the next, a no-nonsense, pokerfaced businesswoman.

"Call me later, girl," Jasmine said.

I walked back to the back of the kitchen to Eugenia's office. "Have a seat," she instructed. I was nervous. All I kept wondering was if she saw me getting ready to drench that old perv. Or, maybe she thought I wasn't ready for nights. I couldn't go back to $60 days. "How did you make out?"

"Not bad," I replied, "but not like the rest of the girls."

"It takes time," she said. "You gotta let the regulars see you more, then you'll build up your own clientele. And loosen up a little. Didn't you say Jasmine told you about the night shift?" I shook yes, but what she didn't know was Jasmine only told me that it was better pay at night. "Just get more confident, and put on a show. Sooner or later, you'll have everyone wantin' a taste of your Chocodrop."

"Tini."

"Whatever." She laughed a little, which broke the ice for me to raise a question.

"What goes on in the freezer?"

"I don't care to get into the specifics of what happens in there," she firmly stated. "But I think it's about time you take the full tour of Eugenia's Secrets." I followed her out of the office, through the kitchen, and back to the freezer. Once she unlocked it, I immediately felt the arctic air penetrate my skimpy clothing. I could see my breath in front of me as I trailed behind Eugenia. There were ribs, pork chops, steaks, chicken breasts; nothing out of the ordinary for a restaurant freezer.

Eugenia began to turn the thermostat dial, similar to a combination lock. "32, 38, 30. Remember that," she said. Two wall panels that appeared freezer-burned split to display a sensuous, red-lit hallway. Along the hall were five shiny doorknobs. "Have you heard of the 301 Bordello?" she asked.

"I thought it was just a myth," I said disbelievingly.

"I want you to look in each room. If you choose to stay, this may be part of your duties someday." The first two rooms resembled typical bedrooms: Queen-size beds with two pillows, a coat rack, and a dresser with a vanity mirror. The third room was an office for those who fantasized about screwing the hot intern or secretary over a desk, copy machine, or file cabinet. Room number four was a brick room similar to a prison. The floor was damp, chains hung from the wall, and a single leather chair sat in the middle of the room. Spray-painted over top of a rack holding a whip read "The Punisher". The last room was for the voyeurs who liked sex outdoors. There were trees as tall as the ceiling that swayed to gentle winds. Playing in the background was a corny thunderstorm track.

"I can't believe this is right in my own backyard," I said, still astonished.

"This is the oldest profession in history," Eugenia said. "I ain't doin' nothing that these men haven't been doin' to us for years. This way, at least us women are in it for ourselves."

"So what about the police?"

"Oh, we treat our boys in blue well," she said with a smirk. "Free lunch, keep 'em on the payroll, and they get their pick of the pussy when they stop through at night."

"So, then that makes you our-"

"Now I'm nobody's pimp. I'm not chasing you around town in some suede red outfit skimming money off the top," she corrected. "I treat this as a restaurant. Whatever you make from what goes on in the freezer is 'tips'. Some days you have good tip days, and some days you don't."

She walked out of the last room and I followed. I still couldn't believe that I was part of some covert whoring scheme. My happiness over my $125, quickly turned to embarrassment. Could I dare drop an offering in the collection plate with this dirty money? What if my boys grew up and found out where their mother was working?

Eugenia could see how troubled I was with the idea of staying employed at her so-called restaurant. When we exited the freezer, she pulled a stool down from the counter to rest. "Now I know this may not be the dream job you imagined with that fancy degree of yours," she started, "but everyone starting out has got to pay their dues."

"This is a little more than paying dues," I said with one hand on my hip.

"Look, I hired you not to be just another chick in here shaking and doing whatever, but I see something in you. You're smarter than these other girls. I hired you for something bigger."

I sighed. "What do you want from me, Ms. Eugenia?"

"I want you to start from the bottom, and learn the business inside and out. I'm not gonna be here forever. Hell, I'm already 58. But when I'm gone, I'd rest in peace if I knew I had someone with a business degree in charge." I was hesitant, but Eugenia did have a good hustle going for a soul food joint. "Just say you'll stay," she said with a look as if I was her last ray of hope. I nodded, and reluctantly continued.

Now eighteen years later, Eugenia kept her promise. She had passed three years ago after a long bout with lung cancer, leaving me to manage the restaurant. She had taught me more than any school could about managing a business. Best of all, I became more managerial than "waitress". With her death, I was able to change some things without taking away from her dream.

First, I added males to our Secrets staff, but after numerous complaints from women not getting what they paid for, we went back to ladies only.

Next, I hired some young, fresh-faced workers who were in the same situation I was when I started. Over the years, I noticed that there was a difference in those who were doing this until something better came along, and those looking for a quick fuck with a side of bacon string beans. On top of that, the older girls were leaving to pursue other dreams and start families. So it was goodbye to Screaming Orgasm, and Sexy Alligator, and Top Shelf, and welcome Champagne, Virgin (which I doubted from her interview), and Hot Tottie, just to name a few. Jazz stayed with me however, and I promoted her to assistant manager. With the new ladies, we catered to everyone from guys who didn't want to start college still wet behind the ears, to army recruits, and even married couples.

Last, but most importantly, we changed the way our guests got into the "freezer". I noticed it was raising a few brows when customers entered and exited the kitchen freely. Someone even made a comment in the suggestion box how "unsanitary it is to allow patrons in the kitchen". To take away suspicion, if anyone wanted something that wasn't on the menu, they could enter through the closet marked Cleaning Products in the bathroom. The waitresses still went through the back entrance.

It was 11 o'clock on a summer Friday night as I prepped the ladies for a bachelor party. Even in these rough times, business was booming. You'd be surprised at what some folks would pay for a pussyburger. After serving the last of the soul food guests, I switched the sign to Secrets and it was on.

The new young ladies came out uniformed in black fishnet stockings, spanx, white button-up collar shirts, and black belts. Mai Tai, our Asian waitress, hit the music and they began a seductive choreographed number to Ciara's "Ride". I was amazed at the work they put in to come up with this on their own! And from the sound of it, the party enjoyed the routine as well. The dance ended with Virgin escorting the Best Man to the bathroom. The rest of the waitresses took orders and flirted with the gentlemen.

"I think that older guy is eyeing you," Jazz said.

"Ain't nobody looking at us with all this young tail around here," I joked. I looked up, and sure enough, a man who looked about our age was staring at the bar in my direction. Jazz motioned for him to come chill with the grown folks. I wasn't taking part in any Freezer activities, but it felt good to get a little attention.

"Evening, ladies," he began, "I'll take a beer."

"Can I see some ID?" I said with attitude. He laughed, and then reached for his wallet. After a quick inspection I replied, "Thank you, George."

"Hi, I'm Jasmine. You'll have to excuse my friend, Daphne. She doesn't know how to appreciate a fine man like you."

"Is that right?" he inquired with a smile.

"Sure is," I said in a flirtatious manner. "Good thing you're not fine in my book." George choked on a sip of beer, while Jazz clapped her hands as if to say, "BAM, she got you!" He shot me a smirk, and I grinned back. He was into me, and I definitely was into him. His light skin was accented by his autumn brown eyes and a mole that sat beside his left sideburn. His hair was texturized into a short, baby-hair bush. He was thicker than my usual taste, but his swagger, as the new girls called it, was enough to give him a test run.

"On that note," he chimed in, "I'll get back to the bachelor party. You take care, Ms. Daphne."

As he walked across the lounge, Virgin burst out the bathroom with her shirt and stockings ripped, screaming, "Help! He's crazy!"

"Bitch, get your ass back here and finish the damn job!" yelled the belligerent and obviously drunk best man. I ran over to assist.

"What's going on here?" I questioned harshly.

"This ho left me hangin."

"Nigga, I ain't your fuckin' ho," Virgin said, "and I can't get with all them bumps and shit on your dick." This infuriated him. He lunged forward and slammed Virgin into a wall, shattering a hanging picture frame with Eugenia's picture in it. He wrapped his hands around her neck like he wanted to choke the life out of her.

"You ain't have to put my shit in the streets," he said through his teeth while shaking her. Jazz and I attempted to beat him off of her with anything we could find, but it was no use. Suddenly, George rushed in and pushed the enraged man into the bar, jabbing him once in the jaw, and again in the gut, causing him to throw his liquor up. Virgin ran into my arms on the brink of tears.

"Ok gentlemen," I yelled, "and I use that word loosely, party's over!" Two other men came to carry their beaten friend out of the club.

"Man, damn! Tiffany is gonna be pissed this nigga got a black eye in the wedding pictures," the groom said. "Let's roll. George, are you coming?"

George looked at the mess, looked at me, and then told the groom, "Nah. I'll stick around and make sure everything's cool here." He was winning me over, slowly, but surely.

I let the ladies leave for the night after counting their money and cleaning up the brawl evidence. George agreed to give me a ride, so Jazz used my car to take Virgin home. He sat at the bar, icing his knuckles.

"Thanks again," I said graciously. "Do you need any more ice?"

"I'm good," he said.

"Well at least let me get you some coffee." I sat the half-and-half and sugar on the bar counter, and searched the dishwasher for two clean cups. I even sweetened the deal with a piece of Eugenia's famous sweet potato pie. Hmph, if he played his cards right I had another piece of pie for him. "So, you must be new in town."

"What makes you think that?"

"Cus everybody that's anybody has been to Eugenia's."

"Well, I'm not real big on soul food," he answered. "Plus, I've never seen you at my hangout spots either."

"And where would that be?"

"Church." I looked at him with uneasiness. "Just joking. That's for you getting me earlier." We both laughed. His sense of humor was appealing. We had spent hours talking, laughing and getting to know one another. This was the most fun I'd had in awhile. Unfortunately, I had to bring the night to an end so that I could help Jazz open up in the morning.

"We can leave after I hit the bathroom," George said. While I was washing the cups out, it hit me. This was the chance to make a move. I followed George into the bathroom, opened the "Cleaning Products" closet door, and gently massaged his back as he walked in. This was more than just some skanky service that we provided. I was into this man.

We went into Room 1: The Bedroom. I laid him on the bed and massaged his back. I undid my ponytail so my hair could sway freely. After helping take his shirt off, we shared our first kiss. He pulled me in so that I could sit on his lap, but I pulled away. I had a few tricks up my sleeve.

I ran into Room 2: The 2nd Bedroom. By the time he caught onto following me, I was completely undressed and awaiting his arrival. He kissed as though there were a treasure map on my body, starting with my forehead, and ending on the "X" that marked my spot. Just when it started getting good, he looked at me and said, "I wanna know what's behind door number 3." Guess he had some tricks, too.

He carried me into Room 3: The Office. George placed me on the executive desk, lowered his jeans around his ankles, and strapped up. I admired his respect. A chill ran up my spine as he slowly entered. He took his time as if he wanted this to last forever. I did, too. After all, there were two more rooms to go.

I had to refer back to my Chocotini days to prepare for Room 4: The Dungeon. I commanded George to sit in the chair. When he was out of line, I used The Punisher on him. The whip scraped his chest, but I could tell the pain was pleasure. "Shut up!" I demanded as he moaned. He really enjoyed The Dungeon, but my favorite room was next.

Our last and final love-making destination was The Rainforest. I wrapped my legs around George's waist, pressed my back against the bark, and let him nail me to the tree like a poster on the wall. The motion-sensing misters that I had installed activated, creating a euphoric sensation. Our bodies pulsed to the beat of the simulated thunderstorm until we climaxed together.

We sat naked in the mist for awhile until I realized it was 5am. It was no point going to sleep, but George took me home to shower and change. I sent Jazz a text to let her know she could bring the car to work; my boo would be dropping me off.

George pulled into the restaurant parking lot about a quarter after 8:00. Maybe I was tripping from not sleeping for twenty hours, but I didn't remember the place being surrounded by squad cars and my morning shift being placed in hand cuffs by the bachelor party guests when we left last night.

"Stop the car, George," I said frantically. "Open the door."

I turned to George and saw a shiny badge with my reflection staring back at me. "Daphne Williams, you're under arrest for running a prostitution ring," he said. "You have the right to remain silent." Damn, this nigga set me up!

I was heated, but I had to remain calm and think straight. I got out the car to speak to an older officer. "Excuse me, are you the one in charge?" He nodded. "I'm Ms. Williams, the owner of this establishment. Is there a problem?"

"Ma'am we were given an anonymous tip that you were running an undercover whore house in your restaurant. Is this true?" Anonymous tip, huh? I looked back at George, flipped him the bird on the sly, and put my acting to work.

"Whore house?" I said with dramatic disbelief. "Officer I'd never disrespect myself, or the memory of Ms. Eugenia Gray like that. The only thing we're selling here is down home cuisine, just like Mama used to make."

"Well in that case, you won't mind if I take a look around, will you?" I handed him the keys, and he led the undercover team inside.

Thirty minutes went by. Then forty-five. Then an hour. Finally, the officer came back, handed me the keys, then ordered, "Release these women. This is nothing but a restaurant. Very sloppy bust gentlemen. I expect a full report on my desk, George."

"Don't be too hard on the boys, sir," I said. "They were just doing their job. Here, let me get you some coffee to go."

I went into the kitchen to pour some coffee into a carry-out cup. As I snapped the lid on, I heard commotion coming from the bathroom. I peeked around the corner and saw George in the bathroom closet, throwing bottles of kitchen and bathroom cleaners off shelves, searching for access to the rooms we visited earlier. His frustration amused me.

"Looking for something?" I asked sarcastically.

"Where is it?" he asked angrily. "Those rooms didn't just disappear."

"Why don't you come over to the bar and we'll talk over some cof-"

"I don't want any fucking coffee!" he shouted. "This isn't a game. You made me look like an idiot in front of my lieutenant."

"And you tried to shut me down and lock me up," I interrupted. "And you almost had me with that bachelor party stunt, but I knew it all along. That's why after we left, I had Jazz come in and 'fix' the place up." He was puzzled.

"So, you knew I was a cop?"

"Please, you think you're the first to try to take down Eugenia's? I knew you were all cops. I've spent almost 20 years serving pork chops and ribs. Don't you think I know a pig when I see one?" George paced back and forth, with his hands on his waist.

"So then what was last night about?" he asked.

"What, the sex?" I said as if it were nothing. "Can't blame a sista for thinking you're cute." All jokes aside, I wondered if he was into me like I thought, or was it part of the elaborate sting operation. "So was last night just part of your job?"

"Was it just meaningless sex with a random, cute nigga?" he countered. He approached me and grabbed my hands. "I think we have something going here, or at least had something. But you know I can't be with a woman who runs a whorehouse and I'm a cop." He kissed me on the cheek, which only added to the disappointment. He grabbed the lieutenant's cup and headed for the door. "If you ever decide to go legit, look me up."

"And if you ever need a quick bite, stop in," I threw out there. "I've always got a special piece of pie for you." He grinned, winked, and left.

I played it cool, but inside I was crushed. It had only been one day, but it felt like we were on the start to something special. Maybe I should just stick to the restaurant business and leave the side gig behind. Then again, maybe not. Poor, stupid heart: don't you know money beats love every time? Guess it's back to business as usual.

E is for Evan

Friday: a blissful ending to a long and exhausting work week. However, this wasn't a normal Friday night for me. This was date night, and not just any date night, but second date night. That means she was feeling me so much I get another chance.

I know you're thinking, "What's so special about this girl?" It was rare that anyone as beautiful as she showed me attention. Truth is, I've never really had much luck with the ladies. So, after thinking long and hard, I finally set up a profile on one of those online dating sites. I had been signed up for two weeks, and it didn't look promising. But after searching through the young girls with tattoos and cabaret poses, and the big girls oozing over spaghetti straps like string on Christmas hams, I found Candace.

I still remember the first day we met. That is, the first time I saw her profile. She had glistening dark brown skin, brown eyes, and dark shoulder-length hair. She was wearing a complimenting brown sweater and was holding a pink martini. I admired her for putting her best foot forward, unlike some of the ladies who had chosen cookout pictures of themselves downing malt liquor and giving the camera the finger. Her picture had elegance written all over it, the qualities a 30-year old brotha like me was interested in.

Next, I clicked on her personal info. She had her own car, own house not too far from my place, no kids, and makes over $50,000 a year: so far, so good. Her interests included going out to eat, African-American literature, comedies, and scary movies as long as she had someone to hold onto during the "scary parts". I clicked on "Message Me" to see what she thought. *"That is a beautiful picture you have up. It looks like we have a lot in common. I usually do happy hour at Shay Lounge around 6pm. Would you care to join me?"* Send.

The following morning I checked my profile, but there was no response. I checked again when I got to work, still nothing. I did one more check after my lunch break, and still nothing. I was nervous. Maybe that picture of me in a wifebeater wasn't as flattering as I assumed. Maybe those yellow lines around the arms weren't invisible like I thought.

I did one last check before leaving for the night. To my surprise there was one new message. It was Candace! *"Hey cutie, work has been so busy."* Which really meant she was asking her girls what they thought about me. *"Thanks for the compliment. You seem cool. I don't get off until 6, but I could meet you there around 6:30. See you soon.:)"* Hell yeah. Your boy's gotta date!

I was ecstatic, yet uneasy. I hadn't dated in three years, or had a serious relationship in five. On the way to Shay Lounge I just kept hoping I wouldn't say or do anything stupid.

I pulled into the parking lot 6 o'clock on the dot. Candace strutted through the entrance a few minutes before 6:30 wearing red dress with a black jacket to downplay the outfit. She was killing the competition with her matching black and red heels. I reached in my pocket and sprayed another hit of cologne, then waved to let her know I was here. She opened the door, said, Hello, Ev-", then broke into a coughing fit. One too many sprays, perhaps?

"Yes, I'm Evan," I said. "Nice to meet you, Candace." After catching her breath, we shook hands and were off to my happiest hour in years.

During the wait, Candace shared how she was a Clark Atlanta University alum, a sister of some sorority, and a member of the track team. I on the other hand, shared stories of graduating from Drexel, being a debater, and attending an occasional party. Just as the ice was breaking, one of the burgundy plush booths opened up and we were seated.

I was tense. If you could see the splendor on the opposite side of me, you would understand. All I could do was pray the sweat wasn't seeping through my shirt. Luckily, the smooth jazz in the background helped me relax and enjoy the outing.

We had been there fifteen minutes, and Candace was already sneaking glimpses of the time on her watch. Thankfully, the server came. "How are you ladies doing today? My name is Donald, and I'll be taking your order."

"Excuse me, Donald," I butted in, "but I'm a man."

"Oh, my bad, dawg." Candace bowed her head to refrain from laughing at the awkward moment, but her bouncing shoulders gave it away. Off to a great start. "Can I get you two something to drink?"

"I'll have an apple martini," Candace said.

"Just a beer for me."

"Ok, and would you like an appetizer?" Candace looked at me as if to ask was it ok. Guess that means I'm paying. It was the first date, so it wasn't too big a deal.

"I'd like to try the spinach dip," she said.

"And I'll have the boneless buffalo strips." Candace made a nauseating look in my direction. I looked behind me to see if something had occurred that I was unaware of. "Is something wrong?"

"You eat meat," she stated with disgust. "How could you eat an animal?"

I thought she was joking to strike up conversation. I answered with, "Don't tell me you're one of those tree huggers, are you?" Her mouth dropped, but with a twisted smile. "And I bet you had plenty of chicken at an HBCU." She looked away from the table, slid a strand of hair behind her ear, and sipped her martini without ever looking in my direction. *"Smooth move,"* I thought to myself. This date was going up in smoke before the appetizers even hit the table.

I don't know what it is about Black people and food, but once ours arrived, the conversation ceased! After the two of us had a chance to put a few bites in our stomachs, the date resumed with less hostility. "Hey," she began, "I'm sorry about that whole meat thing. Let's start over." Perfect! The best thing I could ask for was a second chance. "Would you like to try my dip?" she asked with a smile. I grabbed a chip and dunked into the steaming hot, cheesy spinach dish.

"Would you like a chicken strip?" She looked up as if she were thinking, *"Did he not just hear me five minutes ago?"* "Gotcha," I said. She giggled innocently. It was amazing: the same date that was near death, had bloomed into a possible friendship with a bright future.

A couple drinks and a few stories later, it was time to go. Candace informed me that she had to prepare for a presentation tomorrow. I was having fun, but the quicker the date ended the better. I had redeemed myself, and didn't want to chance screwing it up.

I walked Candace to her car in the parking lot. "Let me get that for you," I said, referring to her door. I wanted to show my gentleman side, but was also setting myself up for the goodnight kiss. She climbed into the driver's seat, adjusted her jacket, and closed the door with the window rolled down.

"This was fun," I said.

"It was," she confirmed. "And funny, too. We should hang out again." I leaned in, closed my eyes, and waited for her to meet me halfway. Suddenly, I felt a palm on my back, followed by another gentle palm. Ouch, the dreaded hug. And through the window at that. "It's nothing personal," she explained. "I don't kiss on the first date." That was somewhat reassuring, but she could have at least given me a peck on the cheek. Oh well, I got a second date. My work was done!

Which brings us to tonight. As soon as work was over, I hurried home to get ready. I showered, shaved, and ironed up a pair of Levi's jeans with a red button-up shirt (you know, something that really made this khaki-colored brotha stand out).

Just as I was leaving out, I noticed that my cell phone had a voicemail. It was from Candace. "Hey Evan, I'm really sorry, but I'm going to have to cancel tonight. I'm feeling like I'm coming down with something. Don't be mad. We'll get together soon." Son of a bitch!

I was ripped. I stood in the living room wondering what I could have done or said for her to blow me off at the last minute. She mentioned all week how she was looking forward to this, and now literally a half hour before we were supposed to meet, she pulls this?

I played the message back again. After taking some time to cool down, I could hear how sick she really was. How could I have been so insensitive? Candace really liked when I calmed down, and showed my mature, chivalrous side. I figured that if she was too sick to come out, I would surprise her with some chicken noodle soup, orange juice, and a few DVDs. You the man, Ev.

"4-1-1, what city?"

"Glenover."

"What listing?"

"Candace Ellison."

"Thank you, please hold for that number."

Now that I had her home telephone number, I plugged it into the Internet for an address, and then printed out the directions. I was sure my romance would impress her, yet. I could imagine the look on Candace's face when she saw me outside the door with "feel good" food and entertainment. If the night went the way I planned in my head, I would be covered in sick kisses by the time I left.

I arrived at Candace's shortly after stopping by the video store. Her house was beautiful and well-designed, just like her. It was a traditional rambler with a brick bottom and tan siding on the top. Her backyard was fenced off by a stained cherry oak fence. I walked up her sidewalk, opened the glass door, and then knocked.

I heard footsteps coming down the steps, followed by her unique giggle. The door swung open, and there stood a shirtless, muscular, dark-skinned, familiar man. It was Donald, the waiter! "Damn, did you get lost?" he asked. "Baby, the carryout is here." He must not have recognized me.

"Well, it took you long enou . . ." Candace came to the door in a pair of tight workout pants, and a long white-t. "Evan? What are you doing here?"

"I called myself surprising you, and you up in here with some other dude." Candace looked at Donald so that we could speak privately.

"Handle your business, Candy. I'll be downstairs," he said.

"Candy? That must be your slut name," I said angrily. "So you fuckin' the waiter behind my back?"

"Slut?" she questioned. "Evan, you have got some nerve showing up here unannounced, uninvited, and did I even give you my address?"

"No," I started, "but I thought women liked to be surprised and shit. I thought you said everything was good, and you wanted to see me again."

"It is, Evan," she explained, "well, it was. You're crazy. That's beyond stalker. You're crazy." Candace rolled her eyes and exhaled deeply before telling me, "You need to leave." I looked down at the soup and movies I had in my hand. My heart was crushed. Out of nowhere, a rage came upon me.

"No," I said calmly.

"Excuse me?"

"Nooooooo!" I shouted, while attempting to pry my way into the house. Candace and I began a tug-of-war match with the door as our rope. "Open the door!"

"You're fucking psycho!" she screamed. "Donald help!" Donald rushed to the door, assisting Candace in shutting me out. I tried to fight, but I was no match for their combined strength. I was at a low point. Still infuriated, I hurled the soup at her glass door. Even if all she did was clean it up, it made me feel better.

I finally turned to leave, and saw the neighborhood kids snickering as I walked away. I envisioned them laughing that she chose some waiter over me. I stopped dead in my tracks in the middle of her driveway, and dashed for her backyard fence. I wouldn't let these kids see me just give up on my girl.

I climbed over, ripping my jeans on the splints and staining my shirt. My plan was to show Candace how much better life would be with me than with him. I grabbed a few hundred dollar bills out of my wallet, popped a stick of chewing gum in, and walked up to the patio steps to the back door. Either Candace didn't have one, or I failed to see the Beware of Dog sign, because as soon as I placed my left foot on the first step, a huge, steroid taking rottweiler appeared from underneath the deck. He was growling viciously as I stood paralyzed in fear. It wasn't until that moment that I realized going home was a much better course of action, but not an option.

I tried to walk slow and calm to the fence, but the beast charged, barking incessantly. I had no choice but to run laps around her spacious backyard. I finally raced to a tree low enough that I could climb, but high enough to be out of harm's way (and the dog's mouth). I took out my cell phone to call the police for help. Just then, the dog caught my shoe in his mouth, causing me to drop my phone. I was stranded.

Finally, Candace came to the rescue. "Baby, come here boy." There was nothing about that beast that looked like "baby". Unwillingly, he left me up in the tree. "Good boy, Baby. That's a good boy."

Candace was glaring at the tree I was held hostage in, while she petted Baby. If her eyes were fire, this tree would be in trouble. "It serves you right, idiot," she yelled from the patio. "I'll be sure to call the police on your monkey ass, AFTER my date." Donald came behind her, grabbed her by the waist, and pulled her back inside. Shit, I hope he's a minute man so I can get out of this tree.

F is for Felicia

"Hi, Mrs. Andrews. No, she's in the shower. Did you want me to take a message? Uh huh, uh huh. Oh ok. Really? Wow, that's a long time! Well, congratulations and I'll be sure to give her the message."

I could hear my baby coming up the steps, followed by a knock on the bathroom door. I hated when my showers were disrupted. I had the water set on scald, the steam was thick, my jazz was blasting, and my vanilla scented candles were the only lights on. It was serene.

There was a second set of knocks. "What is it?" I asked irritated.

"I just got off the phone with your mom, Felicia," Meer said. "She wanted me to remind you not to forget your speech for your parent's 30th wedding anniversary dinner this weekend." My heart started racing. "Any reason I wasn't told about this?" I shut the water off.

"Baby, I just didn't think this was your type of function." Meer paused like I needed to come with something better than that. "Ok," I said, giving into those angry, brown eyes staring back at me. "I wasn't sure if we were ready for you to meet my parents. My father has run off every man I've ever dated, and my mom isn't any easier to talk to. I just didn't think this was the right time to show up with a new date."

"Leesh, as important as it is for me to meet your parents, I don't care what they think about us. As long as you're cool with me, then we're cool. Besides, I'm not like those other guys you've dated in the past." Meer was right about that. I was a sucker for dark-skinned thugs with cut-up abs and baby mama drama, but I traded all that in for Ameera, an exotic, Moroccan woman. I peeked from outside of the shower curtain.

"So, you really wanna go to this thing?" I asked playfully.

"I wouldn't wanna be anywhere else," she said. I nodded with a smile, and Meer expressed her gratitude by joining me in the shower. She kissed my lips while gently lathering my breasts and flat abs in strawberry body wash, creating a pink bubble wonderland. I ran my fingers through her hair and down her back, stopping to cup her ass while we kissed. Our bodies became entangled, repeatedly sliding past each other like finely moistened hands.

*   *   *

Have you ever noticed how fast time flies when something you don't want to do is right around the corner? Saturday was here, and my week was spent pondering how the dinner would go and if bringing Ameera was the right decision. I had yet to tell my parents that I was bisexual, let alone that I was in a lesbian relationship. How would they react to their dreams of grandparenthood being destroyed by something I doubted they believed in?

Aside from being a female, she was everything my parents had raised me to look for in a mate: educated, financially stable, 0-1 kids, someone who provided a sense of security, and overall, someone I could spend my life with. And it didn't hurt that she was cute. Meer was just about 5'9", and 160 pounds solid. She had a phatty, but she hated me commenting on her ass. Her brown hair was thick and rich without ever requiring perm. Her eyebrows were like two bushy caterpillars, and below them sat two sienna eyes. Her skin had been baked a beautiful copper tone from early exposure to the Middle Eastern rays.

"Meer, are you almost ready?" I asked, while sliding into my slip.

"I'm always ready first," she said sarcastically.

"Ok smart ass, give me like five more minutes." I hoisted my black, cross-strapped evening gown up and took one final look in the mirror. The dress complimented my body's petite silhouette perfectly, but what set my attire off were my shimmering half-karat diamond earrings and 4-inch heels, gifts from Meer, of course.

I gathered my purse and jacket and met Ameera at the door. My eyes bulged at the site of her outfitted in a black pantsuit, white button-up shirt, and a tie. We were a couple, but I assumed she would doll herself up until my parents knew what was up. Immediately, I began hyperventilating.

"Felicia, what's wrong baby?" she said. "You look pale."

"Nothing. I just swallowed my gum by mistake and needed some air." Ameera looked suspicious about my answer, but didn't press the issue. "You look nice," I said in an attempt to change the subject. She opened her suit jacket and imitated a runway turn. Poor Ameera; she did her best to put a positive spin on a guaranteed awkward situation and I was considering no one's feelings but mine. I quickly turned my frown upside-down, posed seductively, and inquired, "Am I killing 'em in this dress?"

"Mmm. I just can't wait until dinner is over, so we can come back home for dessert." Meer was corny, but her jokes always made me laugh. We exited the living room corridor and headed for dinner.

After an hour of traffic, we finally made it there. Ironically, the celebration was taking place at the ballroom of my parent's home church. I walked in first, hoping that my dress would take the attention off Ameera. "Is that my little Felicia?" I heard my mother say in excitement. She and my father walked hurriedly to greet me at the door.

"Hey Mom. Daddy." We embraced each other with a hug. "You guys look good." Dad had on a standard black tux and a navy vest that matched mom's sleeveless, midnight number. The two were very fashionable.

"Thank you, Sweet Pea," said my father. "Dining alone again this year?" he joked.

"Um, actually no Daddy."

"Oh, Felicia I wish you would have told me you were bringing a date. No big deal, we can just add a chair to the head table. So where's the new hoodlum?"

"No more thugs, mom. Believe me. In fact you'll be quite surprised." I had broken as much ice as I could break. It was now or never. "They're right outside if you would like to meet them." My parents followed me out into the hallway. Naturally, I was fearful; this was a big step for me, but if I was serious about Ameera, it had to be done eventually. "Mom, Dad, this is Ameera," I exhaled deeply, "my girlfriend."

You would have thought the devil himself made a guest appearance, slid down the handrail, and stuffed his mouth full of mini-quiches the way Mom stopped dead in her tracks. "Oh my God!" she shouted. Dad nudged her so that she could attempt to rephrase her comments. "Oh my God . . . it's . . . lovely to finally meet you." I rested my forehead in the palm of my hand. Ameera reached out to shake my father's hand, and shockingly he accepted.

"Mr. and Mrs. Andrews it's a pleasure to finally meet you. I've heard so much about you."

"Really?" questioned my mother, "Because we haven't heard anything about you. Felicia was probably too ashamed to talk to me about this mess, as she should be."

"Mary," my father admonished. "Nice meeting you as well. You'll have to excuse my wife. We're just caught off guard." My mother folded her arms, staring carelessly into space. "Ameera, maybe we should give the two ladies some space."

"Dad!" I loudly whispered with embarrassment.

"It's cool," said Ameera. "He didn't mean anything by it. I'll see you on the inside."

"Yeah, the inside of Hell," my mother added.

As my father and Meer became better acquainted, I prepared myself for the wrath of my mother. "You think your little charade is funny? You didn't think it was right to tell us in advance about this?"

"I didn't think it mattered," I butted in.

"It doesn't matter?" she shot back. "Why the hell not mention it then if it doesn't matter?" My mother paced back and forth in the hallway. "And you can forget about him, her, whatever 'it' is sitting at the head table with us. That's out!"

After listening to all that I could stomach, I raced to get a word in. "Mom, you raised me to think for myself. Meer means a lot to me. And if she can't be a part of this family, then maybe I shouldn't be either."

"Well, that's fine with me and your father," she concurred, "because we didn't raise no carpet muncher." I was brought to tears that it had gotten this out of hand.

"Mary!" my father yelled on his way back to the hallway. "I don't need you speaking for me. I had a chance to talk to, not judge Ameera, and she seems like a sweet, funny young lady. I'll admit you caught us with our pants down on this one Sweet Pea. But because I love you, I love her." My mother looked at my father in amazement.

"Fine," she said, "munch away." She stormed back into the dining hall.

"Thanks, Daddy," I said as I rested my head on his chest.

Dinner was served shortly after the blessing. We had the typical church banquet cuisine: roast beef and gravy, mashed potatoes, string beans that could've used a few extra minutes in the pot, rolls, and sparkling Moscato. Mom continued ignoring me throughout the ceremony, but Dad was very open-minded and welcoming. We talked about how Ameera and I met, how she cut her family ties and Muslim background to be with me, and Dad even found a new football fan to watch the games with.

"Would it kill you to pay a little attention to your wife at her wedding anniversary?" Mom sarcastically asked. Dad paid her no mind and continued the conversation. Mom left the table to mingle with guests who potentially gave a fuck about her attitude.

Dinner concluded with strawberry shortcake and acknowledgements. Mom clumsily approached the podium and knocked a knife against her glass to gain everyone's attention. "Thank you all for showing my husband and me so much love on this special occasion." As if she needed anymore, she took a sip of wine and resumed her speech. "It's not easy being with the same person for 30 years, especially when you throw kids in there. Luckily, Charles and I had a daughter whom we treasured." The crowd adored her speech, eating up every word like it was the missing ice cream to this bland cake. "And after all that spoiling, she still decides to fuck us over." Everyone gasped.

"Mary, please," Dad insisted.

"Man should not lie with man. That's the 'Good Book' right there," she argued drunkenly.

"Judge not, lest ye be judged," countered Meer.

"I don't need some Arabic cuntlicker throwing Bible verses at me!"

"That's it, Mom!" I yelled while furiously meeting her at the podium. "I get it: you have a problem with us and you hate lesbians. Everyone in this room gets it. But can you at least love your daughter? I'm the same daughter you took on field trips, the same daughter you helped get dressed for prom, and the same daughter that helped you're alcoholic ass through rehab."

"If I wanted a daughter-in-law, I would have had a son," Mom rebutted.

"If none of that matters can you just love me for the sake of being your daughter, gotdammit?" Without warning, Mom backhand slapped me. My cantaloupe-colored cheek turned a bloody, brick red. Damn, I wish Daddy had given her the karat upgrade after the party. I could feel the cut of the stone imprinted in my skin. I rubbed my pained face, and looked at Mom through my blurred teary vision.

"You should be ashamed of yourself," Mom added. "Disrespecting your own mother. And in a church! You probably learned that from that fag," she said, pointing at Meer.

"You caustic bitch!" I interrupted, while simultaneously slapping her back. The blow's force combined with Mom's intoxicated state laid her out. The guests were in total awe. I looked back at Dad with remorse. "Happy Anniversary," I told him. Meer grabbed our coats and we disappointingly headed home.

"Yeah, you go ahead and leave," Mom yelled from the floor. "And don't forget to take 'Fahren-dike 9/11' with you!"

The ride home was awkwardly silent. Did Meer not think I stood up enough for the two of us? Did she think I was wrong for fighting my mother? She slid her hand from the stick shift and clasped my fingers. She massaged the back of my hand to ensure everything would be ok.

We had finally made it home. Even after Meer's kind gesture, my heart was burdened. I ruined my parent's anniversary, my mother had no intentions of ever talking to me again, and now I was certain that if my own mother wouldn't accept me then why would a stranger on the street? I began to wonder, *"Was I willing to march in the rallies, attend the court hearings, and protest equal rights? Was I willing to go through artificial insemination and raise a child with lesbian parents, knowing how cruel their schoolmates would be? Was it better to just say fuck it, leave Meer, and start over with my ex-boyfriend, Clay? Yeah, he was physically abusive, but at least that was a sin he had to deal with, not me. What if Mama was right and I'm going to Hell?"*

I barged through the front door, pushing Meer out of the way. "Getting in the shower," I yelled, hoping that would explain my abnormal behavior. I ran into the bathroom and threw up a mixture of roast beef and emotions in the toilet. I locked the door, set-up for one of my relaxing showers, and cried hysterically. The stress and pain were getting to me. I loved my parents, but did I want to give up my happiness with Meer just for them to love me? And I loved Meer, but how long could I front about not caring what society thought? Then, I doubted myself: was this a fad, or was I really into it? I was at a crossroads and as I lay curled up in the bathtub, only one choice seemed fit: suicide.

I jumped out of the shower and went on a medicine cabinet binge, swallowing extra strength this and nighttime formula that. Next, I grabbed a handful of old prescription pills and chased them with cough syrup. The taste was more than awful. The plan was working. I then stumbled over to the soap dish, grabbed a bar, and scribbled, "Judge not. Love always, Leesh," on the bathroom mirror. My mind was slowly shutting down. It was a frightening, yet tranquil sensation.

I ingested a dangerously large amount of medication, but wasn't sure if it was enough to keep me down. To seal the deal, I swallowed some generic drain cleaner with a cherry cough drop for taste. Instantly, I could feel my throat and chest corroding. My head was spinning and I could no longer see straight. I had created the perfect catastrophic reaction.

As I dopily walked back to the shower, I heard a buzz. It was my cell phone vibrating against the porcelain toilet top. I looked at the caller ID. Hmph, it was Mom. I answered the phone.

"Hello? Felicia are you there?" I refused to answer her. "*Sigh*. I don't blame you for not speaking to me. I was completely out of line tonight. I ruined my anniversary, your father isn't talking to me, and I said some things to my baby girl that I shouldn't have said." She was off to a good start, but it would take more than that Hallmark apology to get to me.

"Felicia, I'm not going to pretend that I approve of you being a lesbian, but it could be worse. What I'm trying to say is I'm happy that you're happy and I love you. Always." I could feel that mom's words were sincere. I sobbed as I listened to her. I stared at the medicinal mess I had created. "Well, don't just sit there. Can you forgive me?"

"I'm sorry, Mom," I said through the foam blocking my throat, "I wish you would have told me this five minutes earlier. These kind words may have saved my life." By the time I finished my sentence my hand was too weak to hold the phone to my ear.

I could hear Mom in the background crying and yelling, "What do you mean? Felicia, where are you? Do you need help? Felicia!!!"

Mom's voice had turned from frantic yelling, to a moderate tone, to a whisper, to nothing at all. I had slipped out of consciousness . . . for the last time.

G is for Gavin

One month ago, my beautiful wife, Christine, gave birth to my first-born son, Aiden. He came home a healthy 7 pounds 4 ounces, 10 fingers, 10 toes, unblemished white skin, and a head finely covered in blonde hair. I enjoyed my four weeks at home welcoming Aiden into the family and taking care of Christine, but like all good things, my family leave came to an end.

It's 8 o'clock Monday morning and I'm gearing up for my first day back to work. While Christine nursed Aiden in her ancestral rocking chair, I grumpily prepared for work. She gave me a small surprise by having a fresh pressed shirt and suit ready by the time I was finished showering and shaving. "Thanks, dear," I said, while applying a kiss on her forehead. I grabbed my briefcase, suit jacket, cell phone and started out for a presumably busy return to the advertising industry.

Generally, I caught the Glenmont subway to avoid traffic and today was no different. I found a space in the parking garage that was just five spaces from the elevator. Was this luck or what? Either I was really early, or everyone else was really late. I finished parking and headed for the train.

But some things never change. The train was approaching the Fort Totten stop: a station where many of the "urban" District of Columbia public and charter school students got on. They usually left us clean-cut, young, Caucasian businessmen alone, but there was no reason taking any unnecessary risks. The doors opened and the passenger car added a handful of students in gray slacks and black polos to its inventory. Of the most memorable were a group of young African-American girls who sat right beside each other, but for some reason were engaged in what seemed like a shouting match. Once the old ladies clutched their purses, I took that as my cue to remove my earphones and tuck my music player into my suit jacket.

"I KNOW you ain't just hide that phone," said one of the bigger girls. She had a very intimidating persona, from her scarf wrapped hair, to her gyrating neck, to her unreasonably long fingernails. "Ahhhh," she said, while sticking her tongue out in an unladylike manner, "I'm just fuckin' wit' chu."

"Rayliqua, guuuuuurl you is a mess," one of the other students shouted.

"T'Onna don't dis nigga look like Tommy?" Rayliqua asked. "White Tommy from 'round LoLo and nem way?"

"He ain't no nigga, gurl. He white." T'Onna turned to me, rolling her eyes with every neck roll in my direction. "Oh my God, I am so embarrassed. You have to excuse Rayliqua."

"Niggas can be white!" she argued. "So where you goin' white nigga that look like Tommy?" Thankfully, this was my stop.

"You two have a good day," I said with a fearful smile. *Ding, dong. Doors opening.* The doors slid open and I pushed through seniors, handicaps, and children to flee from Rayliqua. The thought of a grown man running from two high schoolers had to have made someone's day, but I had not an ounce of shame. Rayliqua looked like the type to shoot someone for taking too many sunflower seeds out of her bag.

Before I got both feet in the door, I was greeted by my manager, Audrey, and her excited voice. "Welcome back, Gavin!" she said. "How is your wife and that bungle of joy?" I assumed she meant bundle. Audrey was a meek elderly lady who could fuck up a sentence like only she could. She was the prime example that it's not what you know, but who you know. Yet, her kind approach to managing made her a loveable manager.

"Christine and the baby are both doing well. We named him Aiden."

"Oh, that's a beautiful name," she added. "Well don't forget we have a team meeting today at 3 o'clock. And when you get settled, be sure to come into the conference room. We're having a "Welcome Back" breffus in lieu of your return." There were so many things wrong with that sentence, but I chose not to be a dick on my first day back. I mentally flipped through my Audrey dictionary and found out that there was a breakfast in light of me returning.

"Thanks, Audrey. I'll be back there shortly. Just going to stop past my desk for a second." I weaved through the cubicles, still shaking my head and laughing lightly at Audrey. I couldn't wait to get home and tell Christine about her latest word fumbles.

Doesn't it feel great to feel needed? I say that with sarcasm as I stare at stacks of work that needed to be completed with a note attached to each pile marking it as "Top Priority". There was no way all of this could get done by today. The only thing worse than the paperwork was the infinite voicemails I'd have to listen to, and then answer. I figured I would tackle this on after "breffus".

The eggshell conference room door opened, releasing streamers and confetti in my direction. "Welcome back, Gavin!" my colleagues shouted.

"Thanks everyone. I really appreciate this!" The women of the office crowded around, hoping to receive a wallet photo of Aiden. "Easy ladies," I joked. "I don't have any today, but I have a few of my own to show you."

"Oh, those blue eyes and blonde hair," admired Brianna, my co-worker. "He's going to be a charmer when he gets older."

"Ok, folks, we don't have much time," warned Audrey. "You know how your supervisor is: all work, no play. If he sees us partying it up, he'll have a nerve of the breakdown. So, we have fruit salad, yogurt, strambled eggs, bacon, winglettes, and I made those pancakes with the little crustacean edges like Gavin likes." Damn, somebody should hit a bell every time she messed a word up.

The breakfast party was exceptional. While others gabbed about the economy and world news, Donald, Brianna, and Byron filled me in on the latest office politics: call outs with no leave accrued, drinking on the job, office relationships, and the word count jar. Apparently, they started a game that whenever Audrey messed a word up when talking to someone, they were to put a dollar in the word jar. At the end of the fiscal year, the money would be used for an office party. The way she rattled them off, we would have enough to host a Grand Hyatt banquet. I was intrigued by all of the gossip, unfortunately, I had to cut our catch-up conversations short. My poor, Caucasian stomach couldn't handle the buttery southern-style pancakes that Audrey claimed to have "put her foot in". I made a dash for the restroom in the midst of Donald's sentence.

It wasn't until I sat on the "thinking chair" that Audrey's mentioning of a team meeting hit me. Before going on paternity leave, there was an opening for a new manager, and the sacrifices I made during Christine's pregnancy made me a shoo-in. I was assured by Darren, the department chair, that my countless overtime hours, constant projects, and trainings would not go unnoticed. Maybe the meeting was to announce my new position. I mean, there were plenty of people who were in the running, but they were obviously no competition for my experience. "Gavin McAdams: Production Manager," I said to myself. "Has a nice ring to it."

As I grabbed my electric planner off the toilet paper dispenser to exit the stall, the automatic toilet flushed itself, soaking my shirt and tie in shit water. The pungent smell filled my nostrils with disgust. Reacting to the scent, I turned towards the toilet as my gag reflex kicked in when suddenly "Mount Flushmore" shot up more water up to my face. My first day back was turning into quite a shitty day, literally.

After attempting to dry off with everything from toilet paper to paper towels to standing under an electric hand dryer, I returned to my desk. Christine had left a message that she had been craving a cheeseburger meal and wanted me to stop on the way home, "and pick up a little something for yourself," she joked. I didn't mind. After all, it must be pretty draining to bring a beautiful baby into the world as she had done. It was already etched in stone that for the next few weeks, I was on my own for dinner.

Forty-seven voicemails, ninety-two emails, three document reviews, and four 8-ounce cups of coffee later, it was finally time for the team meeting. The other eight staff members and I piled into the conference room. Normally the space to avoid, I made sure to claim the seat closest to Jerry, the supervisor. Just then, Jerry walked in, closing the door behind him.

"Good afternoon, everyone," he opened. We all nodded in concurrence. "I want to start by welcoming back Gavin. I am sure he knows that I, along with the rest of the team, am glad to have him back, personally and professionally."

"Thank you, sir." He continued the meeting in the usual manner: status updates, next steps, and Q&A. Finally . . .

"Well if there are no further questions, I have an announcement to make. After much thought the other department chairs feel the need to recognize someone who has been a diligent worker since Day 1. He came in at a time of need, and proved himself to be a quick learner, and an outstanding leader. He has made numerous sacrifices to his personal life to satisfy the goals of our mission."

"Here it comes," I thought to myself.

"So, we would like to promote Adrean Leech to manager."

Adrean Leech? The temp who was here while I was out, Adrean Leech? This recent college graduate with a month's worth of real experience that I trained and mentored in my absence nabbed my promotion?" My face was as long as melted candle wax. "You gotta be shitting me Jare!"

"Excuse me, Mr. McAdams?" I must have said that aloud instead of thinking it. I peeked between my fingers and saw a conference room full of faces staring back. "Is there an issue with my decision?" he questioned. It was too late to turn back now.

"Come on, Jare. I have been with this company for four years. Four years! Now, you give my promotion to someone else? On what basis?"

"Mr. McAdams, you have been out of the office for the last month and a half," he responded. "And while we would never penalize anyone for paternity leave, Adrean has been in the meetings, closing the deals, and making the decisions. Not you!"

"But he learned that from me," I argued. There was nothing that could save me from what came next. "Maybe it's true what they say about you people. The blacks are always 'helping a brother out'." Byron turned away to cover his face, while Brianna and Donald slid down in their chairs. Jare was noticeably infuriated.

"That's quite an allegation Mr. McAdams," he started, "one that is both inexcusable and will not be tolerated." He sat there, thinking for a minute. Maybe I had gotten through to him. Maybe he was seeing how ugly this could get if it was brought to court. Finally, he spoke. "How about you take some more time off while we find someone who's willing to accept that management knows best?" Fuck, Gavin what are you doing? This isn't the time to be a bad ass. Is it too late to back pedal?

"With all due respect, sir-"

"No, this isn't your choice. You can pack your things. Starting now, you are officially on indefinite suspension. You will be paid until the remainder of your annual and sick leave runs out."

"But Jare-"

"It's Jerry. And you should leave before security comes."

I was stunned, but pissed. It seemed so surreal. Out of all the do-nothings at this company, the one with the best work ethic gets penalized? Jerry clearly had his mind made up and I was not going to argue. Well, fuck this job and fuck them!

I stormed back to my desk and collected my belongings. I emptied out my briefcase and scattered the papers across my desk. I could care less who was responsible for completing my assignments, or for cleaning this up.

"Gavin?" a soft voice called out. It was Audrey. Realizing today's misfortune wasn't her fault I attempted to calm myself down.

"Yes, Audrey," I said through clenched teeth.

"I couldn't phantom being in your situation with the new baby and all," she stated empathetically. "Now, I hate to be the berry of bad news, but management asked that I compensate your ID badge until further notice." Audrey's word usage only intensified my frustration, triggering a series of eye ticks as I handed over my badge.

"It's confiscate, Audrey. Con-fis-cate! My God, who did you screw to wind up as my supervisor? Listen: go get yourself a fucking dictionary and take a day or two off to just read the bitch. And if you see Byron, Brianna, or Donald, tell them Gavin owes them three dollars." Her eyes bulged as I walked out the suite's glass doors with my middle finger raised. Hey, indefinite suspension meant terminated pretty much, and if they were going to term me, I was going out with a bang!

By the time I had reached the Metro station, my adrenaline rush had subdued. I began thinking clearly again, wondering if the little act I put on back at the office was worthwhile. "Indefinite suspension," I said to myself. How would I tell Christine that I was out of a job?

The lights on the station platform began to flicker, signaling that the red line to Glenmont was approaching. My solemn step changed to a hurried hustle to make sure I was on the next train. As luck would have it, I had mistaken the up escalator for the one going down. About halfway down, I suddenly lost my footing, causing me to land on my back. I was stuck in what seemed to be an infinite tumble as I continued rolling down while the elevator insisted on going up. Finally, a Metro worker pressed the emergency stop button. I plummeted to the bottom of the platform and swatted the worker's hand away. I guess he called himself helping me up, but it was too little, too late.

The train doors opened and I entered the car. I searched for a seat, but they were all taken by out of school students. It didn't bother me as long as I didn't have another run-in with . . . Spoke to soon.

"Yeah, gurl. So I called him and told him that Lo Lo had seent him walkin wit dis ova bitch and he gon' tell me, 'It is what it is,' like I ain't shit. So yeah I was in my feelins off that. Oh shit, ain't that white Tommy twin from dis morning?" Rayliqua and her "crew" as they called it had entered the same car I was riding in. "You smell like shit. You fotted Tommy?"

"How you gonna say that?" her accomplice asked between laughs. This disrespectful, loud-mouthed teen was really pressing my buttons.

"Young lady," I began calmly, "I've had a really rough day at work, and I would appreciate if you and your buddies would entertain yourselves quietly for the rest of the ride." An elderly African-American woman shook her fist in agreement. While the rest of the nearby passengers nodded in concurrence, Rayliqua was less than amused.

"Un un, un un! Who is you? Who is you?" she shouted. "My muhfuckin' mova don't even talk to me like dat!"

"Maybe that's the problem," I mumbled to myself.

"What chu say?" she hollered. Rayliqua's finger was inches from my face. One wrong jerk on the tracks and she'd poke my eye out. On any given day I would have backed down, but not today.

"I'm sorry, am I not speaking your language?" I asked sarcastically. "Try this." I placed my right hand on my waist, cocked my neck to the side, locked my left leg and slightly bent my right knee. "Guuuurl," I began with my neck in full off-beat rotation, "If you want to make it home to your Mammy's hot sausage and Lemonhead casserole wit' a scrawberry soda on the side, you'se best sit your black ass in that chair 'fore I tell the transit police to lock yo' ass up. I'm sure your dad's cell has a bunk bed waiting for you." The poor elderly woman who had once backed me up dropped her head as if to say "Nice knowing ya."

For the next four stops I was Rayliqua's little White bitch. Behind her prep school uniform hid the strength of a corn-fed ox. She effortlessly tossed me back and forth from door-to-door, screaming vulgarities as the onslaught took place. "Cracker . . . ass . . . muh . . . fuckah," she yelled, beating me with every word. It had to have been shameful to let this high school girl pummel a grown man, yet man, woman, boy and girl watched without interruption. Finally, the train operator spoke into the intercom the best news I had all day.

"Fort Totten, doors opening."

"Come on Rayliqua," her henchwoman, T'Onna said. "They callin' transit Po Po's on us." After hitting her one last time with my eye in her fist, the two ran off. The elderly woman from before offered to help me up, but I passed. I wallowed on the floor in embarrassment for awhile, then sorely jumped up to ride out the rest of my commute in a seat. The government may never pay up for slavery, but that day, Rayliqua got her reparations.

I entered my home reeking of feces, unemployment, and humiliation. On top of that, a black eye was forming around the eye that Rayliqua dealt her last blow. I threw my suit jacket over my shoulder and headed upstairs.

I peeked inside the bedroom door and there sat Christine and Aiden in the same rocking chair as when I left. "Oh, you scared me," she said. "How was work?"

"It uh, it uh . . ."

"Is everything ok?" she asked in concern. I couldn't muster up the courage to tell her about the incident on the train, nor that I lost my job. I walked into the room and she immediately knew all was not well.

"Oh, dear," she said, placing Aiden face up in our bed. She ran over to me and placed my head on her chest. "It's ok," she comforted. Even with the stench of bowels taking over the bedroom, she rubbed my head and soothed my ego. She unbuttoned my shirt and took me out of the soiled clothes. Again, she planted my head between her bosoms and massaged my back.

As my love restored my dignity and happiness, I felt that all would once again be right. She kissed my neck, nibbled on my lobe, and then gently whispered in my ear, "Babe, did you remember my cheeseburger?"

H is for Hilary

Los Angeles: the place where everyone who wants to be anyone comes to make a name for themselves. You've got your actors, models, musicians, and the professional gold diggers, like me. Today I decided to have a light lunch like the "commoners" in the business district at the Limelight Hotel. While nibbling on a Nicoise salad and sparkling water, I scoped the room and found a woman leading a business luncheon. "*Aww,*" I thought to myself, "*she's pretty enough to not have to be smart, too.*" It's like, so depressing watching these people who have to work day-after-day just to keep food on their tables. "Check please!" I said while reaching for my wallet. "And here's an extra twenty to cover the poor lady's lunch at that meeting."

Walking downtown in this heat was murder. It was a sweltering, humid, scorcher day. The palm trees had a hazy look as if they were going to like, burst into flames. My designer four-inch heels were expanding with every step on the pavement, but I was determined to use the weather to my advantage. The UV rays gave my ivory white skin a natural tan. The sunbeams bounced off my lengthy blonde hair like stage lights at a rock show. I strutted up the sidewalk to the nearest bus stop. Not that I needed public transportation, but guys loved to save a hot "damsel in distress".

I approached the stop and placed one of my long legs on the bus bench. My super short white skirt, belly ring, and yellow button up tied just below my breasts was sure to attract a ride home. And if a guy didn't look my way, he must be gay. Simple as that.

I removed my Dior aviator sunglasses so that passers-by could take wind of my aqua eyes. Just when I was ready to take a five-minute relaxer, a car stopped at a red light and honked at me. Finally, a little action. The car approached the bus stop and the man rolled down his tinted windows. "*Cute,*" I thought to myself.

"Hey beautiful," he started, "need a lift?" He was driving a boring gray 5-series BMW (two years old, might I add) with a scratch on the passenger side door. In LA, BMWs were as common as Accords on the east coast. I had learned very early that out here, BMWs stood for Bus driver, Mailman, or Worker's compensation. Besides, I had totally stepped my game up and haven't been caught riding in a Beemer since dating that college athlete back in high school. Mommy taught me a little rhyme to live by:

In a Lexus or a Benz,
We could be friends.

But if you're driving something Italian,
You could be my stallion.
Politely, I declined his offer. "As if I'd be caught in that! I'd rather take the bus."

"Suit yourself," he replied. He rolled up his window and sped off. He tried to play it cool, but behind those tinted windows, he was as hurt as the short kid who didn't grow that one extra inch the night before basketball try-outs. Don't hate, I stopped fucking for rides in "college boy" cars a long time ago.

As I got ready to sit next to some homeless geezer, another car honked at me. With irritated written all over my face, I turned around. I lost my breath at the site of the brand new metallic red Lamborghini sports car that pulled up. Hells yeah! The windows rolled down, and a gorgeous man revealed himself to me.

"Excuse," he said with an accent and confused look. "I'm new to L.A. and am needing to find Spencer John Helfen Fine Arts museum. Do you know where?" Hot car, cultured, and cute? Is this like, my lucky day or what? I walked up to the window, and leaned in, putting my new purchased double Ds in clear view.

"Yeah I know where that is," I said. "I'm actually going that way. It might be easier if I just show you. Do you mind?" He unlocked the vertical Lambo door and I pushed up. I buckled myself in as he gave the car a little gas. The engine's roar sent vibrations through the leather seats and up my skirt, sending a gentle tingle between my legs. Or, maybe it was the thought of his money that got me going. He floored the pedal and we were gone.

"I didn't catch your name," he said.

"Hilary. And you are?"

"Giuseppe." The look on my face must have suggested that was an odd name. He chuckled, and then explained, "It's Italian. I prefer Jesse." Italian car and man. I managed to kill two birds with one stone. How cliché?

"This is a hot ride you've got, Jesse," I flirted. I had to stroke this hotty's ego before I could stroke his wallet.

"Thank you. Want to go topless?" I lifted my shirt above my head and freed my perky set. The car jerked in response to Jesse being stunned.

"Whoa, I meant did you want me to drop the top? It's a convertible."

"Oh," I said with an innocently-guilty expression. "It must have been lost in translation."

"My English isn't that bad," he sarcastically replied while letting the top down. We merged onto the 101 freeway towards The Hills. There was still much to learn about Jesse the Italian stallion.

"You're quite a long way from home," I pried. "What brings you out here?"

"I'm doing some modeling. An up and coming artist sculpted me and they are showing it today at the gallery." Wow, he was the total, no, the ultimate package. With looks alone, he had the right equipment for modeling. His hair was deep brown and full like a 2-in-1 shampoo commercial. He could lie straight to your face and make you believe him with one glance into his hypnotizing green eyes. His teeth were perfectly aligned and white as if a latte had never touched his lips. He was wearing a black Giorgio Armani suit with a white summer sweater, and a silver link watch with the six and twelve replaced by diamonds.

"So what are you going to wear?" he asked as we strolled past the shops.

"Huh?"

"To the gallery. If you're going to be my date, you can't go like that."

"Oh my God, shut up. You want me to go with you?" I questioned as if I was oblivious to what was going on. In reality, I so had "Guido" eating pasta out of my hands at first sight. "I so can't be caught in this. Here, take the next exit so I can pick something out." Rodeo Drive, here I come!

"I think I see something," I said while peeking into an expensive boutique.

"Good," he said. "I'm gonna take a cig out here, but take this. Go crazy." I was sooo caught off guard with what came next. He reached into his pocket, opened up his wallet, and pulled out the limitless, baller status, American Express black card. Once my target revealed itself, my mission became clear. By nightfall, he'd feed me, fuck me, and I would leave him alone all before he even knew what hit him.

My eyes were immediately drawn to the seductive little dress in the back. The earth tone gown was fit for a woman on a mission like me. Without straps, it relied on cleave alone to keep it up. On each side there was a floor length split that stopped just below the imaginary thigh/ass line, giving that free-flowing fabric effect. It was perfect for an awards show, but a bit much for an art showing. But it was exactly what I needed to keep all eyes on me. I slipped into the piece, accessorized with gold pumps and earrings, paid the $4800 tab (with HIS card) and we were off to the show.

I opened the door, and struck a red carpet pose. "Well?" I asked seeking Jesse's approval. His bottom lip dropped, freeing the cigarette from his mouth. He was speechless.

He kissed his fingertips, clapped two quick claps, and shouted, "Magnifico." He lifted the passenger side door and helped me in. "We should eat."

"But what about the show?"

"I am the show. I know what I look like. They can wait. Now, where is the authentic Italian?" He was so fun and spontaneous. I loved it, and I loved being with him and his credit.

I felt like a sexy princess as Jesse courted me to dinner, sparing no expense. We easily must have spent what, like, $300? We began with the escargot alla Romana appetizer, and then moved onto our Caesar salads. For dinner, we chowed on market price Australian lobster tails and linguine paired with a bottle of white wine aged thirty years. We couldn't leave until he finished his tiramisu, but for the sake of my waistline I passed on dessert. As if this white girl would be caught with black girl hoochie mama thighs!

With the cash he was shelling out, I figured I was best to dump the whole card-swiping scheme and put "Operation: Trophy Wife" in play. In a typical dumb blonde move, I knocked my fork under the table. "I'm such a klutz," I said, playing in my hair. While underneath the table, I searched his thin suit pants for a raise. Bingo! Bulge on the left. I slid my hands across his inner thigh. He jumped from the tickle, but did not stop me. I inched closer and closer to the trouser bump. Just as I had opened my hand to pounce on him like a snake on a mouse, he grabbed my wrist.

"How inappropriate," he whispered under the table. "Tasteless, and very inappropriate. This is fine dining, yet you behave like this was fast food." How humiliating? I pulled out all the stops, and he totally brushed me off. Like, WTF? "I have to go to the bathroom," he said, still disgusted with me. Just pay for dinner, and try to behave while I'm gone." He handed me his card and excused himself from the table in an angry fashion.

The after dinner car ride was filled with awkward silence. That little stunt at the restaurant may have cost me my chance at joining the Black Card Wives Club. I had just about given up hope until he said, "I'm kind of tired. I hope you don't mind checking into a suite for the evening." I laid my head on his shoulder to show I was sooo with that idea. "I'll take you home tomorrow morning."

He placed his hand on the chromed out clutch, and I placed my hand on top of his. I caressed his hand as his hair massaged my palm. I scooted my hand onto his knee and began a second attempt up his slacks. Maybe he just wasn't into PDA, but there wasn't a man alive who could resist one of my patented highway handjobs. I slithered to his zipper, only to get blocked again.

"This may be hard for you," he began, "but would it kill you to be a fucking lady?" Blown off again! Like a pouting child, I threw myself hard into the passenger side door. He didn't want it in public, nor in private. I was starting to think the rumors about Italians weren't ringing true for Jesse. Big car, big money, maybe he was compensating. I guess that's what they mean by "Little Italy".

While he waited on the hotel valet, I checked us into a suite in West Hollywood. Still ever-so pissed, I entered the elevator with crossed arms. My attitude calmed down once I swiped the key card and lost my breath at the sight of the glam style room: chocolate plush carpet, mahogany walls, copper columns, tan suede sofas, a bronze bedroom set, and a marble electric fireplace. The ceiling-to-floor windows gave a clear view of the Hollywood sign. I kissed Jesse on the cheek, and he smirked. I knew no man could resist me for long.

We walked inside as he held me by the waist. He opened the mini bar and pulled out a whiskey miniature. "You will take the couch," he said between sips, "and I'll wake you in the morning, no?" he asked. That did it!

"No, Guiseppe!" I was heated. "I will not take the couch. What is wrong with you? I have been like throwing myself onto you all day and not once have you returned the favor. I don't do this for just anybody, and I totally don't do couches. You should be flattered. Can't you see I love you?" I poured it on pretty thick. I hope the cameras were catching this one 'cus this was my acting debut.

"You love me?" he asked with his thick foreign accent. "If this is true, then come. We shall make love." He walked into the unlit bedroom and left the door open. Like a true cheerleader, I jumped up at the chance to finally have my way with him.

I walked inside the dark room, hoping to find him on the bed. I called out, "Jesse? Jesse?" but there was no response. He must have been hiding. Suddenly, the door slammed behind me.

"Boo!" yelled out a shirtless Jesse with ripped abs and rock hard chest.

"Oh, you scared me." Glad the lights were off because I was totally rolling my eyes at his corniness. He ran his fingers through my hair, and then grabbed hold of my gown's zipper. He gingerly unzipped me, causing my dress to split like a banana peel. Aggressively, he spun me around. We awkwardly held each other eyes for a moment, then kissed wildly like a scene from a movie. I ran my fingers across his

12-pack as he explored my lower back and hips. *"Yuck, my hips are so fat. I knew I should have stuck with the salad. Focus Hil!"* Once I reached his happy trail, I undid his belt, unfastened his pants, and he stepped out of them. Looks like Italy wasn't so little after all.

I jumped into Jesse's arms and wrapped my legs around his waist. He ferried me to the bed and twisted me so that I was upside-down. He buried his face deep into my walls, slurping like he had a thick smoothie with a broken straw. "Suck!" he yelled in the heat of the moment. This was sooo against the rules on the first date, but I had to give a little to gain a lot! Hesitantly, I inhaled the unbelievably hairy Peter. I never understood what was the deal was with foreigners and hair. Was it like a rite of passage or something?

Anyway, I spit him out when I had finally withstood as much as I could. "Don't you wanna save some for the real thing?" I said seductively. With no hesitation, Jesse lowered my legs and climbed on top, giving it to me like he was possessed. It was as if he'd heard me talking about his package and now had something to prove.

"Grab the bedposts," he whispered forcefully. I was kinda scared in a turned on kinda way. With my legs still wrapped around Jesse, he stood up, and continued to pound away at me in mid-air.

"Oh, right there Jesse. Yeah, you take that cunt." No, it wasn't acting. Jesse was actually giving me some enjoyment. It was almost too bad that I'd only be dating him for money.

"They're almost here," he said, referencing his "soldiers". He began to slow down, but the ride wasn't over yet for me.

"Don't slow down! Keep going."

"No, they're almost here." He pulled out in the middle of a steamy session and looked out of the window in a panicking manner.

"If you're trying to be funny this is so not cools."

"We must leave."

"What? Why? I don't understand."

"No time for that. We must leave!"

"Not until you tell me what's going on here." Jesse collected his clothes and began dressing. He was breathing heavily as he redressed himself hurriedly, putting his briefs on backwards. Suddenly I could hear police sirens approaching our hotel. I hoped there was no connection.

"I'm not a model," he started. "There was no art show and I'm not rich."

My mouth dropped at the sound of his confession. "What?" I asked in total shock. "But what about the car? What about the fancy authentic restaurant?" And most importantly, "What about that credit card?"

"The car: rented. The credit card: stolen. And my accent: fake. I'm not Guiseppe from Italy." His Italian accent was replaced by a country one, as he revealed, "I'm really Jeff from Nashville."

"You're like, some sick perv. You used me for sex! Ugh! I'm like, sooo heated!"

"Who used who?" he countered. "I knew from the start you only wanted me for the money you thought I had. And don't flatter yourself. Maybe if you were more selective over who you fuck it wouldn't have felt like I was throwing a flashlight down a mine shaft!"

"Eh, the nerve. How dare you? That is so not cools! I should rat your ass out."

"Go head," he dared. "You're the one who made all the purchases. YOU paid for the dress. YOU were at the table when the waiter picked up the bill. YOU were the one who booked the room. And it was all on stolen plastic." That little hick totally set me up. With nothing left to do, I began to cry.

"Well what am I supposed to do?" I asked, like, all frantic or whatever.

"The same as me," he replied. "Get out of here as fast as you can!" He opened a window and climbed over the balcony rails. The police cars had begun to pull up to the building. It would be only a matter of minutes before they traced the stolen credit card to our room. In a hurry, I threw on a hotel robe, grabbed my purse and shades, and dashed out of the room. The stairs would be a dead giveaway, and the elevator wasn't any better. I ran to the end of the hallway, and there was my escape: the janitor's trash chute.

"Gross," I thought out loud. Suddenly, the elevator bell rang, and the hall was filled with the sound of police radios. Terrified, I opened the chute, jumped in head first, and plunged down twenty floors into a large garbage can. Yuck!

After my quick, life-threatening escape from the law, all I could think of was a hot shower. I was a crook, and even worse, I had to leave my dress behind. Disappointed, I hopped out of the trash and began my long walk home smelling like rotten fruit and bad Chinese food. Let's see: if it would normally take nine minutes by Porsche to get home from here, then walking I should get there in . . . uh . . . damn! I never could do those "If a train leaves at this time . . ." math problems.

It was three in the morning. My feet were blistering in these heels, I was naked under this robe, and other than dinner and good sex, I came home with nothing. It was like a real relationship. I had just reached the Beverly Hills sign when a car pulled up beside me. As fate would have it, it was the same guy with the BMW from earlier.

"Looks like you've had a rough night," he said sarcastically.

"I'm not a hooker," I snapped back.

"Easy, easy. I just remembered you from earlier. You look a lot better in the sunlight." He thought he was sooo freakin' funny. "Granted it's Beverly Hills, you really shouldn't be out this late. Do you wanna rethink that ride home?" I was cold, exhausted, and reeked of garbage scum. My hair was tangled and had a cheesy smell. My tears had smeared my make-up across my face like a clown. I had hit rock bottom.

"Awww, thank you," I said cheerfully, "but do you mind following me while I walk the rest of the way home instead? It's not too much further." With a confused look on his face, he nodded yes. Was it really that strange of a request? If you thought this was the time to swallow pride, think again. When you settle for less, you become less. And like I said, even on my worst day, you wouldn't catch me riding in that car!

I is for Isaiah

Let's start with a riddle. The first clue: I'm "cooked", but not eaten. Clue # 2: You can hold me, but don't get too comfortable. The third and final clue: Although I may kick, I'll never crawl. Give up? I understand. My mommy did, too.

I wish I had one of those "cutesy wootsy" delivery stories for you, but I don't. Two years ago I was chemically aborted at the request of a woman who was more of a child than a parent. Weighing only 1 pound, 10 ounces, I was vacuumed out fighting for life, gasping to control the flow of air that was forcing its way into my underdeveloped lungs. If only I knew how to shut my veined lids to keep the bright light out of my delicate eyes. It was so cold, and the white gel that once provided me warmth chilled to room temperature. Suddenly, a man in a light blue scrub suit placed me in the palm of his hand, cut the umbilical cord, and watched me give into the poison. I never had a chance to cry. I lay there lifeless. As I died off with open eyes, I watched "mommy" leave out as if it were just another day in the life . . .

Miraculously, I began to breathe again, but it wasn't like the tortured breaths I had experienced before. I was in full control of the air. Then, I noticed my mind was full of knowledge well beyond my brief existence. I brought my hands (complete with all ten fingers) up to my face, and wiped my eyes. I opened them, realizing I could control my blinking as well. I looked around and observed I was surrounded with foamy white puffs of air and magnificent golden blasts that lit everything around me. It was unlike anything my young eyes had ever seen. I picked myself up, and wobbly stood tall. This was the first time I had the opportunity to use my legs. "*Where am I?*" I thought out loud. And where was my mommy? Why did she leave me here alone? Why did she leave me to die?

I walked around the paved streets looking for any other survivors. There were large palaces created out of gold, but still no signs of life. Just then, a red dodge ball tumbled down the golden street in my direction. "Hey, can you bring the ball back?" a soft, child voiced asked. I had no idea where I was, but somehow knew exactly where to return the ball. I could hear the children laughing and playing. I took off running in excitement, ready to meet others just like me. I ran through communities full of golden houses, crossed through sunbeams, and into a field of clouds where several children were anxiously awaiting my arrival.

"Thank you for bringing the ball back," the little child from before said joyfully. He expanded his wings, creating a beautiful fluorescent beam of light. As much as I wanted to gaze at the glow, my eyes were still sensitive to such intense stimulation. He flew over to retrieve the ball.

"Where am I? How? How did you get those?" I asked in reference to his wings.

He laughed. "If you don't know where you are by now, you won't be getting your wings for quite some time. My name is Dylan. What's your name?"

I looked at the miniature hospital bracelet still wrapped around my wrist and replied, "Isaiah, I guess."

"Come with me. I'll show you around." After touring the endless boundaries of Heaven, as Dylan called it, he brought me to the field where the rest of the kids were gathered. Heaven was full of children whom had either been aborted like me, hit by drunk drivers, died suddenly as infants, and plenty other reasons. However, there was one noticeable difference between them and me.

"Dylan, why does everyone have wings except for me?" I asked.

"We have been here long enough to forgive those who have put us here," he explained. "Your heart is still full of anger, especially towards your mother. Once you learn to forgive, your wings will begin to grow." It wasn't just my mother that I was angry at; it was my father, my family, the doctor, and anyone else who had a hand in my death. As mad as I was, my wings would be a long ways away. My moment to ponder was interrupted suddenly by a loud trumpet.

"What's going on?" I questioned.

"We're making a trip down to Earth," he said. "We have a responsibility to guard those that pray for guidance and protection." Finally, an opportunity to confront those who sent me here. While they were serving up blessings, I planned on dishing out revenge! I was boiling mad, yet afraid of how I would handle myself once I was in their presence.

"Isaiah, my son, you are not quite ready to go back," a deep voice echoed from a distance. I was fear-stricken by the sound of the man calling me. "Do not be afraid of your Father," he said calmly.

"*Father?*" I thought to myself. "My dad is here?" I asked Dylan. He shrugged his shoulders with a grin, implying that I see for myself. As the other angels, young and old, descended towards their assigned beings, I ran through the streets searching for the man who claimed to be my father. If he was here, he'd be sorry he was once I met up with him.

I turned the corner and feasted my sight upon the biggest mansion thus far. It was all white with four giant columns spiraled with thin golden stripes. In the center of the roof and between the two center columns sat a cross encircled by beautiful stained glass. The tall staircase was carved out of stone, and without wings, I had no choice but to climb each one.

"*997, 998, 999, 1000 steps,*" I thought to myself. If this was paradise where was the easy way up? Before I was able to knock, the doors slowly opened, releasing gusty winds and a light brighter than the wings of the angels.

"Enter, Isaiah." I was fearful. His voice was so deep, but gentle. I was afraid to step into the unknown, yet at the same time I couldn't resist. The doors closed and the lights dimmed. The inside was even more decorative than the outside. I was standing on a thin strip of red carpet that appeared to hold itself in place without a floor underneath. There were choirs on my left and right, singing praises of some man named Jesus. He must have been pretty popular up here. I shrugged my shoulders and continued on.

At the top of a much shorter flight of stairs was a man. Even as I looked at him, He was indescribable. "Welcome, my child" He said.

"Are you my father?" I asked with uncertainty.

"I am everyone's Father," He answered. "I created you, everyone here, everything you see, and everyone on Earth. I am almighty. I know all and see all." I was amazed at this man's power, but I was angry for what this meant.

"If you know so much, why did you let my mother kill me?" I yelled while crying. "Why did you let her do this?"

"People tend not to question me," He said with a chuckle, "but I'll let this pass since you're the new guy." He grabbed my hand and escorted me through the home. "You are furious. You have let your anger block what good has become of this situation." I was puzzled as to how there was any good in being aborted. "Do you see the people down there?" He pointed to a zoomed in video of Earth. "The people down there must make the choice to honor me. You died before you were able to stray from the right path."

"So?"

"The Earth has a saying that 'God watches out for babies and fools.' Consider yourself watched out for." God laughed a mighty laugh.

"What makes this place so great? I'm sure Earth is just the same, but I have parents!" I answered sarcastically.

"Count your blessings, Isaiah. You don't want to be down there. And you certainly don't want to spend even a second in the other place you could have ended up." I was so angry, but couldn't stop the tears from flowing.

"There is a purpose for everything," He told me. "You may not understand now, but one day you will. If you can learn to forgive you will see that there is a much deeper purpose for your short existence." As He consoled me, I silently submitted to His demands.

I spent the next four years crying, learning, and forgiving. Dylan had become my mentor and friend, teaching me the rules of "angelhood". As my wisdom grew, so did my wings. One random day, as I meditated in prayer, the trumpets sounded for all guardians to descend to Earth.

"You're up, Isaiah" Dylan informed me. I was shocked. I had seen this done day-after-day, but finally my turn had come. "Your first trip is always the hardest. Just know it gets easier after this one."

Dylan handed me a list of names that I was expected to visit by the day's end. The excitement left when I viewed the three names. I had watched these people for years, and although they would not be able to see me, I would be staring them in their faces. They were Julian Davis, and Evelyn and Sylvia Goode, also known as my birth dad, grandmother, and birth mother.

"I can't," I said to Dylan, tossing the list out of my sight.

"We've all been where you are," he said. "You cannot fully heal until you've confronted those who have loved or hurt you most." He picked up the list and placed it in my chest. It was irony at its best: for the past six years I did nothing but talk about visiting my family, and now that the day had finally come it was too soon. Without enthusiasm, I began my trip towards Earth, which was much quicker than expected.

The list started with paying a visit to Nana Evelyn. She lived in one of the two-story brick homes in a quiet Greensboro, North Carolina community. Underneath her kitchen windows was a row of bushes with azaleas planted in front. On each side of the walkway were five bulbs that lit the path to her front door. I floated over her roof for a short time, then phased inside.

My nose was instantly hit with a sweet smell once I entered her home. There were fresh baked cinnamon rolls on the counter and another batch cooking in the oven. Hmm, I wonder will she take these out before they are done like my mother did to me.

"Yeah, girl," I heard someone saying. That must be her! I turned to hide, but then remembered that she wouldn't be able to see me. She turned the corner and there stood my Nana. Grandma was a full-figured woman but looked like on a good day, she would "hurt 'em". Today, she was dressed in a green silk pajama set, holding the phone to her ear while mixing up more goodies. Her hair was tied up in a cheetah print scarf that was stained from her black dye. I listened in as she continued the conversation with her deafening voice.

"Yeah, so you know the new girl, Amanda, right? White girl? Just got promoted? Yeah, her. She gon' tell me that I'm taking too long to do what them new folks are doing. So I told her I'm two years from retiring, I'm doing the best I can, and if that ain't good enough then tough. They not finna work me to death in there, OK?" Her laughter and happiness brought tears to my eyes. I placed my hand on her forehead and went in for a deeper look.

Nana's mind was full of memories from being raised in the Civil Rights era, to the assassination of Dr. King, to marriage, to having Sylvia, my so-called mommy, and more. I flipped through and saw a memory tucked away of her and mommy talking days before I was aborted. She was 47 then, while mommy was 19.

"Are you sure you want to do this so late in the pregnancy?" Nana asked.

"Oh my God, Ma. Can you just drop it? It's my choice. I just can't live with this." Sylvia got off the couch and walked to the front door. "For once could you just be a mother?" She slammed the door, while Evelyn lay there stunned in disappointment.

"At least Nana wanted me," I thought to myself. I floated out of her memory and was ready to meet my father. I looked at Nana on my way out. She had a hand over her heart a smile on her face, and shed a single tear. She knew that day she had been touched by her grandbaby.

Following my brief visit with warm-souled Evelyn was an appointment with Julian, I mean, Dad. He was not at his home, nor his job, but a bar rather. A patron of the tavern opened the door and I ran in before it closed. The bar was dark and a cloud of cigarette smoke hovered between the ceiling lights. The only two pool tables were scuffed and had rings on the wood finish from guests who forgot to use coasters. Behind the counter was an older Black man who looked as if he didn't have much time left to put in (and I don't mean at this "fine" establishment).

"Another shot of 1800, Julian?" the old man asked to a much younger man. I looked down the bar counter and laid eyes upon a man drowning his pain. It was my father, up close and personal! Julian was a 32 year-old Black man that made a living as a junior high school science teacher. He was average height, dark-skinned, and wore his hair low with waves. His eyes were brown, but hidden in red due to the smoke. His facial hair was low, but unkempt. He had a frown as long as Nana's smile was when I left her. He raised his glass, gulped the tequila shot, and raised his finger for another round. No wonder Sylvia left him. I was hesitant to journey through his mind. Reluctantly, I pressed on his head and entered.

It was a challenge to find any memories of me. His head was cloudy and full of pain that seemed to block out any good times before he hit rock bottom. Navigating through his hundreds of intoxicated moments and weekends spent in jail for countless DWIs, there was a memory of him teaching a class on reproduction six years ago that surfaced.

"The second trimester is usually what most people look forward to," he explained. "This is when you'll be able to determine the sex of the baby. You can also feel the baby move and kick around in there."

"Did you find out what kind of baby you are having?" asked one teenage female student. The class looked on, interested to hear.

"Well, we've decided to wait until it's here to find out. But I'm shooting for a boy." The fresh girls smiled as he showed his excitement about his baby. "Yup, Isaiah Davis."

"Aww, you have a name for him." He smiled, forcing his dimples to appear.

"Mr. Davis is soft," one of the boys yelled, causing a roar of laughter to spread the students.

"Alright, alright, let's get back to work."

It was weird; if he wanted me here, then why wasn't I? He wasn't young and dumb, nor was he married trying to hide an outside pregnancy. On my way out I stumbled onto a memory of him and Sylvia arguing.

"This wasn't your decision to make," she yelled.

"We were in this together," he yelled back. "It's just as much my decision as it was yours. You took my son from me!"

"592 West Avenue, Suite 3100. You want your son? Go check the dumpster behind the building!" She hung up. He yanked the phone out of the socket and chucked it across the room. Dad was furious! Breathing heavily, he trekked the perimeter of his living room before finally falling flat and crying.

I left Daddy's mind, gave him a hug and whispered, "I forgive you," and flew onto my last stop. I looked back and saw the old bartender coming Julian's way.

"Top you off?" he asked.

He wiped his scruffy beard, looked at himself and his surroundings, and then replied, "Nah, I'm done. And you can close my tab; I won't be back." He paid his bill and left with the same smile he had that day when he discussed me with the class.

All these years I blamed my dad when in fact, he was not the culprit. His painful past brought back the resentment I had towards Sylvia. If it wasn't for these wings, I'd let you know how I really felt! Just this once I wish I could set off a stroke while in her head.

It was getting late, and thankfully Sylvia was the last stop on my list. This trip down "Memory Lane" was draining, physically and emotionally. I landed in a classroom full of young girls, some quiet, some loud and hood. I looked around for the loudest, trashiest girl whom was sure to be my mother. Just then, a young, beautiful, and well-dressed woman entered the room wearing a gray skirt suit and pink blouse that perfectly matched her golden apple complexion.

"Ok ladies, let's settle down," she said while strutting in her black heels to a desk to place her purse. "We have an interesting topic that's sure to spark some conversation."

"What we talkin' bout tonight, Ms. Goode?" Goode? As in, Sylvia Goode? I couldn't believe this classy woman that stood before these girls as a role model was my mother.

"Tonight's Share Session is on abortion."

"Why are you giving this lesson, Ms. Goode?" another one of the girls asked. "Aren't you too snooty for this?"

"Actually, I volunteered to host this session." Yeah she was perfect, alright. Perfect for teaching what not to do. I grabbed a chair and listened to what she had to say. Looks like I would be able to hear her memories without delving into her mind.

"I got pregnant when I was 20 by a man that was six years older than me," she started. "He was educated, had a job, and despite the age difference my mother loved him. When I told him I was pregnant, he was overjoyed."

"So it sounds all good," another girl said while sucking her teeth. "Shoot, I wish I had a man like that when I got pregnant."

"Looking back, it was good," she continued. "But back then it was all about me. My boyfriend and I had been arguing because he had reached a point in his life where he welcomed the idea of children. But I was still young and enjoying college life. It ended with him storming off to party with his boys all night. I called and called, but he ignored my calls. So, to get even with him, I hung out with my ex-boyfriend.

"He was high when I showed up, but that didn't bother me back then. We talked, watched a movie, and just chilled. It felt good just to have a back-up shoulder to lean on. When I got ready to leave, he grabbed my arm and playfully begged me to stay. I laughed and told him it was getting late. His playful mood turned into aggression. The more I fought, the more forceful he was. Finally, he threw me on the couch and tore off my sweats. I yelled and fought until he suffocated me under a pillow.

"I went home full of guilt, wondering had I brought this on myself. It was my fault I went over there, and it was my fault I laughed and giggled off his advances. I decided to keep quiet and let it eventually go away on its own.

Night after night for two weeks, I tossed and turned. I became reclusive, backing away from my friends and my boyfriend. Finally, I took a home pregnancy kit, which came up positive. I threw the test in the bottom of the trash can and went to school. This would take more time to handle than I had to give.

"When I got home my mother and my boyfriend were sitting in the living room, trying to hold back smiles. Mom ran to me excited, expressing I was a little young, but she was excited nonetheless. She had found the test kit when she emptied the garbage that day. There was a slim chance that I was carrying my boyfriend's child, or that I could have gotten pregnant by my ex. Instead of telling them what happened, I panicked and played into their assumption. I figured this was a secret that I would take to my grave.

"For six months I let my family and friends go on believing it was his. They were stocking up on baby clothes, diapers, and planning the shower. One day, when Mom walked in with a fancy stroller, I broke down and told her what happened. She held me, and then assured me that it was not my fault. I told her how I was battling to keep it a secret, or if there was a secret to keep at all. She had hoped I would keep it, but respected whatever choice I made. I couldn't keep something so important from him, nor could I raise my child with a cloud hanging over my head. So, two weeks later, twenty-four weeks into the pregnancy, I had my abortion. I was so angry with myself, I couldn't even look at the baby. I jumped up as soon as it was over, ran out of the office, and knew that was a place I would never see again."

The girls, even the "ghetto" ones sniffled and wiped their faces. Her story was as eye-opening for them as it was for me. I was at a loss for words. I had spent six years heated, walking everywhere because my temper prohibited me from growing wings. Now, I had discovered that she wasn't just some pro-ho as I once assumed, she had a legitimate reason. I wish she had kept me, because I did turn out to be Julian's son, but my heart felt for her. I felt comfortable calling her Mom.

"I shared this with you girls not because I'm anti-abortion. I'm still very pro-choice. I just wanted you all to make sure if you were ever in this situation to think it through. I had a loving boyfriend, supportive mother and family, and had I gone full-term I'm sure now that I would have made a great mother."

"So you think I should keep my baby?" asked one noticeably pregnant teen.

"I don't know your situation sista," Mom continued, "so I can't tell you what's right for you. But I know if I could do it again, I'd be checking my son's homework right now. It may seem overwhelming now, but if you have a strong support system like I did, I would rethink it."

"Do you think your baby is in Heaven and waiting for you?" asked one teenage girl, who cried harder than the others. She, too, had just undergone an abortion. Mom looked at the window and noticed a vibrant rainbow in the sky. It was a peace symbol left as I floated back home to show all was truly forgiven.

Though my life was short, there was purpose to my existence. If I were born, Mom would have been at parent-teacher conferences, soccer games and karate matches instead of being able to help these young women. My life gave her an experience that would allow countless others to think before they acted. Now, I understood what He meant by "everything happens for a reason".

J is for Janice

I still remember that frigid December morning when our family got the devastating call. I was in the dining room setting the table, while Mama whipped up cheese eggs, sausage links, grits, and a batch of her famous vanilla battered French toast. Suddenly, the phone rang, changing our happy home forever. Mama answered, listened, and then burst into a screaming fit of tears. If you lived a life as rough as my Daddy did, death should come as no surprise, but it did.

With Daddy suddenly leaving us when I was only twelve, I lost my best friend, my man model, my king, and my ability to get everything that I could possibly want. I also lost my innocence, and was forced to grow up to compete with the fast girls. My name is Janice and I was the youngest of Mama and Daddy's four girls. There was Jada, Jade, Jocelyn and me. We all had "J" names like Daddy—ain't that some ghetto bullshit? With my honey pecan skin, shoulder length dark brown hair, hazel eyes and a body to die for (no pun intended), I felt that I was the prettiest of the girls and that I deserved to be treated like the princess that I was. Oh Daddy made such a fuss over me that sometimes even I grew sick of hearing of my greatness.

To me, twelve was the age that my mind, body and soul started to become interested in what boys could do to me and for me. Oh, don't act like twelve is too young to "have such thoughts" cus it ain't, and it wasn't. I was always searching for some boy, and eventually, for some man, to fulfill my purpose and to provide for me the same comforts like my daddy did. I floated from man to man, aimlessly like a piece of tissue paper dropped off the top of the Empire State Building. I made a home wherever, or on whomever, I landed.

Talk about consequences for your actions. My consequences were my two babies by two different daddies by age 22. I guess two is my lucky number, huh? But that's alright, cus someday, somebody is going to realize how fine I am and they will feel jackpot lucky that they are with me, Dayvita and Daqua'n (that's D-A-Q-U-A-wit' a comma in the air-N).

Finally, when no more shit could have possibly hit the fan, I met Dave. On a whim, I asked Jada, Jade and Jocelyn to do happy hour after work when I was in serious need of a girl's night. Jocelyn spotted a guy watching me from the bar. "Go check him out," she said. He was actually cute: designer black suit, brown shirt minus the tie, and accessorized with what appeared to be a Kenneth Cole watch and a pair of bangin' shoes. Oh, and his face and body weren't bad either. Still, I was in my feelings from my last relationship, so I didn't entertain the idea.

"I'm just here to hang with the girls," I told the ladies. Aside from that, he was light, and I had had enough experience dating light-skinned men to know that never in a million years would I ever go back to those high yellow, overly cocky, arrogant, self-centered, better than you, rules don't apply to me, "God's gift to women", pink dick niggas. Before I had a chance to avoid him, he came up to our booth.

"Good evening, ladies," he started, "I couldn't help but notice your beautiful friend here. Do you mind if I steal her away and get to know her?" I rolled my eyes flirtatiously.

"All this 'getting to know me' and you didn't offer to buy me a drink?"

"Don't you think you're worth more than a drink?" he bounced back.

"Ok, buy me two then, shit." He laughed, but I was serious. He offered to spend money on me like he "knew me" knew me, so why not let him? To patronize me, he bought the two drinks and a round for my sisters. Jade scooted out the booth so I could join Dave at the bar.

The more we talked, the more of a connection we established. No matter how cool I tried to play, it was lust at first sight. Just thinking about what he could do to me made me moist: you know, take me out to dinner, buy me brands that people like you would put on layaway for months, and let me drive the sedan while he pushed the sports car. As our conversation continued, we learned that we worked in the same building, but on different floors, and he was willing to date a woman with two kids and baby daddy drama out the ass. I gave him my number, and he called the next day. He didn't have time for those little nigga games, calling me a week later trying to not come off "pressed."

After three months, I gave Dave the pleasure of taking me, Dayvita, Daqua'n, and Mama to the pancake house. Instead, he took us to some uppity brunch spot. It wasn't all that. I mean, they didn't even have strawberry syrup and whipped cream for my pancakes. And the waitress looked like she never heard of nobody asking for ketchup for their eggs. Anyway, Mama really liked him. He was different than the usual men I brought home, if I brought them home at all. I could see Mama's soul smiling as he talked about earning his MBA, being a section chief for a federal government agency, and being more interested in settling down than shacking up. Every time he mentioned one of Mama's key words, she nudged me under the table like, "Don't fuck this up!"

Weeks later, I still had Dave's nose wide open. He would leave me his credit card just in case I needed to pick up something for the kids. So, I treated myself to a mani/pedi, hair appointment, and a mini shopping spree. I'm sure my kids wanted me looking right. He ain't even trip when he found out about the charges.

Let's see, Mama approved: √. Good with kids: √. Balling: √√! He was the only man that knew I was the shit, put up with my shit, and would come back for more of my shit. It seemed perfect, so where did it all go wrong?

Now months later I'm sitting out here in my hot ass car. It's egg-frying-on-the-sidewalk kinda hot out here. Come on Dave, pick up the phone. Consequences, yeah I got some consequences for this bastard—some more consequences that is. I'm gonna get this nigga one way or another. I thought we were a fuck away from happily ever after, but I found out he's dating a 30-something white chick that works in our building. Guess it was just one big happy family, except I didn't get the memo!

When I found out about the heffa, Dave said, "She's more mature than you, she doesn't have any kids and she wants more than Prada tops, Gucci shades, and Dolce & Gabbana bags out of life. She's got more in common with me." When did he realize all of this commonness, when he was putting it in, or pulling it out of me every night for the past six months? But today, no, no, no. Not anymore. I thought about it for all of two days and Janice is not having it.

The closer I got to his office, the more my mind was flooded with what if's. *"Come on, Janice,"* I said in a self-coaching manner, *"keep it together."*

As the tears and mascara streamed down my face, I rationalized that public humiliation has got to be dealt with publicly. I mean, how many other people knew about this? How many people just continued to speak to me and snicker behind my back while keeping Dave's dirty little secret? But I got something for that ass cus if my Uzi don't kill him, then my "dirty little secret" would! I could give a fuck and half what you think about me, but it's about respect and I'm left with no option.

I tried to talk to him on more than one occasion, but he was always unable to come to my house. He said he had to work late on a "big project" and he would see me later in the week. Yeah, he had a big project alright. His project weighs about 240lbs, is a white bitch, and later in the week never came.

It's going on 12:30. Dave's lunchtime. I can just picture that nigga swiveling around in his big black Italian leather chair behind his cherry wood desk to face the afternoon sun. He basks for a moment in the warmth of the blinding rays. Then, as Miss White Bitch soothes his cock (as they call it) under the desk, his thoughts are invaded by memories of us last night, listening to, dancing to, and making love to Maxwell's "A Woman's Work". How could Dave trade my love for that trash? I don't mean to brag, but Janice screws a brother like it's a job and she's up for a promotion! OK?! I even used to let that nigga drill me anyway he wanted: missionary, from the back, pretzel-style, anally, and beyond. He thought it was sexy I could take the pain. It hurt like hell, but hey, if he didn't go deep he'd never catch what I was pitching, right?

I pulled into the parking lot and tried calling Dave one more time. If he knows what's best he'll answer that phone before I have to come all up in and through there. Hmph, what?! At last, he picked up.

"Hey Janice," he said innocently.

"Hey? Where have you been? I called you five times."

"Baby, you know I've been busy with that big project." Here he goes again with the bullshit.

"Well, we need to talk so meet me in the parking lot. I know you don't want me to come up in there!"

"You read my mind," he said. "I was gonna come past your place tonight. I been doing you wrong lately. I'm ready to put that mess behind me and move forward." He spoke like it was his decision if we moved on or not. It would take a lot more than a *"Baby you're right"* to get back tight with Janice!

When he hung up, I saw him peek out the window from his office blinds. I flashed the high beams so he knew exactly where I was. As the glass doors swung open releasing Dave from the building, I reached in the glove compartment for my piece. This thing had become real.

As he lightly stepped out on the parking lot like he was on "Cloud Nine", I went into panic mode. Damn, what's going to happen to my kids if I do this? What's going to happen to my Mama? What about all my clothes and stuff? I never got to wear those earrings. Hold up, isn't this payday Friday? If he dies, who pays the rent? I quickly hid the Uzi under my seat, spruced up my bangs, and threw a smile on my face. *Honk, honk.* "Hey, over here, baby. Want to go to lunch?"

As much as I wanted him dead, I needed Dave's supervisor status income. If I couldn't kill him the quick and easy way, I would settle for his slow and painful death by my HIV. Oh well, he can't say I never gave him nothing.

K is for Kerrington (Part I of III)

"Dearest Kerry,

How have you been? If my memory is right your college graduation should be coming up next year. Are you ready? I know you'll be fine. You always were the smart one. I am so proud of you. I know it seems like forever since my last note, let alone our last conversation. It took me awhile to finish this one. Half the time I was hiding it so "you know who" wouldn't tear it up again, and the other half I was scared to tell you the truth. The last time I saw you face-to-face I felt uncomfortable, but not in a bad way. I realized that I had feelings for you that were deeper than a best friend and it terrified me to think of you in that way. I have known you for years, but I had that first date feeling in my stomach. You've been there when I was going through all of Omar's bull, through all of the exes, and I'm beginning to realize you were the only man who has treated me right. I remember you saying you would be right there waiting whenever I figured I deserved better. So, I told myself that when I got the nerve to get on my feet and move out of this situation, I would tell you how I feel.

Here's where the fear kicks in. I was ready to break free, Kerry, I really was, but O started complaining about me not wanting to give him any. So, just to shut him up, I did. I didn't even enjoy it, but I was tired of the fighting. That one slip up triggered all these old feelings and got me reconsidering getting back with him. It's like I know he's bad for me, but I can't move past how much history we have. Now you know why I was avoiding you so long. I couldn't deal with hurting you after we made plans to see how our friendship would be on the next level. I'm sorry if I hurt your feelings, but maybe this was a sign in some weird way.

You're the only guy that's never done me wrong. I feel like I can share anything with you and be myself without ever wondering what you'll think of me. I would never want to give that up for a relationship, Kerrington. You're a good guy and I know you'll be a great man. You don't need to waste your love on someone STUCK in drama like me. I love you, and always will and hope that you understand.

Love always,
Tierra

Xoxo"

I hadn't spoken to TiTi since she sent that letter, so you can imagine how surprised I was when her little sister, Janelle, decided to give me a ring tonight out the blue. "What's goin' on, baby girl?"

"Hey, Kerry," she said. "I didn't think you would pick up the phone."

"I always have time for your calls. What's up?"

"Nothing, just called to say congratulations on graduating."

"Thanks," I said sarcastically, "you're only what, about five years too late?" Janelle was up to something. "What did you really call about Janelle?"

"If you must know," she said with a playful attitude. I could picture her eyes rolling through the phone. "Tierra's birthday is tomorrow and . . ."

"Good talking to you," I interrupted. "Take care of yourself."

"Kerry, both of yal need to stop faking!" she yelled. "You know you miss her. If she ain't mean so much to you, you wouldn't be trying so hard to forget her." There was dead silence on my end while Janelle finished chewing me out. What bothered me most was some of that was true. Not a day in the last five years went by without me wondering about "my girl". Who was she dating and was he treating her right? Did she get her shit back on track?

With a deep exhale into my cell phone, I grumbled, "What do you want me to do, Janelle?"

"Just show up in your best chill club attire," she said. "TiTi thinks we're going to a lounge for her birthday. It's the only way her nigga would let her out. Once she meets over at my place, you'll be here to surprise her." It reminded me of old times: sneaking behind some dude's back to spend time with a friend. "Now I don't do this often," she added, "but she deserves a good night with an old friend. I'll set the place up real 'grown n' sexy' like, cook dinner, and leave you two alone for a couple hours."

It sounded like a gift that could be a pleasant birthday shock, or a night of never-ending silence. We hadn't spoken in so long, I was afraid there may be nothing left to say. For Tierra though, I would take that chance. "I'll be there," I agreed. "Text me the time and your address."

"Thank you, Kerry," said Janelle in a baby voice. "I knew I'd have the best gift for her." She was really playing me up, but I liked it.

I tossed and turned in bed all night thinking about this birthday surprise. Would she be as happy as Janelle and I both thought? It felt like I was waiting on the other side of Mother Love's door. Then I remembered that I wasn't the one needing forgiveness. She was the one who bailed on me! Then I flipped back to how I could never be mad at Tierra. I felt like a straight bitch the way emotions were going back-n-forth.

Eight sleepless hours later, tomorrow became today. I hit the gym to work off some of the tension, and to get one more workout in before our reunion. I wasn't the same Kerrington that TiTi remembered before I went to college. Back then, with my scrawny legs, bird chest, and glasses big enough to be the windshield on a tractor-trailer, I could have easily been mistaken for Urkel's stunt double back in the day. Who knew that majoring in athletic training would do me some good?

By the end of my freshman year, I had ditched the glasses, lost the braces, and filled into my basketball player-like stature, going from a puny 160 pounds to a fitting 210. Those college girls went crazy for us almond colored niggas with brown eyes and perfect teeth.

It was eight o'clock, just an hour before I was to arrive at Janelle's. My plan was to show up in a suit with roses and show what she missed out on. *"Forget her,"* I thought out loud. *"I ain't gotta impress her!"* Immediately, I placed the blazer back on the hanger and pulled some sweatpants out of the drawer. *"That might be too nonchalant."* Finally, I settled on a midpoint. I threw on a red Lacoste polo with a pair of loose jeans and a fitted red and black cap. And toss the roses idea. A simple birthday card would do.

I drove into Janelle's apartment complex a little after nine. I wanted to make her know I'm glad for reconnecting us, but I wasn't pressed either. I gave three knocks to Apartment 203. "Coming," Janelle called from a distance. The floor thumped slightly as she made her way to the door. There was a silence as she examined me through the peephole, then a series of loud clicks to unlock the door. "Kerry!" she yelled while giving me a hug. "Oh my God. You look like a whole different person. I shoulda saved you for myself!"

"Thank you?" I said with a chuckle. "You don't look so bad yourself."

"You know how I do," she joked, flaunting her jeans and sleeveless ruffled blouse with a runway spin. Janelle was a dark-skinned, petite young lady that stood as tall as my chest. She followed the recent hip-hop trend wearing one side of her hair curled to her cheek with blonde highlights while the other was shaved low. Her squinty, Asian-like brown eyes gave her an exotic look. She could have easily snagged someone on her level, but she was a sucker for the thugs. I still remember sticking up for her when those knucklehead niggas used to drop by the house unexpectedly. "Come on in."

Janelle had her living room laid out as if it were some romantic restaurant. Smooth jazz, dim lighting, and pleasant smells coming from the kitchen. Her dining room table was covered with a red silk tablecloth and one long-stick candle sat in front of each plate set. It was the perfect stay-at-home date night, but this was a bit much for a friendly encounter.

"Janelle, you don't think you got too carried away?" I asked, but it was more like stating the obvious.

"Damn, I was just trying to create a lil ambience for yal," she replied. "Anyway, can you check on dinner while I finish getting ready? There's homemade lasagna in the oven and garden salad." As she headed to her bedroom, I brightened the lights, and switched the jazz to the 90s R&B channel. What's a reunion without "blast from the past" music?

"Homemade?" I yelled once I peeked inside the oven.

"It is homemade!" she yelled back. "If I sprinkle cheese on top of a frozen dinner I made it! Don't get knocked out boy." My laughter only increased once I saw the bag of salad chilling in the crisper. To be only twenty-two, out on her own, and putting this thing together, she had done pretty decent. Promptly at 9:30, there were two knocks on the door. If my memory served me right, TiTi was a stickler for being on time.

"Just a minute," Janelle yelled while thundering through the apartment once again. She took a look through the peephole, and then whispered, "It's her! Hide in the kitchen." She opened the door, and in came the soft, angelic voice I hadn't heard in years.

"Hey Nelly," greeted Tierra. "I'm surprised I got here on time."

"Nigga problems?"

"Girl, to say the least. You know I had to get approval on my outfit and permission to go to the club. Speaking of that, I thought you said no jeans? Why aren't you ready? We're not gonna make it in time for "Free Before 10.""

"Ok, ok," Janelle brushed off, "I was trying to decide on which pants to wear with this shirt. Can you come see?" I could hear Tierra grunting in disgust at the thought of being late. She obliviously walked past the candlelit dinette set, ignored the cheesy scent floating through the apartment, and made her way to the bedroom without even a glance in my direction. She did a double-take after seeing a shadow against the wall, and there I was. She was even more beautiful than the fair skin, hazel-eyed, long-haired mental picture of her I had tucked away in my mind, never to be forgotten.

"Kerrington," she let out with an exhale. Janelle smiled a toothy grin as she watched her master plan unfold. I opened my arms in preparation for a much missed hug as Tierra walked up, but instead, received an open-handed slap across the back of my head.

"Ah, shit!" I yelled. "What's wrong with you?"

"Seven years!" she yelled. Then, as if the slap attack never happened, she ran into my arms. "Don't ever do that to me again! I missed you! We have so much to catch up on. I thought you had forgotten about your best friend!"

"Never that," I assured her.

"Janelle, I am gonna kill you," she joked. Janelle stood there clapping like a cheerleader. Her birthday surprise unraveled just as we had hoped.

"I know, I know. You're welcome." Janelle walked over to the coat closet and pulled out a light jacket. "Well you two enjoy your catch-up time. I'm going to catch a movie in the meantime. That should give you all plenty of time for 'whatever'." Janelle was a trip! Like most people, she saw our complex friendship as a pitiful attempt to cover-up something more serious. TiTi and I just had a platonic closeness that was hard to come across between friends of the opposite sex. It was an unexpressed agreement that no matter what people thought, we knew what was up. She left out, and we began what would be a very memorable night for both TiTi and me.

Over our "home-cooked" meal, "fresh" salad, and "fine" champagne (still marked $6.99), we shared what we had been up to during our hiatus. I talked about how I was working in a sports medicine clinic and she told how she finally got her Associate's in veterinary assistance after "dropping in and out of the program." Following small talk, high school memory flashbacks, and some old school jamming, we dug into the personal questions.

"So, are you dating anyone now?" she asked.

"Here n' there," I casually stated. "Nothing serious." Then, it was my turn to do the diggin'. "So are you still messing with that same nigga?"

She sighed, then energetically answered, "Hell no! I been through with Omar."

"That's wassup, TiTi! So, you kicked him to the curb, he moved out, and . . ."

She sighed again, and then unwillingly answered, "We still live together, unfortunately." At the sight of my disappointed face, she felt the need to add, "but we're nothing to each other but roommates."

"Hmph," I scoffed, "heard that one before."

"Kerry, don't tell me you're still on that." She wiped her mouth, threw her napkin into her plate, and placed her purse strap over her shoulder. "It was good seeing you." She was about to leave, but I couldn't let her walk out of my life for another extended period of time.

"Wait," I called in desperation. I flipped to the recent Hip-Hip mix channels and tried to dance for a final attempt at a laugh. "What you know about this?" I joked, doing an off-beat dougie. She cracked a smile, but tried to act as though she was still upset. I kept dancing, pretending to slick my hair back. She roared with laughter as my lanky limbs tried to stay on beat.

"Please," she begged, "my stomach can't take anymore."

"Remember that time where we danced at the freshman prom?" I tried my best to keep her entertained. It appeared as though my off-colored statement was slowly fading.

"Yeah, and everyone was laughing at you trying to 'freak'. Nobody thought you could dance like that. If I recall, I was too much for you back then." Once the flirty jokes were back on, I knew I had won her over.

"Oh really? Sounds like a challenge to me." She squinted her eyes, sat her purse on the couch, and rhythmically bounced over to my direction. We started with an innocent two-step, then inched closer with every song until we finally scooted nut-to-butt.

Maybe it was the cheap champagne that was finally taking over, or maybe it was a taboo desire that crossed our minds simultaneously, but our friendly dance took the next exit off platonic. I positioned my arms around her waist, and she moved them to the lower front of her dress. We continued swaying to the music while she grabbed the back of my head, pulling me close to her neck. I blew a gentle breeze across the back of her neck, sending chills down her spine.

"Mmm, Kerry," she whispered, "I, I . . ."

"Shhhh," I said. I kissed her neck until I had positioned myself to face her. She closed her eyes and I did the same. Our faces drew nearer until finally, our tongues collided. The moment we had spent fifteen years pretending to avoid had finally presented itself. Her kisses were sweet as if the taste of champagne lingered on her buds. My mind drowned out the rap music blasting from the speakers and replaced it with the mellow sounds of Maxwell's "Til the Cops Come Knocking".

Suddenly, there was a thud at the door as if the cops had really come. "We probably upset some neighbors with the music that high," Tierra reasoned. She lowered the volume and then came back to pick up where we left off. Then, there was another set of pounding at the door.

"Damn, it never works for us." Something always seemed to keep us from crossing that line.

"I should probably get that so Janelle doesn't get a fine. But you stay right there." TiTi walked to the door annoyed at whoever was on the opposite side. Once opened, our magical night would be forever ruined.

"So, this is the club with your sister?" asked a familiar angry voice. Janelle was flung inside, and that's when a muscular man entered, carrying a child that was TiTi's spitting image. I hadn't seen the guy in awhile, but an asshole always looks the same. It was Omar, and he was obviously furious that he was not made aware of Janelle's set-up. "Didn't I tell you I was hanging out tonight? You were supposed to be home watching your son!"

"It's my birthday," TiTi cried.

"I don't give a damn," he argued. "And then you're not even at the club. You hanging out with . . . I know that ain't Kerrington!"

"I don't have to explain shit to you O.!" Tierra argued back. I had never seen her so angry before. The TiTi I had come to love had an innocence about her, and was shy unless she knew you. But that night, I had heard her call Omar everything from a "shitty ass father", to a "no good motherfucking motherfucker". She even had the nerve to add, "And you're lucky you brought my son or I'd tell you how I really felt!"

"Son?" I interrupted.

"Son!" Omar said confidently. "A six year old son." I looked at Tierra wondering when she planned on filling me in about her and Omar's child.

"I am so sorry, Tierra," Janelle said. "He saw me at the gas station and didn't see you with me. I tried to lose him, but he followed me back here."

"Shut the fuck up, Janelle," Omar butted in. He knocked Tierra's purse off the couch and sat their son down. He looked around the apartment and stopped once he noticed the candlelit dinner. He was pissed! "Oh, so you fuckin' wit' Mr. College Degree now, huh?" He snatched the tablecloth, causing everything to spill over onto the floor. "Justin," he called over to the kid on the couch, "do you see your mommy being a slut?"

Tierra was becoming more and more upset. Her birthday was spoiling before her eyes. All I kept thinking was I should have known. I wasn't for all the drama, so I grabbed my fitted cap, and figured it was about time for me to leave. I would hate to have to show Omar that I wasn't the same scrawny nigga he used to know. "Thanks Janelle, for a 'great' evening. TiTi, get my number from your sister. Keep in touch, OK?"

I walked over to get one last hug and a bold in-your-face kiss, but was thrown off by a shove from Omar from behind. "You just gon' disrespect me like that?" I bounced off the wall, and turned around swinging.

"I ain't wit' that pushin' shit!" I grabbed him at the waist and rammed him into a wall. Justin was crying for his daddy, TiTi was crying for the police, and Janelle was screaming about not getting her security deposit back. Even with all the noise, I was focused on whipping this nigga's ass for tonight, and for all the stuff I knew he had put Tierra through in the past.

Omar clenched his fists together and pounded on my back, while I delivered shots to the gut. With the adrenaline flowing, neither one of us was slowing up anytime soon, but I had a trick up my sleeve. As he raised his arms once again to slam on my spine, I chin checked him with an uppercut, putting all of my weight into the blow. As he attempted to readjust his jaw, I scoped the room for something to end to this. I laid him out with a champagne bottle to the temple.

"Tierra, I can't leave you with him," I said in desperation. "Do you want your son to grow up like this? Do you want him to think it's OK to treat women like this?"

"What about all our stuff?" she asked.

"Forget your stuff! I'll buy you all new clothes, new toys, whatever. You can't go back to this."

"But Justin is in the middle of school. We can't just transfer."

"It's summer, Tierra!" Janelle interrupted.

"What kind of man would I be if I left you with him? I love you, and I would love Justin as if he were mine. Please, I'm begging you."

Tierra's eyes were red from all the tears she let loose. She glanced over at Omar as he tried to regain consciousness, and then back at Justin, who was still crying on her shoulder, covering his eyes to drown out the fight and the arguments. "I can't."

I was heartbroken, again. "I don't understand."

"Dammit, Kerry. It's not for you to understand," she explained. "This is my life. Yeah, it may be a fucked up mess but it's MY fucked up mess. I need a plan. I can't just walk out on my family cus you say it'll be better."

The foggier it was, the clearer it became. No matter how much love I had for her, how promising a life I could guarantee the two of them, she would never leave Omar. Tierra suffered from the disease known as "stuck woman syndrome" where it would take something serious before she realized he wasn't good for her. I just hoped she caught on before that something serious is death. Her mind was made up and there was nothing I could do.

"Whatever. Enjoy your life."

"Kerry!" Janelle screamed. Blinded by my crushed feelings, I failed to see Omar had reawakened, grabbed a vase, and was heading full speed at me. He cracked it over the top of my head and I went down hard. I could feel shards of glass sticking deep into my skull. He continued his beating, kicking me in the ribs as I lay on the ground. His boots to my chest lifted me across the room like a rag doll.

"You'll never have her!" said Omar. He lifted my lifeless body up, held me against the wall, and yelled, "Never!" one last time before punching me back down. "Now, come on Tierra!"

Omar walked out of the apartment while Tierra gathered their son and her belongings. "I'm so sorry, Kerry," she sobbed.

I was still rolling in pain, clenching my stomach from Omar's sneak attack. There was blood, glass, and food everywhere. Janelle came to the rescue with a bag of ice, but I was less than accepting. I snatched the bag from her hand, slowly stood to my feet, and left the apartment without saying a word.

It was at that moment I had remembered why we hadn't spoken in seven years. The sad thing is that even after tonight's fiasco, I could never give up on Tierra's friendship, or that small ray of hope that we'd be something more. For her, I'd always be there. Always . . .

L is for Lovette

Where all my Libras at? That's right! It was a late Thursday night, the eve of my 40th birthday. This was a milestone unlike any other. It was a lot more grown and experienced than 30, but wasn't quite 50 and over the hill. To me, 40 marked the realization that you really couldn't tell me shit! I mean you could, but the question was would I care?

To celebrate my Fabulous Forty, I wanted to do something that surpassed a romantic dinner with the hubby. He had suggested a trip back to Maryland to see my parents and then dine at Eugenia's Secrets, but ever since that police raid last week you couldn't pay me to eat there again. Besides, I was thinking more along the lines of lettin' loose with my Aces. That's when my other girl, Winona, came right on time with news that a Vegas spa resort was practically giving rooms away. I knew this recession would work in my favor eventually. Winona, my other girl Regina, and I met over drinks and came up with the bright idea of renting an SUV and taking the four hour road trip there from our hometown of Bakersfield, CA.

It was time to do a run-through of my suitcase. I hate that feeling that you never really have everything. *"Let's see: I got my travel clothes on the iron, my bathing suit is hanging in the bathroom, my suitcase and headphones are by the door . . ."* Suddenly, my house phone went off for the fifth time in a half hour. It must be Regina again. Hold on.

"Hello."

"Lovey, this Las Vegas getaway could not have come at a better time. So what time should I be at your place tomorrow?" Regina seemed more excited than me, calling every five minutes talking about clubs to visit, drinks to order, how many pairs of shoes I was bringing, and what was the SPF of my sun block. She was buggin', but I know how happy she was to get away from her drama.

"We're going to meet here at eight," I answered. "That will give us enough time for yal to be late, but early enough to get a quick nap in before we start the party." I could hear Regina snickering through the phone.

"Girl, how you plan on being tired tomorrow?" she asked.

"I ain't young no more," I responded. "And you know you're gonna want a nap too before we go out that night."

"OK!" she said in agreement.

I entertained her for a few more minutes, but I had to get some sleep in. I don't know why I volunteered to take first shift driving. It was midnight, and in eight hours I would be on the road to memories I'd always remember with girls I hope to never forget.

<u>Friday</u>

"Where in the hell are these heffas?" It's 8:10 and not a word from neither one of them. I'm sittin' on the couch burning up in my navy sweats and black tee, sipping on my "for the road" travel mug of coffee. Just then, I saw Winona's little sage crossover car turn into the cul de sac. I ran out to the rental truck to let her know she need not get comfortable.

"Sorry I'm late" she said, running up to the driveway in her stretch jeans, movie star sunglasses, blue peek-a-boo heels, and matching blue shirt. She wore a short Halle-esque hairstyle which complimented her tall, toned figure from her religious workout regimen.

"Hey Nona. You know it's a four hour drive right?"

"Yeah, but that don't mean we gotta look like we got our asses beat on the way down," she said making fun of my sweats. We both laughed as she loaded her suitcase into the truck. Winona was my party starting, keep it real, you swing I follow-up girl. "Is that Regina turning in?"

"It is," I replied, "but who else is in the car?" I hoped maybe it was her daughter dropping her off and taking the car back home, but it's never that easy. The passenger door flung open and out stepped Charlene, Regina's outspoken cousin. "What is she doing here?" I thought out loud.

"Heeeeeey Miss Birthday Girl!" she yelled. "Look at you lookin' all prosperous," she added, grabbing hold of a love handle I had acquired over the years. As Charlene prissily strutted over to the truck to load her bags, it became apparent that "Cutie on duty" had joined the birthday bash. She was cool when she wanted to be, but she also had a knack for drawing attention to your less than flattering qualities, and then calling them out in front of everyone. Then, she would fix it by adding her patented, "Stop being so serious girl, I'm just playin'." She was uninvited, annoying from the minute she got here, and at this very moment I felt like telling her to kiss my "prosperous" ass!

"And you must be Winona," she said with a hug. "Girl, I love your hair. Uh huh. Lookin' like a ol' cockatoo." Her shoulders shook as she laughed a silent, uncontrollable laugh. Winona rolled her eyes and tried to ignore the comment. "Aww stop being like that, you know I'm just joking."

Winona mocked her shaky shoulders before answering, "Well, you ain't funny so I ain't laughing." She slammed the backseat door and looked back at me as if to say, *"Who is this bitch?"* I could see those two bumping heads all weekend. I pulled Regina to the side before we got going to see what was up with the surprise guest.

"Regina, what were you thinking?"

"I know, I know," she said while waving her hands, "but we needed a fourth in order to upgrade to the suites without paying too much more. If she gets too out of line, I'll step in. I promise." Sweet spirited, easy-going Regina was hardly the one to step up in a confrontation. She could find the good in the worst of situations, and when she couldn't she just sat there and made the best of it. She wasn't necessarily the life of the party, but as my best friend and voice of reason, she had to accompany me in case the celebration got a bit wild.

I shook my head in disbelief as I helped Regina shift luggage in the trunk. Looks like our trio was now a foursome.

Despite the minor tiff between Winona and Charlene, our trip started off great. About halfway into the trip we ran into some traffic, but we kept the party going by taking a karaoke journey through musical history, from Mo-Town classics, to a Michael Jackson mix, to En Vogue, Mary J., and of course, Beyoncé. We were tearing them songs up, sounding like a group of alley cats who had gotten their tails stepped on.

"Well, I was saving this for dinner," Winona began, "but this traffic is perfect timing." She took a deep sigh and began her story. "Terrance and I filed for divorce last month." Regina lowered the speaker volume, and we all turned to comfort her. "Now don't go getting all sad on me now."

"I thought you all were so happy," I said. "You two and your son seemed like a perfect family."

"I'll always love TJ," she responded. "It's just I've been losing my attraction to him." She stared blankly out of the window as she continued to explain herself. "I used to feel so head over heels in love with Terrance, but after five years it all seemed cheesy, like I was trying too hard just pretending to love him."

"Did he cheat on you?" asked Charlene. Winona looked as if Charlene wasn't cool enough to ask questions yet, but she kept the story going.

"No, it was nothing like that. It was all me. He genuinely loved me, but I was done with it. I wasn't happy, so I had to do what was best for me."

"So do you think you'll get married again?" Regina questioned.

Winona smiled, chuckled lightly, and then stated, "Yes, if they ever pass the law in California again." The truck was full of silence as we all tried to figure the meaning behind her riddle. It seemed we all figured it out within a matter of seconds.

"Well no wonder you weren't happy, girl," Charlene jumped in. "Your G-spot gets hot for the twat."

"And last time I checked Terrance ain't packin' no pussy," I added. "This didn't just jump on you overnight though. When did you realize this?"

"Lovey, I've been feeling this way since high school, but you know my parents weren't goin' for that. But 40 means fuck 'em, right? I'm living and enjoying it." There was an awkward silence that filled the car.

"Well," started Charlene, "as long as you ain't rubbin' up on me and peekin' at me in my two-piece you cool to me." We all laughed at her breaking the ice and continued onto our destination. Maybe they would get along after all.

We should have gotten there by one o'clock at the latest, but between the traffic, Regina's frequent pissing, and my pullovers from nonstop nausea, we didn't arrive until after three. Everyone was moody, grouchy, sweaty, and tired. The only thing that was able to calm these bitches was the sight of the synchronized fountains rhythmically shooting water high into the air. We checked into our 39th floor suite at the Springbrook Casino Hotel. Haven't heard of it? Of course you haven't. That's how we roll. The pad was a laid out, interior design marvel: the gray carpet matched the plush gray sofa, loveseat, and coffee chair perfectly.

Regina tugged on the burgundy curtains to unveil the famous Las Vegas strip of bright lights. With it being my birthday, I immediately claimed the king's quarters overlooking the fountains as my Queendom.

"So, I'm thinking we can get some sleep and get up around seven for dinner?" I proposed.

"Girl, this is a party," said Charlene, "I'm getting up out this room. You take your nap, but I'ma slip into this two-piece and find me a boy toy by the pool. Come on Regina." Winona and I simultaneously looked at each other as Charlene and her flunky left to change.

"And you can come scoop me from the hotel bar when it's time to go," added Winona. "I came to do everything but relax."

I dived deep into the covers once the ladies left. My head was pounding, the nausea was coming back, I had sensitive, achy breasts, and my feet were so swollen from driving that they felt like sandbags. Even with all the symptoms of the period from Hell, I couldn't help but picture the hardcore partying that lay ahead of us this weekend. As I closed my eyes and buried my head under the comforter, I imagined me and the girls having the ultimate Vegas experience: eating at an expensive steak buffet, catching a cast of lounge singers cover all the Mo-Town classics, then drinking and dancing at a premiere night club all before finally ending the night at a casino where I hit the slot machine's million-dollar jackpot.

*   *   *

"Lovey, it's 7:30," said a hesitant Regina. "We're ready whenever you are." I don't blame Winona for sending Regina in to wake me. I had a reputation for waking up more violently than a sleepwalker. After I got my bearings, I took a quick lights-off shower, threw on my skimpy black dress, and diligently applied my subtle pink lipstick and charcoal/pink eye shadow blend for the smoke effect.

"Lay-deez," I yelled out in a ghetto voice, "the queen is ready."

"Not til' 'the queen' stops playin' and puts some leggings on to cover her ass," Charlene said.

"Whatever," I argued. "What do you think Regina?" I tugged at the seams trying to bring it lower, but the dress wasn't budging.

"It is a little short," she said. "I mean, but do you like it?"

"Nevermind, Regina," I said. Before I could look in Nona's direction, she reminded me why she was my "partner-in-crime".

"Lovey, don't listen to these haters," she began. "If you wanna wear your shirt as a dress, then do you. Cus 40 means what?"

"Fuck 'em!" we said in unison with a loud laugh to follow. Charlene rolled her eyes in embarrassment while Regina stood there in her usual keep the peace style and stayed neutral as she grabbed her jacket. I grabbed my clutch and we hit the town.

We stumbled upon a wild west themed casino and buffet that had land and sea options. Everyone jumped at the idea of a surf-n-turf dinner. Well, everyone except Charlene, that is. "I mean, I know it's your birthday," she winded up, "but can't we try to find something we all want?"

Brandon Hairston

"What do you want to eat?" I asked in a bother.

"I was thinking sushi maybe."

"Where in the fuck have you seen a buffet with sushi on it you would eat?" Regina jumped. I couldn't believe she had snapped at her girl like that. I guess she was as tired of Charlene as the rest of us. "It's Lovey's birthday and we're eating here."

As we filed into the restaurant, Winona purposely held the door open for Charlene to make sure she could add extra salt to the wound. "Do I detect dissension in the ranks?" she asked sarcastically. Charlene rolled her eyes and reluctantly walked inside with her nose in the air, stiffly bent wrist, and scowl on her face that let everyone know how beneath her this place was.

We had a good laugh at Charlene showing her crazy ass at dinner, but she wasn't through. Charlene complained that the spiced shrimp on the buffet didn't look fresh, the crab legs were dry, there weren't enough menu options, the salad bar didn't look cold, and when the waiter brought her hot tea, the water wasn't "hot-hot". She didn't stop us from taking part in the meal though. In fact, the waiter brought a saloon pale full of shrimp to cut back on the three of us standing in line.

"Now that's customer service!" joked Regina. "He's gettin' a tip."

After we got our guts full, we dragged up three blocks to Club Gamble. Our old asses shoulda known better than to pig out right before the club scene, especially me in this small dress. I looked like a stuffed pig. Only person still bouncing around ready to party was Charlene, and that's cus she ain't eat. Feeling like a fool, she did try to redeem herself.

"Did I ruin your night?" she asked innocently.

"Everything's good over here," I responded in a hurry. I brushed her off and kept jammin' to the club beats to show ain't nobody trippin' off Charlene but Charlene.

"No, for real," she pleaded, "let me make it up to you." Charlene danced her way over to some handsome stranger, and came back with four shots and a lemon. "I had to work my magic right quick." We laughed as she continued to break the ice. This was no time for childish beefing. We were here to have a good time. Passing out the shots, she toasted, "To Lovey: may God bless your 40th birthday and may you have 40 more." We bit the sugar-dipped lemon wedges, and chased its bittersweet taste with a mysterious mixture that reminded me of chocolate cake.

"Now let's party!" I yelled. Winona led us to the dance floor and I followed with drink number two in hand. She seductively swayed her hips to the bass of the Reggae tunes. The fellas had no choice but to put all eyes on her, which meant no attention on Charlene.

"I smell a friendly competition," joked Regina.

"I got your competition," said Charlene, "but ain't nothing friendly about it." She sat her drink on the bar, grabbed the generous gentleman from before, and hit the dance floor. She scooted Winona to the outskirts and pressed up on the man. Charlene pulled out all the stops to bring the focus on her: she unbuttoned his shirt, devilishly slid her nails down his chest and did not stop until she reached just below his belt buckle. She continued her burlesque routine as she grinded, and winded on the lower half of his body. The only thing she didn't do was pull his dick out and fuck him right on the dance floor.

70

"I'm gonna get another drink," I told Regina, "but watch those two fools." As I danced over to the bar, I cracked a smile thinking of Winona and Charlene's 40-plus asses trying to out-ho each other as if they were back in their 20's.

"Sex on the beach," I told the bartender. As he poured and shook the ingredients, my sight was drawn to a sexy dark-skinned man on the other end of the bar. He caught me staring, and nodded his head with a smile. "*Don't even think about it,*" I thought to myself, attempting to shoot down any and all unfaithful ideas running through my head. I was doing good until that little voice whispered in my ear, "*It's not cheating if you're just talking.*" I persuaded myself that this was true, tucked my wedding ring in my clutch, and joined him on the other side.

"I know you didn't come here just to stand at the bar," I joked. He smiled the same cute smile he gave me before, but it looked much better up close.

"Well maybe I'd be out there if you were dancing," he said. "I'm Curtis."

"Lov . . . Linnita." Linnita was the name I used out of town so I wouldn't get linked to no mess. He kissed my hand as his way of saying nice to meet me, but the pleasure was all mine. Curtis stood tall with biceps that were so cut, it looked like one big sneeze would bust that polo into confetti strips. With his brown eyes, chiseled jaw, and Hollywood goatee, he was every single Black woman's dream and every married one's little secret. Shit, if I wasn't taken, he'd be the reason I stuck two extra dollars in the collection plate. He knew exactly what he was doing with his arrogant, chocolate self. His cologne was faint, but even the scent of his club sweat got my downstairs plumbing flowing. "So, how about a dance?"

He raised an eyebrow as he watched the crowd partying, swiped at his nose with an index finger, and then turned back just to say, "I'll pass."

"How you gonna play me on my birthday?" I asked innocently.

"Two reasons: your tan line on your left ring finger let's me know you're married, and from the looks of the tie-dye swirl that suddenly appeared on your dress I'm pretty sure you just 'came on.'" I looked down and saw the big stain on my birthday outfit, and several small drops of blood between my heels. Curtis reached for his wallet and sat a ten dollar bill beside me. "Enjoy your drink."

I was so humiliated. It felt like I couldn't find the exit quick enough. I barged through the crowd, pushing and shoving anyone who stood in the way. The sooner I got to Winona, Regina, and Charlene, the sooner I could get out of here. Suddenly, an angry voice called me out over the music.

"Damn, watch who you pushin' you fat bitch!" said some woman, followed by a shove in the middle of my back. The last thing I needed was some bitch trying to fight. "Don't act like you can't hear now," she said while tugging on my hair.

"What the fuck is your problem?" I asked with frustration. We got into a shoving match, followed by a "Who Can Say Bitch the Loudest and Most Times" contest. Right when I had reached my breaking point, a fist flew from behind me and the girl fell back on the rest of her friends. Once again, Winona was there when I needed her. She could hear a fight brewing like a dog could hear a high-pitched whistle.

"You don't want no trouble," Winona bucked, "so just go on about your day! You aight, Lovey? And what's that on your dress?"

"Girl, I am too through. Let's just get outta here before-" I couldn't even finish my sentence when a slap landed on Nona's face. I guess the girl from before didn't have enough because she was back, and this time with her three friends. She didn't know she wasn't the only one with a crew. Winona pounced on her and they went down. Once the other girls tried to jump in, Charlene, Regina, and I each picked a girl and it was on. For what felt like an eternity, we had a four-on-four, hair-pulling, face-scratching, and dress-ripping good time. Security finally reached us and pulled the girls from under us.

"Alright out," he said. "I saw the whole thing. You four, let's go. Ma'am we're gonna have to ask you to see our nurse in the back."

"Why?" I asked. "I'm fine."

"Yeah, but we had an incident where we let someone leave because they felt fine; they were found by hotel housekeeping the next morning. It's club policy that anyone with that much blood on them has to see the nurse before we let them leave."

This weekend was turning into more of a headache than a getaway. I sat and waited fifteen minutes before some blonde, young-looking training nurse came to check me out. "Hello, sorry I'm late I was just getting a drink." I hopped off that table and headed for the door. "Just kidding," she started, "just a little lounge nurse joke. So what brings you to Vegas?" I wasn't in the mood for all the small talk.

"It's my birthday," I answered, "and I'm not having a very happy one. So, can you just do what you need to do so I can get out of here?"

"Temper, temper," she giggled. She grabbed a clipboard with a symptoms checklist off the counter. "I need you to touch your abdomen just so I can check for any internal bleeding, OK?" This was stupid. I had never heard of any club going through all of this for some bar brawl. "No bleeding up top. Can you lift up your shirt?"

"It's a dress!" I said with attitude. Unphased, she continued her questionnaire.

"Are you feeling any nausea, unusually painful cramping, or spotting?"

"Yeah, but that was before the fight."

"I see. And how far along are you?"

"Are you calling me fat?"

"No, I'm calling you pregnant." Pregnant? There was no way this could be happening right now.

"I can't be pregnant," I argued. "I'm just having an unexpected cycle. I'm forty, I'm . . ."

"Forty?!?!" she interrupted. "Whoa looks like someone's having a miracle baby." I was ready to whip her ass in that examination room. "Look, I'm pretty sure you have the symptoms, but if you don't believe me, you can take one of our pregnancy tests with you."

I could see Nate looking at me with that dumb look going, *"How did this happen?"* Nigga you were there! We were at a good place in our lives and a baby was not what either of us needed right now. I peed on the indicator, and walked out with the cup and strip in hand. I was ready to go.

"Took you long enough," Regina said.

"Is that what I think it is?" questioned Winona.

"Let's just get back to the hotel and go to bed," I said. "The quicker we go to sleep, the faster we can have a better tomorrow."

"Girl, that baby is gonna come out looking like somebody's grandfather with them old eggs," added Charlene. I knocked her with my shoulder and headed for the club exit. "Stop being like that girl. I'm just playing."

We made it to the hotel a little after 1:30am and were stopped by the concierge. "I'm afraid that you will not be able to return to your room ladies."

"Why the hell not?" I asked.

"We received a call from Club Gamble about a fight and we were willing to look past that, but the pool staff said that one of the guest in your party gave them an extremely difficult time." We all looked at Charlene. "I'm sorry, but we're not going to be able to honor your weekend reservation anymore."

"The hell you won't," said Winona. "That suite was $2300." I was too exhausted to fight this bullshit.

"Fine, we're gone."

"Lovey, come on now," said Winona.

"I said let's go! We just need to get our stuff."

"Oh, we've taken care of that for you," he said with a smile. "It's all packed and waiting for you on the luggage cart. Thank you for choosing the Springbrook Casino Hotel."

The car ride home was eerily quiet: no radio, no karaoke, no stories, nothing. I didn't care at this point so long as I could get some rest. "So did you have a good birthday?" asked Charlene. Winona swerved hard towards the median, causing Charlene to knock her forehead into the window. "Ow!"

"Thank you," I said with my eyes still shut. I didn't need to see Winona's face to know that one was intentional.

"No, really," she persisted. "So your weekend shebang was cut a little short. You accomplished everything you set out to do in one night: you had a road trip with the girls, slept in a top floor suite, had some Vegas buffet, got one good wear out of your short-short dress, and after that fight I don't think you'll ever forget your 40th birthday." It might have been the sleep deprivation, but she was actually making some sense.

"Did yal see the way Nona punched that bitch?" I asked. "And Regina, who taught you to fight like that? Gurrrl . . ." We all died laughing. After I caught a second wind, I turned the radio back on and the party resumed.

"You better lay down," said Regina. "You know you're not feeling well."

"I can sleep when I get back to Bakersfield. Right now, it's time to rock this SUV."

"Are you sure?" I grabbed the pregnancy test from the cup holder, took a deep breath, and smiled.

"Positive."

M is for Maurice

"Thank you all for agreeing to participate in our wedding," said my beautiful fiancée, Michelle, from the head of the table. We made reservations at the Shay Lounge to treat our wedding party to dinner. "It took us three years, seven months, ten days, and a whole lot of hint throwing to get us to this point," she joked, "but we're here."

"You never told us how he proposed," said Zakia, the maid of honor. Michelle and I looked at each other and then looked away at the ceiling, trying to hold our laughs in. I noticed a couple of my groomsmen who already knew how it went down were also hiding behind their cloth napkins.

"You know, it was like any other proposal," I stated. "We had a fancy dinner, some roses, champagne, and then I popped the question. Nothing big."

"But what about the details?" she insisted.

"Yeah, I'm interested to hear this story, too," agreed Jeff, my best man. He was well aware of the story, but thought it would be a great anecdote to get out there. I looked at Michelle for her approval. She shrugged her shoulders with a smile on her face.

I took a deep breath, looked at our friends, and smiled. "OK, here it goes." . . .

Last Friday, I woke up to a pile of bridal magazines stacked up beside the bed; one of Michelle's many "subtle" hints left in the house that day. I walked into the bathroom, disrobed, pulled the shower curtain back, and jumped at the sight of several magazine covers that featured recent celebrity couples taped to the tiles. I cleared the shower with a smile, then jumped in. I threw on a designer black suit, white shirt, and left the top button open, creating the look I coined as, "Business, pleasure, or both?" It looked good on us tall, lean, dark-skinned brothas. I approached the door and found the last hint: a veil from a costume shop hanging from the knob. Shell was funny (and apparently crazy), but she was right. We had been dating since forever, loved each other, and were already living together, so why not do the damn thing?

After catching her drift, I determined that tonight was the night. I called my supervisor and let him know that I needed the day off. It almost didn't fly until I gave him the reason. He even asked if there was anything he could do to help. I thanked him for the offer, but this was something I wanted to do on my own.

Shell always said I wasn't big on showing affection, so today was the day to prove her wrong. My first destination to create her dream proposal was a stop past the seafood section in the grocery store. I had them pack two fresh lobsters up that I would steam at home myself. Next, I hit up the produce section for a box of giant strawberries, a tub of microwaveable chocolate fondue, and some whipped cream. On the way home, I stopped at florist to order three dozen roses: a dozen to be delivered to her office with a card that read "Just because. With love", a dozen to lead to the bedroom, and a dozen to spread over the dinner table, along with a bottle of wine from the restaurant of our first date.

Once I got home, I covered the strawberries in chocolate, and placed them on a sterling silver dessert tray, surrounding the whipped cream. Steaming those lobsters was the challenging part. They put up quite a fight once submerged in the boiling water, but eventually they gave in. I loaded the CD player with a mixed CD of her favorite slow jams, spread the rose petals across the table and chairs, and took the final dozen to create a trail to our bed and shower.

When I reached the bedroom, I crossed two wine glasses across the bed, and sat the wine in my electric chiller. By the time she got off work, the bottle would be perfectly chilled with drops of mist running down its label.

"Come on man," Jeff butted in, "get to the proposal."

"I'm getting there, nigga," I said, pretending to be annoyed. "Haven't you heard of building up suspense? Anyway . . ."

Time was winding down. It was now 2:30pm and Michelle usually came home everyday at four o'clock like clockwork. I was becoming more excited as the time drew near. The suspense was killing me. She hadn't called about the flowers yet. I decided it was best to swing through her office and make sure she received them.

"Aww, she wasn't cheating on you was she?" asked my boy, Erick.

"Let him finish the story," Michelle said. "Go ahead baby."

"Thank you boo. So . . ."

I got to the receptionist's desk and asked if she could page her to the front. Michelle turned the corner wearing a knee-length black skirt, a white ruffled blouse, and a pair of heels that gave her legs for days. I loved when she would wear her hair down and give it that shiny effect. She had the body of a dancer and the glow of an angel.

"Hey, Shell," I said while leaning in for a kiss. She turned to the side, giving me cheek only.

"Baby, not at the office." I forgot she was up for a promotion. It was rare that her boss promoted Black women, but she let her merit and accomplishments speak for her, not her race. "Why aren't you at work?"

"Just on my lunch break," I answered. "Did you get anything out of the ordinary?"

"Oh, the flowers. Baby, I completely forgot to call. But thank you. It was really sweet. You know all the ladies here were hatin'."

"They're going to hate on you even more after tonight," I hinted.

"Moe, don't be getting' all nasty in here," she said suggestively.

"Nah, not like that. Just wait and see."

"Can't wait! Oh no, baby did you say tonight?"

"Yeah," I said disappointedly. "What's wrong? You're not working late again, are you?"

"No, I got invited to happy hour with the girls after work." My face dropped at her reason. "I know, I know, but I haven't seen Destiny in awhile and she sent a last minute email about meeting up."

"Shell, you choosing your friends over me? I think you would really want to come home right after work."

"Moe we can do that anytime. You'll still be home when I get there, whether it's four or nine."

"Don't worry about it. Hang out with the girls. I'm cool."

"Are you sure?" she asked. "I can cancel." I knew she didn't mean that.

"Nah go ahead. Have fun. Maybe I'll call Jeff and the crew and have nigga night. But, do you." I angrily stormed out of the lobby to leave out. It was one thing to not have any plans, but what's worse was knowing that Michelle knew I ain't have shit else to do either.

The whole ride home all I kept thinking was how she postponed my perfect proposal for "girl talk". That's some teenage bullshit. I thought women had an intuition for things like marriage proposals. I mean, she was throwing it in my face how all her girls were engaged, leaving pictures in my shower, and shit. If I ain't love her, I woulda thought she was one crazy bitch.

Then, in mid route, an idea hit me. Why was I so concerned about Shell chilling with the girls? With her giving me some space I had a chance to reconnect with my old ways. I'm talking about a good old-fashioned session of "self-love". Don't act like you're too good for it. Every nigga has done it, still does every so often, and those who say they don't do it the most. Anyway, since getting with Michelle, I hardly had the time or the opportunity. But tonight, after crushing my lobster dinner, strawberries decadently covered in chocolate, and a frosty glass of expensive wine, I was going to prove that "bad" habits really do die hard.

I rushed through the door grinning from ear-to-ear, excited for what would soon take place. I may seem overexcited, but this was a rare occurrence. Seldom does a man in a relationship get the privilege to fire one off without the excessive pillow talk and cuddling afterwards. I went in the fridge and grabbed the dessert tray, then headed upstairs.

I placed the tray on my bed, and then went into my closet. Underneath a pile of too small clothes was a locked safe containing my porno collection. I remembered the combination was set to memorable dates: 29 was for my birthday, 17 was for Shell's, and 9 for the number of months before we became official. The door popped open and DVDs galore sprung out, along with one of Shell's thongs she let me have when we first started out! I threw them out my way and began searching for my material. What would I choose? There was "Aladdin and the 40D's", "Mortal Cumbat", "You Got Served: The Interracial Orgy Edition", and plenty more. *"I think I'll go with this one,"* I thought to myself. I loaded the disc, climbed onto the bed, and bit into a couple strawberries while the DVD player loaded.

"Wait a minute," interrupted Angie, "I know you're not about to-"

"Girl, you got to hear the whole story," Michelle said with a smile. "It only gets better!"

So, I'm getting' ready to beat "Moe, Jr.", when I got that awkward feeling someone was watching me. It was an aura coming from a picture of me and Shell on a cruise.

Whether I laid on the left or right side of the bed, her eyes in the photo seemed to follow me. I faced the picture frame backwards and grabbed a bottle of lube and a rubber on the way back to the bed. Why the rubber? Have you ever seen the end result of a nigga who hasn't jerked off in months? Cleaning that shit was a task I wasn't up for.

After several minutes of delay, I was finally ready. I rolled the condom down, lubed up, clutched my shaft, and went to work. Five minutes had passed, then ten, then twenty. I was working up quite a thirst. Good thing I had that wine in reach. Twenty-seven minutes into "Living Sing-ho: Asian Volume 2" I popped. "Mmmm," I moaned from being overwhelmed at the tingling sensation of the release. I exhaled deeply in pleasure as my abs contracted and my eyes rolled back.

It was about 5 or 5:30 and with Shell hittin' the lounge with her girls, I had time to clean up later. I was sweaty, exhausted, and needed to be refreshed and rejuvenated with a piping hot shower. While I was in there, I kept thinking about how I should've waited instead getting myself off. With dinner and the proposal, I was guaranteed some ass, but I chose the selfish way out. Then, I got a thought that was probably the best idea I'd had all day. Shell was oblivious to everything that just went down. I could clean up, throw a few more berries on the plate, smooth out the whipped cream, nuke the lobsters, and go with the original plan. Immediately, I shut the water off and threw a towel around my waist. I opened the door, and felt an incredible force knock me in the face. I looked up wide eyed and mouth open. It was Michelle!

"So this is what you do when I come home late, nigga?" she asked in an uproar.

"Baby, I know you don't approve but you ain't have to slap me. I ain't even dry off yet. That shit hurts!"

"Fuck your feelings, Moe!" She pushed me into the bathroom, knocking shampoo, toothpaste, and a hairbrush off the counter. "So where's the bitch?"

"Huh?" I asked in confusion. She ran to my mounted flat panel television and grabbed the edges as if she were threatening to smash it. "Ay, chill Shell!"

"Oh, you wanna play dumb?" she asked. "Where's the ho you were screwing behind my back!"

"What are you talking about? Wait, I thought you were going out after work?" That must have been the wrong answer, because my 42-inch, high definition screen came crashing down. "Damn, what the hell!?"

"So that gives you a reason to cheat? I hate you!" She stormed out of the room and raced downstairs, dragging her keys along the walls in the hallway.

"*Cheating?*" I thought in perplexity. I scoped the room and noticed that through the eyes of a woman, it did appear rather sketchy: the empty wine bottle with two glasses, the half eaten plate of strawberries, the bed in disarray, the condom wrapper in the sheets with matching used condom in the garbage, and her picture facing backwards.

"Shit!" I chased after her, hoping to catch her before she drove off. "Shell, wait up! Listen to me, baby!"

She was halfway to her parking space when I hollered, "Baby, I know you don't want to hear this but it's really not what it looks like." She turned to face me with tears streaming from her light brown eyes.

"Why, Moe?" she asked. "Was it worth it?"

"Baby, all that was for you: the strawberries, the anniversary wine, the lobster, everything. There wasn't anyone in there but me."

"Well what about the filled up condom, Moe?" It was hard to admit, but it was do or die. I could either tell her the truth, or lie to cover my dick, but lose my heart.

"I was masturbating and didn't want the 'kids' going everywhere." Shell's face turned upside down in disgust, then she laughed.

"And I'm supposed to believe that? Niggas are dirty. Yal don't care about shit like that."

"But it's the truth," I insisted.

"Goodbye, Moe."

"Shell if it wasn't true then why would I have this?" I pulled a ring box from under my towel. I put it there as an ace up my sleeve in case she didn't buy my story. "Baby, we have been through way more than this. I can look in your eyes and know when you're sincere and you can do the same to me. We've built trust over these last few years. I know it's hard to step out and believe me, but I need for you to trust that I'm telling the truth. Not accept it, but know in your heart that nothing happened." I attempted to get on one knee, but the towel's knot wouldn't hold. "Will you marry me?"

"You can't even get down?" she asked, still crying softly.

"But baby, the towel." She turned in the direction of her car and began to walk. "Ok, Ok, Ok," I begged. I removed the towel, exposing all my glory. My dick had shriveled from a combination of the shower water and the cold air. I think I even heard some of the neighborhood kids screaming at the sight. I got down on one knee and blocked out everything else around me. "Now, will you marry me?"

Michelle giggled at my shrunken package, wiped her tears of anger, and released her tears of joy. "Yes! Yes I will!"

I jumped up in excitement, nakedly kissing her to show my appreciation. "B-b-baby, c-can you hand me that t-t-t-towel?" I asked between shivers.

The bridal party died of laughter. Everyone was either wiping tears, or holding their stomachs from the pleasurable pain of laughing too hard. "That is definitely a unique proposal," Zakia said. "Girl, no wonder you told me it was just dinner."

"To Moe and Michelle," toasted Jeff. "May they have many years of happiness so that this nigga never has another minute alone!"

N is for Nina

I woke to a beautiful summer Friday morning. I rolled over, kissed Neal on the cheek, and threw on a pair of sweats—no shower, no make-up—and started up the Corolla. This was a chill day, and I planned on doing just that. But there were a few errands to take care of first.

On my way home, I stopped past Cre8ive Hair and Nails for a quick gel fill-in. I felt a tap on my shoulder while my girl, Lynn, hooked me up. It was Kim.

"Nina?" she said. "Girl I haven't seen you around here in forever."

"Hey chica," I started. "I've been so busy working."

"Mmmhmm, busy working that white man you got. Yal still together?"

"Yes, Neal and I are still going strong," I said between laughs. "What about you? What's up with you and your boo for the weekend?" Kim made a devilish grin and asked the nail technician if we could have a minute. Once she left, Kim told me her juicy plans.

"Actually, we're hosting one of our 'parties'." I wasn't sure why she used quote fingers around parties, and my expression must have illustrated my confusion. "I thought I told you Josh and I swing?" she clarified. I was stunned.

"For real?!?! I've never known a real-life swinger. I mean, I know they're out there but damn this hits close to home."

"Girl, it's a lot more people swinging than you would think: married, dating, single, and especially them church folk." We laughed at the idea of some random Pastor and First Lady McGee getting' their freak on. "But seriously, if you're not doing anything tomorrow you should check it out."

"That might be a little too extra for me," I said nervously. "Plus, Neal isn't hardly going for no swinger's party."

"Well, let me leave you a flyer," she pushed, "just in case you change your mind. I hope I see you there. We could use some Latin flavor to spice up the party."

The flyer was pretty captivating. Looking at the models dressed finely in business attire and holding wine glasses, you would think it was nothing more than an entrepreneurial mixer. Neal and I didn't have any set plans for tomorrow night, and I honestly was a little curious to participate in swinging. This was my once in a lifetime chance to fulfill a naughty fantasy. Hey, I'm young: why not? The hard part would be getting Neal to keep an open mind.

Later that evening . . .

"I'm not doing that freaky shit," Neal contested furiously, "and neither are you."

I tried to appeal to his fantasies. "I thought you would like a girl willing to hook up?" I asked. "We don't have to do anything, but we can just go and check it out."

"I'm not into letting my girl get felt up by anyone other than me. Shouldn't I be enough for you?"

"Of course you are, Papí."

"So just drop it then." I could tell he was taking this personal. I loved Neal, and would never want to lose him over one night of infinite temptation. As I got ready to toss the flyer in the trash, he grudgingly asked, "So you really want to go to this thing, huh?" This was my chance to win him over.

"Just to look around, and say I've been. I wouldn't do anyone or anything you wouldn't want me to. It'll be fun. Maybe you will meet a sexy little something there. Come on, I thought 'you people' were into trying crazy new things." Neal walked over to me and threw the flyer in the trash. I knew that was the end for sure.

"So who's holding this thing anyway?" he asked with interest.

"Remember my girl, Kim? Well, she and her boyfriend, Josh, have been hosting swinger functions for awhile and they were looking for new couples to keep the excitement up. She thought it would be good to add an interracial couple to the mix." He looked away for a few seconds, scratched his head, and chuckled as if he couldn't believe what he was about to say.

"OK," he said.

"OK?" I asked in confirmation.

"We'll go." Before I could celebrate he added, "But I get to pick who you do anything with, I have to be in the room if anything happens, and if there's a sexy Asian in there, you have to let me go for her."

In my mind I was thinking, *"Yeah fuckin' right,"* but I shrugged my shoulders and accepted his negotiations. Overall, I had won, and would get the opportunity to swing with the best of 'em.

After a good night's rest and a trip to the mall for the perfect little cocktail dress, it was time to get ready for my "date" with Neal. I stepped into the seductive tight red dress with a slit on each side. My blonde hair was finely crimped from removing my cornrows. While applying my eyeliner, I could see Neal putting the final touches on his black suit, sky blue shirt, and black and blue tie. I guess he finally got into the idea of swinging because he was looking good! Just thinking of women pushing up on him got me a little jealous.

We arrived at Kim's house around 11; fashionably late, of course. Neal and I were greeted by a dark chocolate butler with a bald head, a bulging, greased up 8-pack, and wearing nothing but a black speedo. He welcomed us with two champagne glasses filled with what appeared to be a mimosa. Neal declined, so I downed mine, then held his to appear classy around the other guests. The butler then proceeded to take us to the party room.

Kim's house was exquisite, to say the least. The hallway we were guided through reminded me of a palace with its polished hardwood floors, high ceilings, and white walls adorned with elegant paintings. Hidden speakers played soft music to create a sexy, yet classy ambience. Finally, we were escorted through a set of white wooden double doors.

"Nina," I heard Kim's voice over the music. She walked over to us with Josh. "Looking caliente, Mamí. I'm glad you two decided to show up. This is Josh. Josh, this is my girl, Nina and her boyfriend, Neal."

"Nice to meet you both," Josh said. "Hey Neal, there's a couple of ladies I'd like to introduce you to. How about we go to the theater downstairs?" Neal looked hesitant to leave me unattended until Josh mentioned, "I have the NBA playoffs on, and a kegger." He gave me a kiss on the cheek, and was gone to party with the game watchers.

"Man, you're a lifesaver," Neal joked, "because some guy in a thong up there was handing out punk drinks. I'll pass." The two walked in the direction of the basement until I lost sight of them amongst the crowd.

"Come," Kim said, "let me introduce you to the other guests." The party was a lot more sophisticated than I had expected. Everyone was engaged in political conversations, handing out business cards while either swirling wine, or slowly sipping the drinks we had received at the door. I felt uncomfortable in my dress. I ordered another Mimosa from one of the servers to help me relax. "You better slow down on those," Kim warned.

"I'm a big girl," I answered. "This is only my third one. How much damage can juice and champagne really do?" Kim giggled at my ignorance.

"Girl, do you think people would be getting loose off Mimosas? You're drinking X's & O's." I was still unaware of what she meant. "You've never heard of ecstasy and orange juice? X and O? Get it?" Talk about mind over matter, cus as soon as I was conscious of what I was drinking, the room began to swirl to the beat of up-tempo jazz jams, blending the colors within the party into an aesthetic neon presentation.

"WHOOOOO!" I shouted out. "Ow! Ow! Party over here!" I stumbled into a wall, laughing uncontrollably.

"OK, just sit down and calm yourself for a minute," Kim laughed, "I'm going to go find Neal."

"Let Neal have his fun. I'm ready to get the real party started!" I yelled, causing a hush over the mingling attendees.

"OK folks, you heard her," Kim concurred. "Grab one, two, three, or however many you desire and let your fantasies run free."

Within minutes of Kim's announcement, every corner had two or more people kissing, fondling, licking, sucking, and eventually fucking. It was peculiar watching the couples mix and match sexual partners while their spouses looked on, or engaged in their own activities. Maybe it was the drugs, but I think I had even seen Neal and his "Asian delight" walk past holding hands and heading upstairs. It bothered me, but the blame was on me if anything happened. I was the one that persuaded him to come. Not to mention I was a preying on that sexy ass naked doorman.

I looked to the left and saw him serving up more cocktails. He seemed to be in reach, but the ecstasy had me trippin' hard. I extended my hand and fell face first, chipping my tooth on the wood floors. I had finally succumbed to the X and was out cold.

"Nina, Nina," Kim said in an echo, "Nina are you alright?"

"Where am I?" I asked groggily.

"She's OK," Kim yelled out, as if anyone gave a damn. It was almost three o'clock the next morning and the party had cleared out significantly. Kim helped me to my feet. My head was throbbing and my balance was still off.

"Where's Neal?" I asked. "I just wanna find him and go home."

"I don't think you want to see Neal right now," she debated.

"Why? Oh, he's still with that Asian bitch?" Looks like Neal had a blast. "That no good bastard didn't even come check on me?" I unbunched my dress, took my heels off, and went upstairs searching for him. At that moment, no headache could keep me from kicking one of two asses, hers or his!

I opened the first door on the right and entered a pitch black room. After flicking the lights on, I saw that this was Kim's bedroom, and was noticeably off limits from any "partying". The next door on the left was the guest bathroom where there was moaning coming from the shower. "Neal!" I yelled, pulling the shower curtain open. Inside the tub were two people going at it as if the curtain were still intact. Damn, where could he be?

As I exited the bathroom, I saw Kim blocking another door. Clearly, the prize was behind Door #3. "Kim, move." She looked like a kid that got cut spilling juice on the carpet before having a chance to clean it up. I shoved her out of the way. I didn't have time for this shit and was beginning to lose my patience.

I turned the knob and immediately exclaimed "What the fuck!?!?" No amount of ecstasy could prepare me for the sight of Neal sucking Josh's dick while that sexy doorman pounded his ass into the wall. And the Asian girl was there too, masturbating and filming everything that went down.

Between mouthfuls, Neal had the nerve to say, "Baby you were right. This was a great way to keep things fun and exciting between us!"

I was paralyzed with disbelief. I closed the door, because at this point, there was no way I would ever feel comfortable being intimate with Neal again. I slowly walked down the staircase and headed for the double doors. "I'm so sorry," Kim said. "Call me when you get home, OK?" I looked Kim up and down, grinned, then jabbed that Black bitch right in the eye.

Experimenting and excitement, huh? Next time I'm in the mood for some excitement I'll try something safer, like bungee jumping without a cord!

O is for Omar (Part II of III)

Ring, ring, ring . . . Come on Tee, pick up. *Ring, ring, ring . . .* "Hi, you've reached Tierra and Omar . . ." Shit! "Sorry we missed your call, but leave a brief message and we'll call you back." *Beep.*

"Ay Tierra, *sigh*, it's O again. Yo, how long are you gonna be trippin'? I said my bad, baby. Damn. I hate when you get like this. Hit me back when you get this. Aight."

This is one of them days when even a nigga could use a shoulder to lean on. No homo. It's midnight; I'm high, I'm tipsy, and I've been racing up and down the highway for the past 2 hours trying to figure out the right thing to say, but the only thing that comes to mind is, "I fucked up, yo." I can't just let her throw away two years of history. Two years; shit that's a long time. I still remember the beginning like it was yesterday.

I was standing in line for breakfast at the soul food carry-out on 23rd, starving. As I approached the counter my eyes came across the prettiest hazel eyes I had ever seen (and they were hers). Her hair was brown, shoulder-length and wavy. Her skin resembled that of a perfectly cooked Belgian waffle (I musta been really hungry). She smiled, but I could tell that there was sass behind that smile and it drew me in. I walked to the counter and placed my order.

"Welcome to Fill Up on Soul, how can I help you?"

"Ay sweetheart," I said as I leaned on the counter, "what you think about the pancakes?"

"Umm, they're round," she answered. I could tell she was feelin' me just from that short back-n-forth. My authentic suit and cologne must have led her to believe I was about something when in reality, I was just leaving an interview for a bank teller position.

"Oh, damn it's like that?" I joked back. Her cheeks turned a rosy red as she smiled and enjoyed the flirtatious exchange.

"Boy, what do you want?"

"You mean to eat?" She bulged her eyes as if to say hurry up, while pointing at the line of angry patrons forming behind me. "Aight, aight. Lemme get the three pancakes with two strips of turkey bacon, and scrambled cheese eggs. Oh, and a medium fresh squeezed orange juice." Before she even mentioned the total, I pulled out my wallet and flashed a stack. I counted the three hundreds, two fifties, few twenties, and several tens, fives, and ones. Even though that was my nothing but errand money, I could feel her staring at the wad of cash. "How much did you say, again?"

I sat near the back so I could eat in peace, away from the church service let-out. Just as I poured the syrup over my pancakes and bacon, the thick cashier from before decided it was time to wipe off the open tables. Maybe I was hoping for something that wasn't there, but she poked her ass out more than I had seen any girl do when washing tables. Once she looked up at me, I mouthed "Delicious," to which she rolled her eyes. I laughed, and bowed my head for grace.

"Oops," she said, knocking my elbow off the table with her butt.

"C'mon man, I'm praying," I joked.

I had unlocked my door when I noticed those familiar hips standing at the Metro stop. I walked over, stood beside her as if I hadn't seen her there, and pretended to look down the street for the bus. "I can take you there," I offered.

"No thanks," she replied, "I don't take no rides from strangers."

"Well, maybe you should give me your number then," I suggested. "That way, I won't be a stranger the next time." She smiled, and gave it to me (like I knew she would), and I waited with her until the Metro came. Tierra, with a heart over the "I". Classic.

Step 1: Make Her Love Me

I called her later that night just off some "get to know you" type shit. Yeah, I knew about the two-day wait, but there was a 3-step method to the madness. I wanted it to come off as her having this old head sprung, wrapped around her finger, and all that. I was just baitin' her, and she'd fall for it. They always did.

"Hello?" answered an unfamiliar feminine voice. This musta been Moms.

"Can I speak to Tierra? This is Omar." It was quiet, as if she wondered what a man with that much bass in his voice wanted with her young daughter.

"Hold on," she said with an instant attitude. It sounded like the phone went on mute for a second. At least Moms had the decency to dog me where I couldn't hear it. After a long break, Tierra came to the phone.

"Hey O," she said.

"So I'm O now?" I joked.

"Is that a problem?" she playfully fought back. "But can I call you back?"

"My bad, I didn't know you were busy."

"Yeah I gotta finish up this homework."

"Ok, ok. So you a college girl, huh?"

"Not til next year," she answered. "I'm a senior at Park Arbor High." Damn, what are they feeding these youngins' today? "I mean I am 18 though." That right there let me know she was feelin' me. "So, what are you, like 21?"

"23." Which was really code for 25.

"Really? Wow, you don't even look that old." There was a break in the convo while we both did the math. In reality, there was a seven year age difference, but in her mind, we were only five years apart.

"So you still gonna call me back right?" It seemed like she had to think on it real quick before she could answer.

"Yeah, I'll call you back," she said with hesitation.

Tierra and I talked every night for the next month. I would pick her up from school, come through the restaurant just to see her, and even if I didn't ask, she would slide a waffle or a wing over to me. Eventually, she warmed up to me enough that we could start going out to restaurants, movies, and late drives just to talk.

As I turned down her street, she grabbed my arm and laid her head on my shoulder. "Why are you so much better than the rest of the guys I've dated?" she asked.

"That's because you be fuckin' with them high school boys," I said. "All that ass belongs to a man that can handle it."

"Oh my God," she laughed, "you are so inappropriate." I was so "inappropriate" she never took her head off of me. I pulled up in front of her house and kissed her goodnight. She slid her tongue in for the first time. "Five after twelve," she said in a panic. "My parents are gonna kill me!"

"Be easy, it's just five minutes," I said.

"You don't know my parents." TiTi unfastened her seat belt, kissed me one last time, and ran up to her driveway. I had a good school girl breaking mommy and daddy's rules after just two months. I can't imagine how she'd be if I woulda gave her the dick. Step 1 gets a check.

Step 2: Us Against Them

TiTi and I had been hanging out almost everyday. She had pushed her homework aside, called out of work, and every free minute she had she either spent with me or on the phone talking to me. I even got her to fall back from chillin' so much with her best friend, some nigga named Kerry. I never understood that opposite sex best friend shit. My guess is he prolly wanted her, but played the friend role too well and ended up as her brother. Sucks to be you, nigga.

One day, may have been a Tuesday, I had her out at Pentagon City mall to find a white dress to go underneath her graduation robe. After we got that out of the way, we just window shopped, and chilled in the food court. "You my girl now, right?" I asked as we stood in line for a cinnamon-raisin pretzel. TiTi was looking like the question was so left field. "Don't play with me," I joked, punching the air in front of her face.

"Boy, don't play," she jabbed back. She placed her finger on the corner of her mouth, and stared up as if she were in deep thought. "Yeah," she said, "I'm your girl."

Unphased, I replied, "That's wassup," and nodded my head.

I dropped her off around the time that the street lights cut on. "Aight call me later," I said. TiTi looked like something was on her mind.

"O my parents want to meet you." I rested my head against the window of the driver's side and blew out the smoke from my blunt. "See, that's why I ain't wanna tell you. They just wanna see who I've been spending so much time with. Are you mad?" It was all an act. I had no problem meeting her parents, but I had to keep them out of what I had planned. See, older muhfuckas knew the drill, but as long as I preyed on her youth and ignorance, she'd be mine.

"I don't see why we can't just wait until the graduation, but if you want me to meet 'em, let's go now."

"Oh, thank you, baby!" she said with a long kiss. I tossed the blunt out the door, and started up the driveway. We reached the door and my nerves began to take effect as she turned the key. No matter how many times I had gone through this, the first meeting was always tough.

"Mom? Dad?" she yelled back.

"They're in the basement," a younger voice called back that sounded as if it were approaching us. "You want me to go get . . ." In mid-sentence, a girl jumped back behind the comfort of the hallway wall. She couldn't have been any older than 14, but she covered up as if I was interested in seeing under her long, white-turned-beige t-shirt. "Tierra why didn't you tell me someone was out here?"

"Hey, I'm Omar," I said.

"I'm Janelle," she said. "Are you Tierra's boyfriend? You look kinda old."

"Janelle, can you just go get Mom and Dad and mind your business?" TiTi interrupted.

"We're already here," said a gorgeous, but stern woman. Tierra's mom must have had the stronger genes, and thank God for that. As small as her mother was, dad was as big. He might have played football or something back in the day. "It's nice to finally meet you Omar," she continued. "We're Mr. and Mrs. Johnson."

"Nice to meet you, too," I said, extending my hand. Dad shook my hand, but mom continued her harsh introduction, brushing past my hand as if she hadn't seen it.

"Sure did take you a long time to introduce yourself, young man," she said. "I was beginning to think you were hiding from us. Do you have any reason to hide? Scared, perhaps?"

"Mom," TiTi butted in. I continued playing the "Good Guy".

"No ma'am. I just wanted to make sure Tierra and I was serious before we took this step." Dad acted as though this was unnecessary, but Mom looked as though this were just the beginning.

"Well, that's an interesting five o'clock shadow you have there. Don't see too many high school students with a full mustache and goatee."

"Mom he's not in high school," explained TiTi. "He's . . . 20." Damn, got her lying for me, too.

"Don't lie to your parents," I said. "Ma'am I'm 23 years old." Her eyes damn near jumped out of the sockets.

"It was a pleasure meeting you," she started, "but our daughter will no longer be seeing you."

"Mom, I'm 18 years old," TiTi argued. "Why do you keep treating me like I'm a child? Oh my God!" All the yelling was falling on deaf ears, as Moms paid her no attention, and showed me the door. "I'll call you later O."

"Like hell you will," said her mother. I hated to leave her there, but she had to go through it. This was essential in beginning the process of severing the ties between her and her family.

I drove real slow around her neighborhood, anticipating a call from her. Like clockwork, I was right. "Hey Tee." She sounded as though she had been crying. "You straight?"

"Can you come get me?" she said between sniffles.

"What happened?"

"She gone tell me that she don't care if I'm going to college next year or not. While I'm in her house, I won't be calling some 23 year old man my boyfriend. So, I said I don't need your house. Then, she called me stupid for believing you were serious about me, so I got in her face and defended you." I could hear her voice trembling again. "And she pushed me. So, I pushed her back. And we started fighting. Right in front of Janelle and my dad. They couldn't break us up for ten minutes." Her shaky voice turned into a full out cry. "Can you just please get me. All I have is the clothes you bought me. Just come get me."

I circled back around and scooped her up. "Did you tell them where you would be?" I asked, pretending to care.

"Janelle knows where I am if they need me."

I took her to my apartment, wrapped my arm around her neck to show her I cared, and she curled up on me on the couch. I ran my fingers through her hair, turning her cry to gentle sniffles. She rubbed my arms to show her appreciation. My dick showed its appreciation as well, raising up in my jeans. She ran her fingertips across my imprint, and slowly unzipped me. We began kissing, sliding down the sofa until she was positioned under me.

I undid her pant's button with my teeth, slid her zipper down, and realigned my torso with hers. I could feel her pushing back as I tried to slide in. "I'll pull out," I whispered between kisses.

Her pushing grew less and less intense until finally I was inside. I had guessed I was the first nigga she let beat raw, and later on she told me I was right. That night, I gave it to her like she never had. I had her thick thighs wrapped around my neck. Coulda called her pussy Berlin the way I pounded at her walls. We had the couch rockin' on two legs a couple times. Hahaha, nah I'm just remembering how she was screamin' out for me.

She spent the next week and a half with me until her graduation the following Friday, never calling home once. To her, we had made passionate love nonstop, but in my mind, I just called it fuckin' til my pipe was cleaned.

* * *

August had come around a lot sooner than I had expected. Tee would be going off to college soon, leaving me behind. She had dreams of becoming a vet or some shit like that, but I needed her here. I couldn't have them college dudes all up on her. So, a couple weeks before she moved on campus, I asked her out to dinner to propose something to her.

"You want me to move in with you?" she repeated.

"Yeah, baby," I responded. "These last few months have been good. I don't want you to leave me in the middle of what we're building.

"But what about school?"

"School will always be there. But what are the chances of you finding love like this again?" She squirmed in her chair at the thought of blowing off college.

"Can I think about it?" I was pissed, but I had to give her time.

"Of course, baby."

The ride home was jy quiet. She stared out the window the entire way to her parent's house. Right when I pulled into the driveway, she turned to me with concern in her hazel eyes. "Are you for real?" she asked again.

"If you're real, I'm real." She smiled, kissed me, and gave her final answer.

"Then yes!" I smiled back at her, but tried to keep it cool too. "But, I need to enroll in community college to get my pre-reqs over in case I wanna transfer next year." I was cool with that, but her parents weren't.

They fussed, fought, and even offered a car if she reconsidered, but Tierra's mind was made up. She moved in and there wasn't a damn thing they could do about it. Mind and body, she was mine!

Step 3: I'm All You Got

Time passed and we were celebrating our one year anniversary. What would have been Tee's second semester out-of-state had instead turned into another year of community college. She had spent her days out of class applying for part-time jobs, but no one was hiring. So, she went back to doing hair, using my kitchen as her salon. She had built up a steady flow of income, plus she had a student loan rebate check to hold her over. Turns out the community college classes weren't as much as the four-year schools, so we, I mean she, had a nice lil' check coming back. Eventually, I went from full-time manager, to part-time, to calling out so much I got fired. I would just put my suit on and chill for eight hours at my boy's gettin' wasted, at my mom's eatin' and sleepin', or at some bitch's house doin' whatever.

On my way home from "work", I stopped by the movie store and rented a couple of Tee's favorites for a romantic night at home. I walked into the living room and saw her on the couch, phone to her ear, with homework sprawled over the coffee table. "Workin' hard, huh?"

"O I forgot how hard algebra can be," she said flustered. "I'm glad Kerry was taking math too cus I needed some help."

"Kerry?" I asked. "I thought you stopped talking to him."

"Awww, don't act like that baby," she played. "He's just my friend. You know I only think of you like that." I played it off but I was blown. I threw the bag of rented DVDs to the ground, walked to the phone outlet, and pulled the cord out of the wall. "What's wrong with you?" she asked.

"Is this what you do while I'm at work?" I yelled. "You think I'm dumb or something cus I'm workin' to keep your ass happy instead of being in school?"

"Whoa, whoa, whoa! Where is all of this coming from?" She looked so dumbfounded, but she wasn't gonna make some fool outta me. "I was just doing homework."

"You ain't gonna keep throwin' that homework shit in my face." My temper was growing every time she opened her mouth. I was furious. She had begun to pack her things as my frustration had scared her. "Where the fuck do you think you're going?"

"OK," she said calmly, "you need to stop cussing at me first of all. Second, I'm goin' to my parent's house until you get yourself together." Get myself together? This bitch had the game wrong.

With the phone cord still in hand, I ran in her direction and wrapped it around her throat. "You want the phone so bad, well here it is." She was gagging and struggling for a breath of air, and I wasn't letting up. "Here," I said sarcastically, "ask Kerry for help. Go ahead." I could hardly feel her scratches on my arms and face, but I dropped to my knees when she threw her foot back to my nuts. "Ah, fuck!"

"Oh my God," she yelled, "you're crazy!"

I ran to the coffee table and started flinging her books and papers everywhere. I made sure to rip some of the pages too. "FUCK . . . YOU!" I walked into the bedroom and slammed the door. When I came out, she was gone. But like all good girls, I knew she'd come back.

A couple days later there was a knock at the door. It was Tierra with her father carrying her bags. To make a long story short, he told me that after she moved out of the house, he and Mrs. Johnson had downsized to something more affordable. TiTi chose to "play house" as he called it, now she has to live with her decisions.

"You don't have to be 'together'," he said, "but you all need to be civil. And I don't ever wanna hear about you putting your hands on my daughter again, OK?" She must not have told him everything that went down. I shook his hand, promised my word to treat her right, and he left.

"Tee," I started, "I don't even know what to say. Sorry just doesn't seem like it's enough. I just wanna move past that."

"Just promise me you'll never do that again," she said with fear.

"I promise. I'm gonna make you love me again." I kissed her forehead, and laid her head on my chest.

For a couple of months, things were back to normal. Every now and then I surprised her with some grocery store crab legs and steamed shrimp. I dunno why bitches, especially black bitches, act like all is forgiven when you break out the seafood. But as you know, promises are made to be broken.

She started writing Kerry since she was too scared to call him, and if he tried to jump bold and call her, that was an argument. If she did her homework while I was tryna smash that, that was an argument. If she wasn't answering the phone when I was calling, that was a guaranteed argument and a possible ass-whippin' when I got home. And let her drink the last cold soda in the fridge without replacing it . . . Well, you get the idea. Basically, I could do whatever and whoever I wanted, and she just had to suck it up. She was free to leave whenever she wanted, but she thought she had nowhere else to go. They always do. Mission accomplished!

Now that you're all caught up, I can get into tonight's issue. I had just gotten off work (for real this time) when suddenly . . . hold up, that's my cell ringing. I knew she'd call me sooner or later.

"Hello." Nothing but breathing. "Hello? Tee you there?"

"Come home," she said sadly. "I miss you."

"You had me worried girl," I said. "You know I luh you, right?"

"I know, O," she said, "it's just so hard sometimes to love you. It's like you're saying it, but not really meaning it."

"I'm sorry, Tee. I can't see myself without you, and would never want to mess that up. Let's talk it out when I get home, aight? Is the house clean? You know I don't like coming home to a dirty house." She laughed a little on the other side of the phone.

"Yeah it is. See you soon." See, that's why Tierra was my heart. Through the bull, she was there no matter what. Thick and thin, til the end. Kickin' me outta my own gotdamn apartment. Ain't that some shit? She just better hope her daddy still there to protect her. She needs to learn who runs this house!

P is for Parris

Dear Mom,

It's been kinda crazy without you here these last seven years. I'm sorry I waited so long to write to you, but I didn't know how to forgive you until now. Today is my 13th birthday, but I know you know that already. Anyway, Uncle Floyd and Aunt Deidra bought me a diary for my birthday since I wasn't talking much since you left. Aunt Deidra told me, "It's not good to hold all that in. You don't have to talk to us, but talk to God. And just write. You don't have to share it, but let it out." I thought the first thing I wrote should be addressed to you. I just want you to know how I feel about everything.

I still remember the three of us, me, you, and Daddy, and how happy we all was when things was going good. You would come home from working your shifts at the hospital, looking all tired, and would see me and Grandma working on my homework at the kitchen table. After a quick hug and kiss, you changed out your scrubs and started dinner for Daddy and me.

Once Daddy got home, Grandma would leave so someone could "keep an eye on me" like she would say. He would come home with his tie loosened and his top button unbuttoned, top hat and trench coat, and sigh like every day was a long day. But as soon as I ran to the door, he always smiled and lifted me up. He would carry me over to the stove and give you a kiss to show how much he missed you all day.

I remember one day we had just finished eating some of your homemade spicy spaghetti, with the pepperonis and sausage pieces in the sauce. While you were washing out the pots, me and Daddy snuck in on you and sprayed you with the water guns. "Stop it, now! You as bad as the damn kids!" You were mad and laughing at the same time. We were leaving and you yelled, "Hey!" soaking us with the sink hose as we turned back around. The water fight was back on and we were all chasing each other around the kitchen, slipping and stomping through the puddles.

Later that night, you wrapped me in my pink pajamas and tucked me tight under the covers. You usually read to me, but that night, I remember you telling me how proud of me you were, and that I could be whatever I wanted: a designer, a singer, a doctor, all three if it was what I wanted. "The world is at your fingertips," you said. I said my prayers, and fell asleep, thanking God for giving me such a great Mommy, Daddy, and happy life.

In the middle of things going great, a big change came. I got off the school bus and didn't see Grandma's car in the driveway, but you and Daddy's cars was home. I opened the door, walked, into the kitchen and was surprised to see you two sitting in me and Grandma's homework chairs. I was so happy to see you all home early, but you both looked so sad.

What's wrong?" I asked. Daddy just sat there, like his stomach was in pain.

"Your father won't be working for a little while," you began.

"Like fired?" I had asked so innocently, but when I saw your eyes close and shoulders sink, I knew I had stumbled onto grown-up business.

"It's OK," Daddy said while reaching for your hand. "We should tell her the truth. Come here." I sat my pink and purple book bag on the ground and climbed up his long legs. "Yes, sweetie, I was fired. But, it's not all bad news. It means that until I find a new job, I can take you to school in the mornings, and I'll be here to help you with homework and play with you when you're done." My eyes lit up at the thought.

"Forever?" I asked excitedly. You two just laughed and laughed.

"Hopefully not forever, but it might be a couple of weeks or so. But your mom and I love you very much, and we don't want you to worry about adult problems. You're the kid. We worry about you, OK?" I nodded my head and hurried upstairs. I was looking forward to the little time Daddy and I would have at home.

As luck would have it, and not in a good way, the little time turned into a lot of months. It was going on seven months and Daddy still didn't have a job. He'd drop me off at school and go out in his suit everyday hoping someone would call him, but it never happened. And the more I saw of Daddy, the less I saw of you. Your three twelve hour shift turned into three twelve's and two eights. Your home-cooked meals changed to pizza, fast food, and take-out. Your tired smiles when you got home switched to angry frowns. Things was changing, and it was happening fast.

I remember coming home one day from school and hearing you and Daddy arguing before I even got inside the house. Remember that day? I had opened up the front door and sat my book bag down like normal, and could hear your yells echoing through the house.

"I don't see what's so bad about putting in an application at the grocery store just until you hear back from something else," you said.

"Because I have a degree and a lot of good experience, Charisse. I'm not baggin' nobody's groceries," Daddy yelled.

"So you're OK with sitting there, out of work, unable to take care of your family?"

"You better watch yourself," he warned.

"No," you pushed on, "because while you stay home and play Mr. Mom, I have to work again. Sometimes I'd like to come home and know that I have an off day coming up, but I don't have that simple luxury anymore."

"Do you think I asked to get fired!?!? Huh?!?!" Daddy yelled. I could hear things being tossed around upstairs, and was afraid to go up any further than the third step. I was scared of what I'd see if I went there before you had finished.

"I'm just saying you should be taking care of me, not the other way around. I'm the bitch!"

"I know you're the bitch. Recently, not a day goes by where I'm not reminded how much of a bitch you are." After Daddy said that, it had gone from loud shouting to no noise coming from upstairs at all.

Without warning, you came out the room and slammed the door, running down the steps fast. "Hi," was all you said when you passed me on the stairs. You looked sad, like you was bout to cry, and ran past so I wouldn't see you. You hurried out of the door, jumped in the car, and sped off.

A little after you left, Daddy came to the top of the steps and said, "Get started on your homework. I'll be down in a second." I had hoped that would be the end of the bad days, but as you know it wasn't.

More days went by and Daddy still let his pride get in the way of interviewing at places he was "too good for." He started drinking, at home, and on the way to dropping me off at school. I never knew what was in that brown paper bag back then, but I knew it smelled worse than bleach, and more like something to put on a cut than something to drink.

Anyway, one day you came to pick me up 'cus he was too drunk to drive. We was all wet up from it raining real hard. With Daddy's drinking, we never knew what mood he would be in by the time we both got home so we tried to sneak in as quiet as we could.

"Thank you for getting her," he said walking into the living room. "I wasn't feeling too good so I just laid down for a minute and . . ." Dad crashed into some pots that were sitting on top of the stove and got really upset. "Fuck! Who put these here anyway?"

"Parris why don't you go upstairs and change out of your uniform," you said.

"Yes ma'am." I walked out of the room and up the steps with a cold, hollow feeling in my chest like something bad was coming. I didn't want to leave you, but I knew that you only liked to say things once. I ran up all the steps, then crept halfway back to make sure you were OK.

"So, you gotta job?" you asked, taking off your raincoat and placing it in the closet. "A late interview or something?"

"Don't you think if I had one I woulda told you?" he answered.

"Well, I figured that would be the only thing that could keep you from picking up your seven year-old daughter from school. News flash Ray: when you call the school to say that I'll be picking Parris up, make sure you let me know, too."

"I didn't think it was a big deal. You work fifteen minutes from the school," he said irritated.

"Yeah and you don't work at all." It got quiet again, like that time I had heard you arguing before, and then I heard a clap loud enough to make me jump. I couldn't see, but I knew he had hit you. I didn't hear you fall, cry, or even lose your cool. You just stood there and let him talk to you and say anything that came to his head.

I know now you were just protecting me, but back then I was so mad at you. I couldn't understand why it seemed like everything was OK until you came home. I remember wondering why you always had to bother him about a job and how you always said the wrong things out your mouth. Things sure have changed.

I heard footsteps leaving the kitchen and I ran back upstairs so you wouldn't know I was there. You came out rubbing the side of your face and grabbed your raincoat.

"And where you goin' in this weather?" Daddy asked.

"I forgot to go to the grocery store. I need to get a salad for dinner."

"A salad? With it pouring down, thundering and lightning out?" I could tell he didn't believe you. I didn't either.

You raised your voice and said. "I'll be right back! Come on to the store with me, Parris."

"What she need to go for? I thought she had homework." He wasn't giving up, and I was happy. I was so mad at you for dragging me into it. I was hoping he wouldn't hate me later as much as he hated you now.

"I can stay with Daddy," I said, running down the stairs with half of my coat on.

"No, we're going to the store."

"What's the big deal about her staying here?" Daddy asked, throwing his arms up. "It's not like you aren't coming back, right?" he asked, almost as if he dared you to say you were leaving. "Plus, we've got homework and bath time to start on. Just go on and we'll finish everything here." You hated the idea, especially since you were tryna get us outta there and over to Grandma's or somewhere safe until he calmed down, but you had no choice but to leave me if you wanted it to be peaceful.

"Fine, I'll be back." You tossed your coat on the floor and slammed the door.

"Hmph, guess she's mad about something," Daddy joked. "Why don't we skip homework for tonight and you can go play. I'll just tell your mother we did it."

I remember thinking how much cooler he was than you, and how much more fun he was when you weren't around. I went into my play kitchen and pretended to turn on my stove. I threw some plastic food around in the pan and smiled back at Daddy while he sipped his drink and watched me play.

When I finished cleaning up my pretend mess, I threw the food on a plate and served it to Daddy in the kitchen with a cup of blue juice.

"For me?" he said with a fake surprised face.

"Uh huh. Cus Mommy doesn't cook anymore." He took little nibbles of the food and loud sips of the juice, and faked a burp to make me happy.

"Mmmm, that was good, thank you!" I was grinning from ear-to-ear that I had finally seen him smile again.

Daddy sat his plate on the counter and pulled me up to his lap on the bar stool. His breath still smelled like whatever he had been drinking before we got home. "Well since you're playing house, you know, there are some other things that Mommy doesn't do around here, too."

"Like what?" I asked.

"Well you know she comes home late from work a lot, so sometimes she's really tired. She doesn't feel like cooking, or cleaning, or doing other things she normally does." Daddy began to slide a finger down the buttons on my uniform shirt, while I felt something poking at my back and jumping on his thigh. It was the first time he had ever done something like, and I felt weird, but I wanted us to just be a family again. I was scared, but I didn't cry. It was my Daddy, and I was his Parris; why wouldn't I trust him?

He started to unbutton my shirt and softly kiss my cheek in a way he had never kissed me before. It reminded me of the kisses people had given on TV shows and stuff. "Put your hand here," he said, pointing to the thing in his pants. He brought me in close and put his hands up my jumper. It was so uncomfortable, and I had begun to wish I'd gone with you like you had asked.

He knocked the toy plate and food onto the floor and laid me on the counter like I was getting a diaper change. He took off his shirt, dropped his pants, and showed me what was in his pants. That was the first time I saw a penis, and I was scared! He laid it flat on my thigh and inched closer and closer to between my legs, getting ready to do who knew what. That's when we heard the two loud pops.

Daddy and I both froze to see what it was. He got from over top of me, felt the back of his shirt, and bulged his eyes at the sight of blood covering his palm. I peeked from behind him and saw you standing there, angry, dripping wet, and holding a pistol.

"You shot me?" he asked. You never answered, but the one tear coming from your eye said it all. You had no shame or regret for what you had just done. "You bitch!" He tried to limp over to you, but before he made it you shot him one last time between the eyes. He stumbled back and fell over me and I screamed. There was blood everywhere and I was covered in it.

You ran to get me from under him and threw me across your shoulders, but I fought, punching at your back the whole time. "It's OK, Parris!" you yelled. "Calm down. Everything's gonna be fine now." But everything wasn't OK. You killed him.

You put me in the passenger seat of your car and buckled me in, but I didn't wanna leave him there. We could hear the police cars' sirens as you rushed to the driver's seat. One of the neighbors must've heard the blasts and called them to our house. You backed up, but ran right into a squad car. I was screaming, crying, and scared as I dunno what! Without panicking, you turned the car off, unbuckled your seatbelt, and spoke to me.

"Parris, I need you to be quiet and listen to me. You know I love you very much," you began, "and there's nothing I wouldn't do for you to protect you. What happened in there was to protect you. I know what you think you know, but when you're older, you'll understand."

The police surrounded the house while two more broke down the front door. "Ma'am, step out of the car slowly!" one called out. You did as he asked.

"Just stay in the car until they come for you," you said. "They'll take care of you."

Me, you (in handcuffs), and the police sat there waiting for someone to come pick me up. Finally, Grandma pulled up as they wheeled out his body.

Grandma squealed as she watched her only son being rolled out in a black bag. "AHHHH!!!" She charged towards the door trying to peek inside, but the officers held her back. She walked over to you almost as fast as if she were running. She was angrier than I had ever seen her.

Just before the cops held her back again, she reached out and slapped you in your face. Your cheek turned, but again, you didn't cry. "You never knew how to keep him happy!" she yelled. "Never!" The police called Uncle Floyd and Aunt

Deidra shortly after they noticed that Grandma wasn't the right person to take me home.

So, here's where I've been for the past seven years. Aunt Deidra finally told me that you were in the hospital, not jail. I guess no judge could blame you for what you did. I hear they think you'll be out soon. I hope so cus we have a lot to talk about.

You said I'd understand when I was older, Mommy. Well I'm older and now I do . . .

Love,
Parris

Q is for Quentin

"Damn, six a.m. already?"

"Just five more minutes baby," she pleaded.

"Work calls," I said, throwing the covers up and rolling out of bed. "Kids, wake up!"

I headed to the bathroom to wipe the crust out my eyes, the drool from the corner of my lip, and looked back at the gift from God still lying in bed: my wife's best friend, Janay. I couldn't help but smile when I saw Janay's honey brown skin quiver in her sleep as the morning breeze seeped in through the cracked window. I imagined that she was flashing back to how I wrecked that the night before. I thought to myself, *"Q, you did your thang, bruh."*

I never intended to hurt my wife. In fact, I loved everything there was to love about Kara, from her freckled white skin and blonde hair, to her infectious laugh and sense of humor. She was kind of flat-chested, and would joke around that, "More than a handful was a waste anyway." She wasn't the best looking woman out of her group of friends, but she made up for it by treating me like a king. At least she used to.

Once I got past the physical she baited me in with her ambition. She was determined to be an executive by thirty, and a woman not afraid of hard work sealed the deal for me. Who knew the thing I loved most about her would turn on me?

Not even five years after we said "I do", I noticed that I was missing a spouse to come home to. Kara's consulting firm offered her a chance at a promotion that altered our storybook marriage. Her career became her focus, her co-workers turned into her family, and her subordinates replaced our two children, Clayton and Hannah. She spent weeks at a time traveling to close big deals, leaving me and the kids to fend for ourselves.

I had gotten used to eating dinner with just the kids, and scrambling to the karate matches after work alone, but I needed some help and Janay was the best choice. She was always there when Kara was "too busy", whether it was to drop a pizza past the house for me and the kids, or pick up Clayton from karate practice. But it wasn't just her willingness to help that drew me in. Janay had enough ass and titties to feed a small village with leftovers for days. I knew it wouldn't be long before I broke down and gave in.

Eventually, she stepped in to fulfill some of Kara's other "duties" as well, but she was close enough to Kara that our hanging out wouldn't raise any eyebrows; and unlike any random chick off the street, she cared enough about Kara to keep this thing quiet. I knew I was wrong, but what Kara didn't know wouldn't hurt her. And even if she somehow found out about it, who cares? After all, it's just emotionless sex.

I finished my typical morning routine: pissed, showered, shaved, and threw on my black-on-black pinstriped suit with an indigo button-up shirt and matching tie. Whoever said light-skinned dudes were out of style must've been hatin' on us cus I was on point! I felt so good, I even upgraded from the everyday zirconium to the half karat diamond earring Kara bought me. Doesn't my baby treat me good?

I grabbed my briefcase near the banister and ran downstairs, following the scent of bacon and scrambled eggs with cheddar cheese. Janay must've gotten up while I was in the shower and pretended to curl back in bed before I got out. That girl really knew how to take care of "her" man. "Girl, you keep treating me like this," I yelled upstairs. I turned the kitchen corner and almost choked on my words at the sight of Kara in her travel clothes standing at the stove swirling eggs.

"Shhh, you'll wake the kids," she said with a smile. "Aww baby, I know you're surprised. I could've taken a flight but I wouldn't have been home until this afternoon. So, instead I rented a car and made it home in time to fix my hubby some breakfast before he headed out." My heart was beating through my blazer. If Janay rolled over an inch in our bed, the creaky floors over the kitchen ceiling would be a dead giveaway that someone was upstairs. I tried to talk as loud as I could to give her some type of tip off.

"Thank you, Kara-bear. And you even have the coffee," I said, kissing her forehead. "I can't wait to dig in. Let me run upstairs right quick and see if the kids are ready." She smiled as I squirmed out of the kitchen, exhaling that I had dodged trouble for the moment.

I ran up the steps and into our bedroom, passing the kids brushing their teeth in their bathroom. The running blocked out any conversation that Kara could've listened in on. Janay began to speak when I pulled the door open. "Babe, you're running late."

"Don't speak. We have a big problem!" I whispered. "Kara is downstairs cooking breakfast." Her eyes widened with panic.

"What the hell, Q! Why did you say I could stay over?" She asked in confusion.

"I didn't know! She wanted to surprise me. Just stay up here, but you need to get out of the bedroom before she hears you. I'll try to get her to leave the house with me so you can leave out."

"Clayton, Hannah. Breakfast," Kara called up.

"I gotta go. Just stay still til I get them out."

I jogged back downstairs and tried to act as calm and normal as possible. I kissed Hannah on her cheek, and hugged Clayton from behind his chair.

"Running late again?" Kara asked.

"Yeah. In fact, I'm gonna have to take my breakfast to go. You mind dropping the kids at school?"

"Well, how would they have gotten there if I didn't come home early?" she asked.

"Huh?" was the only answer I had at the time. I could feel my deodorant working overtime as my anxiety took over, but I tried to stay cool.

"I'm just really tired, and was just thinking maybe you or Janay could drop them off."

"Janay? Oh no, she's probably at work already. Because she said she had some work to catch up on?" I asked, almost like I didn't even believe that myself. "So, yeah she's already gone. Are you sure you just can't take them?" She thought about it for a few seconds, and then finally agreed.

"Ok, we're taking breakfast on the road kids. Clayton, take your sister to the car and strap yourselves in. I'll be out in a minute." The kids excused themselves from the table, gave me one last hug, and did as their mother told them. I grabbed my briefcase and headed to the door, hoping Kara would follow behind me. "Q, before you leave," she called. "*What now?*" was all I could think.

"What?" I asked innocently.

"I came across a wine bottle in the trash when I was throwing out the egg shells. You're drinking again?" Shit! I didn't take the trash out last night because I thought I had a couple more days til Kara came home.

"Well, you've been gone so long I just get frustrated and stressed out tryna do it all on my own," I explained.

"But strawberry wine?" she continued. "I remember you as more of a rum and coke man."

"You know they say red wine is good for you. Plus, I didn't want to get too drunk around the kids," I explained further. She wasn't done yet.

"What about the two glasses in the dishwasher?" My heart began to pound so heavy that I could feel it in my ears. My palms tingled as alarm and blood flowed through my veins. I could feel my face turning brick red and my slacks began to tremble as my legs shook with fear. I had to think of something quick.

"I didn't drink it all in one night. Babe, where's all of this coming from?" Kara lowered her head in disappointment. We both knew what she was inferring, and where she was trying to lead me.

"I'm sorry, honey," she began. "I guess I let my imagination run wild and I'm just so upset with how often I have to leave you and the kids for so long. I hope I didn't offend you."

"Come here," I said, grabbing her and kissing her thin lips. "You know there is nothing to worry about. I love you. You do know that right?" She leaned in for a hug and melted in my arms. "Now, let's get outta here before I'm any later." We walked through the living room and made what I hoped was our last attempt out the door and out of trouble.

"Oh, one more quick thing," Kara excitedly said while running to grab the remote for the living room TV. "Have you seen this show before?" The channel looked grainy and the camera was shaking, almost like live taping of a reality show. "Yeah, it's a new show called 'What Kind of Fool Do You Think I Am?'" Kara pushed me back, and that's when I noticed that the couple on the television was us.

"What the . . ."

"The nanny cams you had installed," she explained. "You forgot to uninstall them once we fired the babysitter and Janay took over." She rewound the tape to last night as I gulped and tried to swallow the lump of embarrassment down my throat. "7:35 pm: you, Janay and the kids watching TV, laughing like a happy little family." She fast forwarded. "9:22pm: popcorn and a movie, but no kids this time. 9:27pm: she lays on your arm, feet on MY couch, curled up under MY blanket. Now, here's where it gets interesting." Again, she fast forwarded.

"10:08pm: my so-called best friend is slobbing your neck down like a dog. 10:10pm: you're putting on a condom. And by ten thirteen folks, he's done." The video showed me shaking and cumming with Janay sprawled under me. Even with a condom on, I made the rookie mistake of not pulling out. Kara was furious. Her blue eyes were clouded by anger. I couldn't tell if I was looking at my wife, or some unknown demon from Hell.

"Kara, I . . . I . . ."

"But the funny thing," she interrupted, "is that after your brief performance, the two of you head upstairs. But there's no tape of her ever leaving. In fact, I was home before the two of you were even up. So, with that being said, that whore is still here. JANAY!"

The ceiling began to creak over our heads as Janay made her way out of our bedroom and down the stairs. "Kara, please. Just let her go. We can talk about this ourselves," I reasoned.

"Shut up, Q!" she yelled back. Janay had just reached the banister and Kara instantly lost it. "Oh my God!" she repeated, swaying around as if she were drunk. "Seeing it on tape is one thing, but actually seeing your backstabbing ass in person? Unbelievable. Aren't there enough single men out there that you could've left mine alone? Hell, you could've even wrecked any other home but your best friend's, Janay! Why?" Kara placed her hands over her face and broke down. I could only imagine the pain that I had caused her.

"I'm so sorry Kara," Janay started. "I was weak. We were weak, and we didn't think about how this would mess a lot up for all of us. Please don't cry."

"Crying? Oh, you must have thought I was one of those pitiful white women from Lifetime: the quiet little blonde woman that does everything and puts up with anything 'Daddy' gives her, all while crying herself to sleep, but I'm stronger than that," she said while unbuttoning her blazer. "Eight years of marriage, two kids, nice house and two incomes, and you still turned our American dream into a nightmare. But you sooo won't see me cry over you." Kara threw her blazer on the floor, pulled her sleeves up to her elbows, and fastened her hair into a ponytail. "But let me tell you something, Janay," she began, "if you want my man, you're going to have to fight me for him. You hear me, you black bitch?"

Without further warning, Kara leaped over the coffee table and charged at Janay with full force and tackled her to the ground. She swung her fists wildly, landing blows anywhere Janay wasn't protected. Janay swatted back, but her open hands were no match for Kara's fists. Immediately, I ran to pull her off, but a loose fist caught me in the balls, putting me on the floor for a few seconds that felt like excruciating hours. After I caught my breath, I grabbed Kara from behind and began to pull, but Kara had clenched onto Janay's hair.

"Kara let go," I yelled. "Let her go!" I flung Kara off and accidentally into the wall, leaving a hole from the impact. But that didn't stop her. As I checked on Janay, Kara jumped on my back, wrapped her legs around my waist and began to scream.

"You're gonna defend her?!?! You're gonna defend her?!?! AHHHH!!!" She began to take her anger out on me, violently pounding on my head and shoulders. I spun chaotically until she finally crashed on the couch. She was breathing heavily and had a fiery look still burning in her eyes. Her hair was wild and had come out of her band. I held Janay back from trying to get her revenge.

"Now look, you need to calm down," I said. "We can talk about this, but you need to breathe and calm down."

"I am calm," Kara yelled while flipping the coffee table, shattering the glass top. "Oh, you don't believe me? Why don't we ask your mother what she thinks?!" Kara catapulted herself off the couch and ran madly towards the fireplace where my mother's urn rested.

"Kara, please," I begged.

"In a minute," she said, halfway cutting me off. She lifted the top and began to yell inside the urn. "Mrs. Scott," she began, "Quentin thinks I need to calm down. What do you think?" Kara raised the urn over her head, and hurled it at Janay like a major league baseball pitch. Janay ducked, and the urn exploded on the wall, spreading my mother's ashes throughout the living room. My eyes began to well up as thoughts of my mother and her long battle with cancer began to resurface. Kara smiled and said, "That felt good. No wonder you love smashing other women so much."

Without hesitation, I stormed across the room and slapped Kara to the ground. I picked her up and began choking her until her feet were dangling off the ground. Even being unable to breathe, she had a cynical smile on her face as if nothing could possibly hurt her anymore than what I had put her through.

I let her go, and she stumbled into the kitchen, returning with a half-empty bottle of gin. She sipped slowly, then massaged the strangle lines around her neck with the chilled bottle. "Drink anyone?" she asked sarcastically.

"Kara," I said while trying to control my anger, "you need to leave."

"Fuck you, this is my house!" she argued back.

"Just get the hell out now!" Suddenly, the front door gently opened, showing Clayton on the patio holding Hannah's hand, both with tears in their eyes.

"Mommy, can we go to school now?" he asked innocently. They looked around and saw our living room was destroyed as if we'd had our own personal hurricane attack our house. Kara looked at the kids, then back at us, and then back at the kids one last time. I could tell she was conflicted; she wasn't through with us, but she didn't want the kids to see how much uglier this could get.

"Of course. Let's go to school," she answered unwillingly. Kara cut her eyes at me and exited the room, gin still in hand. I tried to take the bottle from her, but she snatched back. I was concerned for the kids, but as long as she was gone, I didn't care.

"Have a good day at school, Clay," I said, but he didn't answer.

Janay sat on the couch and I rested on the steps. I couldn't believe how this day had played out. It was a shameful mess, to say the least. All I could think about was would my kids ever forgive me for the pain I know I'd caused. Finally, the awkward silence had been broken.

"So what now?" Janay asked.

Before I could answer, Kara loudly screamed from outside, "MOTHERFUCKER!!!", at the same time as her bottle of gin was hurled inside the living room window with a burning paper towel corked in the bottle's neck.

"Oh my God!" Janay yelled in fear. The smoke detector wailed as the flames quickly began to consume the entire living room, leaving us little time to make our way to the front door.

"Follow me," I said. We trekked through the cackling fires to the front of the house. I grabbed the door handle and yelled in agony from the searing heat of the doorknob. I hurriedly took off my tie, wrapped it around my hand and grabbed the door handle. This time, I was able to turn it open, only to realize Kara had locked the storm door. I shook the door frantically, praying that it would miraculously unlock, but it didn't. The fire was rising higher and the heat eventually melted the smoke detector into warped rubber. This did not look good for Janay and me.

Just as I had given up hope, Janay came running and handed me a leg from the destroyed coffee table. I shattered the glass and we both crawled out, gasping for a taste of fresh air as the fire department pulled up.

Janay and I crawled to the sidewalk and collapsed as if we'd finished a 5K run.

One of the firefighters approached me while the others set the hose up. "What happened? Are there others in the building?" he asked. I shook my head no. Just then, I received a text from Kara, probably to tell me we could try and talk, or that it was officially over.

"Don't bother going into work today. I left a voicemail and they ALL know what you did! And if you love that car, I'd park it somewhere safe b4 you find it the same way YOUR house is."

It felt like every quote was running through my head: "It's cheaper to keep her," "It's better to leave than cheat," and definitely "Hell hath no fury . . ." I sat on the curb and watched my house, marriage, family, and life burn to ashes. I had really done it this time!

R is for Regina

These days all I hear is how many unmarried black women there are, how many will never get married, or how high the divorce rate is. But I don't pay those stats any mind cus as I sit here waiting for my boo to pick me up, I realize I got my husband. In eight short months, I've been to three continents, dined at every upscale restaurant in and out of town, been to over twenty-something different bed and breakfast inns, all without ever pulling out my wallet. It wasn't because I couldn't afford it or because I was some golddigger, but because Trent believed a woman should be treated simply like a woman. He pulls my chair out whenever we eat out, offers up his blazer on cold nights, and takes the trash to the curb for me after he leaves out. Even better, he kept it all up after I gave him my goodies for the first time. Yes, I do have the perfect husband, but there was just one thing wrong: he wasn't MY husband.

It was an unseasonably cold November for Bakersfield. The last of the colorful autumn leaves were dying off and I just wanted to take the weekend to relax by the fireplace with a bowl of clam chowder, but my girlfriend, Stacey, invited me to her annual classy charity fundraiser. She told me there would be plenty of eligible men there, so be sure to doll up and stick out. Any man that her bougie ass was into would definitely turn me off. However, I followed her advice, wearing a pleated, sleeveless, plum cocktail dress that tied around my neck and rested just above my knees with silver pumps that flawlessly matched my purple and sterling costume bracelet.

I arrived at the Myleena Hotel a little after the start of the party. I walked in on the red carpet and was instantly blinded by the professional photographers that had been paid to act as if they were paparazzi. Stacey knew how to plan a charity event! "Regina, over here," she called, sauntering over in a pearl colored floor-length dress and diamond necklace that let everyone know this was her function. "Darling," she greeted with a sadiddy kiss on each of my cheeks. "I'm glad you could make it out. And you look gorgeous, too! Who are you wearing?"

"Macy's," I proudly said. She paused like I had instantly brought down the taste of her party, but I told her I wasn't feeling this thing anyway. "Hey, I made it, didn't I?"

"True, true," she answered between breaths. I wish I had brought Lovey and the girls. Now, that woulda been some fun. "Anyway, let me introduce you to someone." We walked through the dark hotel lounge as the hundreds of guests mixed and mingled. I grabbed a red wine glass from a server's tray and continued flowing through the crowd and scenery.

"And here we have the refreshment bar," Stacey concluded. "Feel free to take a few pieces, but not too much. They're hors d'oeuvres, not dinner." I rolled my eyes as she walked to entertain the rest of the guests. I bit into a piece of cheese quiche and immediately coughed it up and spit it into a napkin. "*Hmm, that plant in the corner looks like a good place to hide it,*" I thought. As I inconspicuously strolled to the plant, my path was cut off by a tasty stranger.

"I'm not too big on quiche either," he said. I laughed politely at him busting me.

"Oh yeah. I was just looking for the trash can."

"I'm Trent."

"Regina," I said extending my hand. Instead of a shake, he reached out, grabbed my hand, and kissed it.

"Pleased to meet you, Regina." Stacey was right, there were some good catches amongst this crowd, especially this caramel brotha that stood before me. Another hostess passed us, and Trent grabbed two more glasses from her tray as we got to know more about each other.

"So, how do you know Stacey?" I inquired.

"We represented her company in a recent acquisition. After all that hard work, she felt she owed us an invitation to one of her lavish parties."

"Oh ok. I've known her since high school."

"She's good people," he said. "And she sure has good taste."

"Yeah, she could always throw a good party."

"I'm not speaking about the party," he said. It was something about the confidently humble way he sipped the wine after that statement that had me checkin' him out. I could tell underneath that black Jos. A Banks suit he was built like an underwear model. His bald head glistened when the flashing lights hit it at the right angle. His bold brown eyes left me in awe every time I looked into them. I looked down to see if I could spot any hardware imprints through his slacks. Nothing. Oh well, he could be wearing briefs so I'll give him the benefit of the doubt. Plus with those long fingers I knew he had to be holding something. Look at 'em, all well-groomed, rugged and wearing that wedding ring? I shoulda known it was too good and goin' too well to be true.

"Well, it's getting late," I said with a platonic pat on the back. "You enjoy the rest of the evening." I walked out of the party without as much as a glance back. I just kept thinking how much more entertaining my soup would have been. And I was gonna put Old Bay and oyster crackers on it too. Shit.

The next evening I had planned to meet up with Stacey to tell her how that egotistical fool tried to play me. I sat at the bar with a Cosmo and waited on her arrival.

"Waiting on someone?" a deep familiar voice asked. It was Trent.

"Are you following me?" I asked bothered.

"Not at all," he said with a smile. "Stacey told me she was meeting a friend and once she told me it was her beautiful, breath-taking friend, Regina, I just had to tag along. She was the one who insisted I go and make it a date." That sneaky heffa! "Can I sit down?" I snatched my purse out of the empty seat and downed my cocktail. I needed a buzz to get through this date. "I'll take a rum and cola, and another one of whatever she's having."

"You buy drinks for women who aren't your wife?" I wanted to see Trent weasel out of that question, but he acted like it was nothing new. He sipped his cordial, sat the two short straws on a bar napkin, and continued to watch the game.

"You look nice," Trent responded.

"It's just jeans and a top."

"I know," he said, "but you look even better in your normal clothes." He pushed my second Cosmo over to me. I squinted and hesitantly took a sip. After all, it was free.

As the drinks kept coming, the hour got happier and happier. Trent and I were sharing old stories, laughing it up like we were best friends reunited. "You have to try this crab and cheese dip," he urged. I reached down for a piece of the dipping bread. "No, no, no," he swatted away. He ripped away at the loaf, dunked it, blew it cool, and fed me.

"Mmmmm, that's good. I never would have thought cheese and crab meat mixed." I was lying. That was one of my favorite appetizers, but I wanted him to think he had put me onto something new. With all the fun we were having I didn't even notice it was quarter after nine.

"I had a surprisingly good time, sir," I started, "but it's time for me to go. I have to get up for church in the morning." He looked at my three empty drink glasses and looked back at me. "Yeah, so?" We both fell out laughing again.

"Don't worry about the bill. You have a good evening," he said. The liquor was definitely talking because I was not expecting what came out of my mouth next.

"You're not gonna let this poor drunk lady drive home without at least following behind to make sure she's safe, are you?" He smiled that sexy smile. And those eyes; gotdamn those eyes! If I had my way, I'd take him on the bar counter, the restroom, the parking lot, and underneath his christened marriage sheets. As far as I was concerned, I wasn't doing anything wrong.

He flashed his 7-series Beemer headlights and let me pull in front of him. The whole way home I tried to coach myself out of those adulterous thoughts I was having of Trent, blaming it on the alcohol and what not. "That's my story Lord," I prayed, "and I'm sticking to it."

I pulled into my driveway and he met me at the driver's side door like a gentleman. He escorted me to my front door where we awkwardly stood for some time. "Thanks for the meal," I closed out.

"Are you sure you can make it upstairs OK?" he flirted.

"I think I'll be just fine," I bantered back. He drew near as if he were coming in for a kiss goodnight. In a panic, I searched through my purse and unlocked the door.

"Well, we'll have to do this again some time. Bye." I slammed the door and stood on the other side panting like I had just finished a triathlon. I screamed silently on the other side of the door, kicking air like a spoiled brat. Damn, why do the ones I want always play out this way?

As good as I wanted to be, my hormones were in naughty mode. I convinced myself to go after him. Those were his vows to uphold, not mine. Fuck it, my dusty little kitty cat could use some attention. Besides, what were the odds of me meeting his wife? I flung the door open, hoping I could catch him at his car.

"Trent, wai . . ." Before the "t" even got out good, he passionately lunged at me, intimately sliding his tongue into my mouth as our saliva danced. I pulled him in, shut the door, and felt my way around as I led him to the couch.

"Still worried about this?" he asked holding up his ring finger. I illustrated my lack of concern by sucking the finger that held his wedding band and circling my tongue around his cuticle. We kissed long and deep while I unzipped his pants. Through his boxers poked a head the size of a mushroom. Thank whoever's responsible that the suit pants last night were misleading. Trent helped me out of my shirt while I hopped out my jeans and thong in a single scooch. Like a magnet, I was drawn to Trent's oh so defined pecs and abs when he raised the front of his undershirt over his head and around his neck like a gun holster. The suspense of him being inside was killing me and I couldn't take it anymore.

I let my untamed hair down and jumped on top of his condomless shaft and worked my waist on him like a hula hoop contest. "Mmmm, baby," I moaned. Just when I thought I was winning the pleasure battle, he grabbed my soft ass to bring the rippling to a cease and began to thrust in me as I bounced down. He bit his lip with a seductively devilish look like he was thinking, "*Take that!*" I was so pleasantly powerless that all I could do was grab on and enjoy the ride.

"Wrap your legs around me," he panted. Once I got a good grip, Trent stood to his feet with his jeans still at his ankles, and pounded at me so hard, I swear I could hear my dishes in the kitchen shattering from the sound waves of our flesh hammering together. Once he reached his climax, he flung me onto the couch and unloaded between my sweat-drenched breasts. He fell to my side as we both breathed like two furry dogs left in a car on the hottest day of the year. Once his strength returned, he wiped me with a spare napkin I had laying on the coffee table.

I cuddled in Trent's big arms and started to drift off when suddenly his watch buzzed. "I gotta cut on out for tonight," he said, pulling up his pants in a hurry.

"What?" I asked dumbfounded. "Why? You can't just put it down like that and leave."

"I am still married," he said.

"So, how did you think this was supposed to go down? I was under the impression that you were divorced, or at least separated, but you're cheating on your wife. You can't have your cake and eat me too."

"Look, Shawnte and I love each other," he explained, "but we're not in love with each other. No sex, no dates, no romantic dinners, none of that. The problem is we both have assets to protect. So, instead of getting a divorce, I do my thing and she does hers. It really is cheaper to keep her."

"That's really sick," I said.

"What is marriage anyway?" he questioned. "It's a piece of paper. A business agreement. There's no love in that. I'm legally bound to her but other than that, where's the love?" He walked over to me and rested his palms on my shoulders.

"But what if we ever hit things off?" I asked. "Granted, this is only our first date, but I could never take 'us' seriously with you still being married."

"We can be as serious as you want," Trent said while massaging my shoulder blades. "I can give you all the love and intimacy you need and that's what's important. When I'm on my business trips, you'll be the one on my mind. When I'm making extravagant dinner reservations, you're the one I'm making them for. I'm still a monogamous man, Regina. I just have a 'legal issue' on the side, for lack of a better phrase."

"Could I really be the other woman," I thought to myself. *"Homewrecker: how scandalous? Then again, it ain't much else bitin' at this bait these days."* I turned to face him as he desperately waited for an answer. "I guess we can see how this works," I said. "Every woman has a juicy fling at some point in her life."

"Seeing how this works" turned into two months of expensive nights out on the town, romantic movie nights and takeout, and resort hotels. By month three I was introduced to his mother, who welcomed me with open arms and a bottle of Chardonnay for us to get better acquainted.

By month four, I was traveling to Japan as his guest while he met with international marketing clients. It's always fun when you bring a friend. I think that was the same month we celebrated his birthday at the quaint, late night coffee and dessert restaurant. He had spent it with his wife and friends earlier that day, but I was the one who got the birthday sex.

As time passed, I grew more enamored with Trent. It wasn't just his body and money that won me over, but the respect and dignity he treated me with was almost as if I were the only woman in his life, and I wanted to believe that were true. I didn't need to be the woman he brought around his friends, or the trophy wife he brought to the office holiday parties as a charade, just as long as I knew he was mine. It would've been nice to meet at least one of his friends though.

Anyway here we are, celebrating our eighth month of adulterous bliss on a warm and sunny summer Saturday afternoon. Trent had planned for us to lie out on a blanket in Kern River Valley and light the grill. Next, we'd paddleboat in the river splashing water on each other like kids. To end the day, we were going to watch the sunset and make love until the park police threw us out. I couldn't wait, but it looked like I'd have to. Trent was running a little behind, so I thought I'd call and see where he was.

I picked up my cordless phone and called his cell. It rang once with no answer. It rang again and then disconnected. He must have been in a bad service area. I called him again. After the second ring I heard the receiver pick up. "Hello," said a noticeably irritated woman. It was his wife! What should I do? If I hang up, she'd grow suspicious, but if I ask for him, that would be even more suspect. My heart pounded as my deodorant damn near evaporated from the terror. "Hello!" she yelled as if there were a bad connection. In a panic, I changed to my secretary voice and spoke up.

"Hello, may I speak to Trent . . . on? May I speak to Trenton? Please?"

"Not today bitch," she calmly answered before introducing me to the dial tone. She had her nerve. He doesn't even want her and she acting all jealous. I just hope my impatience didn't mess up Trent and I. Suddenly, I got a text message that put my fears away.

"Hey baby I forgot it's Shawnte's birthday. She invited her parents to the house so I have to be here. Can we reschedule our day at the beach and I'll drop by tonight?" I was so glad that I hadn't cost us our relationship, but I was slowly growing angry for some reason. What does it matter that it's her birthday? I'm the woman in his life now. If he thinks he can blow our date without even the decency of a call, he must not know me like I thought.

I wrote him back: "Have a good time. But remember: if you want me to keep our love quiet and play second, I BETTER come first!"

Trent never did respond to my text, but he isn't the only one who can dip into two candy jars. Just how exclusive does he really expect us to be? Remember nigga, you are still married. With my cell phone still in hand, I scrolled through my contact list and came across George: a familiar "buddy" that I abruptly cut loose once Trent entered the picture. I'll just call and see how he's been.

A quick change out of my cookout sundress and into my casual attire and several hours later I was off to meet George at one of his favorite poetry cafés. He arrived shortly after me wearing dark jeans, a white collar shirt and black blazer. "I was beginning to think you had forgotten about me," he said. "To what do I owe the pleasure of this random call?"

"Just wanted to catch up with an old friend," I replied. "You look good." He did look good, just not Trent good. My phone had suddenly disturbed our getting reacquainted session as it rang through my purse. It was another text message from Trent.

"What are you doing?" he asked.

"Busy. Out." I texted back.

"Out??? Can I come through later?" I'm not responding to that. It's probably best that he sweat a little. "???" he texted again. Obviously, he was going to keep this up the whole night unless I respond, so I played the player.

"We'll see. I'll call you when I get home. It's rude to text on a date." I didn't get another text during the rest of the poetry slam. I was laughing on the inside, thinking of how Trent was probably going off, wondering where I was and who I was with. George rested his arm behind my head as I scooted in to lay my head on his shoulder.

While we listened to the poetry together I fantasized about being there with Trent instead. He loved little places like this and the memories that we create around them. As the poets shared their love poems I would look at George and pretend that it was Trent looking back at me.

Once the poetry night ended, George asked if I wanted to come back to his place for wine, but I had ignored Trent long enough. "Thanks George, but I'm kind of tired. I'll just head home." I had just taken my cell phone out to see where he was when I noticed his BMW sitting in my driveway. I walked up to the driver's side and he rolled the window down.

"Hey," he said. I stood there with my arms crossed and eyes squinted so he could see how angry I was. "Oh, and I brought you a little something." He reached into the passenger seat and stuck a plate covered in aluminum foil out of the window. This man fucked up and instead of bringing jewelry or flowers he brought me a to-go plate from his mother's house? I wasn't getting it. "Well I figured your 'date' took you to eat, so the least I could do was bring the dessert." I slowly peeled the foil from the around the edges, lifted the top, and instantly smiled at the sight of Shawnte's birthday cake.

"Aww an end piece just like I like. Thank you, baby." I stuck my finger into the butter cream icing and indulged on the sweet taste. "Do you wanna come in for a little bit?" he looked down at his watch as if he had somewhere to be, but put his car in park and came in. We watched TV and ate birthday cake, just laughing and talking like our first happy hour months ago. That's what I like about him: Trent takes me out or comes over just because he misses me without expecting anything in return. But when we did have sex, it was mind-blowing. Just the thought of the passion, the positions, and the tricks he could do with his tongue were enough to hold me over until the next round.

Sadly, after a couple hours I had to kick him out. Lovey had invited me to church with her and I had to keep my promise. I figured the fact I hadn't been caught and beat down by Shawnte and her girls yet was nothing short of God's mercy and owed Him my attendance at tomorrow's service. I gave him a long kiss at the door as we said our goodbyes.

The next morning I woke at 8:15am striving to make it the 10am service on time. I ironed up a knee-length black dress and put on my Tiffany's necklace and bracelet from Trent. I grabbed my gum off the nightstand and headed down to the foyer to put on my black heels.

Unexpectedly, there was a knock at the door followed by three doorbell rings. "Just a second," I yelled. It was probably Lovey; we never decided who was riding and who was driving. After I got my last heel on, I grabbed my Bible off the arm of the couch. The crazy doorbell ringing continued and the knocks got louder and louder. "OK, OK, I'm coming."

I swung the door open expecting to see Lovey, but was instead staring into the eyes of an unfamiliar face. She was beautiful peach colored woman that stood about as tall as my shoulders. Without introduction she blurted out, "I'm pregnant."

"Excuse me?" I said with confusion.

"Don't play dumb," she said. "I'm Shawnte!" I jumped back at the revelation. How did she know who I was and where I lived?

"I'm sorry, you must have the wrong house," I said innocently.

"You church bitches kill me," she said looking down at my Bible case. "You go out sleepin' with other people's husbands because you're too pathetic to get a man of your own, then think you have a 'Get Outta Hell Free' pass just because you whip up a batch of stale ass brownies for the church bake sale? Whether we're married or separated, as long as that ring is on his finger he's NOT yours." I didn't know what to do except take her insults. "And you're an ugly bitch at that."

"I know I'm wrong," I started, "but you're not gonna keep callin' me a bitch."

"You're a bitch if I say you're a bitch, BITCH!" Now, she was pissing me off.

Suddenly, Trent pulled up to try and control the situation. "Shawnte, get back in the car."

"I'm running this, Trent," she explained, "not you, and not this tacky bitch with the full coochie pouch poking through the front of that horrible dress."

"Ok look," I said annoyed, "you all obviously have things to talk about so I'm gonna go to church as planned. I don't have time for this!"

"Regina let me drop you off," said Trent. "I'm sorry about all of this." I was reluctant to ride with him, but if it wasn't for me having to get some questions answered, I would have driven myself.

"Yeah, you get in that nice car," Shawnte yelled at me. "He wasn't even able to buy that without me cosigning on it. That's my motherfuckin' car, but you go on and enjoy it!"

We sat in the car while Shawnte continued to make a scene on my lawn. "So is it true, Trent?" I inquired. "Is Shawnte really pregnant by you?"

He paused for a second and then unwillingly answered, "I don't know."

"What do you mean you don't know? What happened to no sex and no romance, and just living together?" My rant was interrupted when Shawnte swung her fist into the passenger's side window as if she wanted it to break.

"You need to get out of my gotdamn car!" she screamed. When she saw I wasn't moving, she started kicking and punching the hood, yelling, "OPEN THE DOOR!" Trent pulled off and left her in his tracks. I looked back and saw her hop in a gray Maxima and chase us down. We took the first exit onto the freeway and the next exit off, hoping to lose her, but she stuck with us. I was terrified.

"Baby slow down," I said, "you're going too fast!"

"Hold on Regina. I'll lose her."

"I dunno how much more of this I can take." I looked up and saw us rapidly approaching the bumper of an eighteen wheeler. "Oh God!" I'm panting, my heart's beating uncontrollably, blood's racing through my veins, and I'm gripping onto anything I can get my hands around just to brace myself for what seemed like an unavoidable crash.

Trent darted through the middle lane just before the truck merged over, however Shawnte wasn't as lucky. She attempted to follow us, but the tractor trailer merged over too quickly, causing her to catapult into the metal guardrail, slide across three lanes of traffic, and then smash into the concrete median.

"Oh shit!" Trent yelled.

"Aren't you gonna go back for her?" I asked.

"Are you serious? We need to keep moving. If we go back, we could be in a lot more trouble than this." It seemed like he didn't even care whether or not she survived that disastrous accident. Even I'm not that malicious. "Baby, I need you to stay focused," he continued. "You know I'm only about you. There's nothing that can explain me lying to you but I'm sorry. Do you still love me?"

"I still love you, but I don't know if I'm in love with you anymore."

"Well, why don't you come with me to Italy next month? I was gonna surprise you but I think you should know now. Remember how much you loved Paris? Maybe a trip overseas will get us back in love again. What do you say?"

As Trent held those plane tickets up, I kept thinking this thing had become much more than simple infidelity. People were getting seriously hurt, emotionally and physically. And if Shawnte really was pregnant, I could never trust Trent again if he still wasn't willing to get a real divorce. After everything that happened today, I was completely over this situation and the drama it keeps bringing. Sorry Trent, but you and I are through . . . right after Italy.

S is for Stephen

"I always laugh when people say they prayed to God for their hardship to end. Well, excuse my language but who the heck do you think you are?" The congregation stood to their feet, shouting praises to the Lord as I continued my sermon. "In every hardship there's a lesson, and once it's learned, He will bring you out of it. Instead of praying for it to end, pray for understanding. Pray you'll become better than you WERE once the rough patch is OVER! Oh, yal don't hear me in here!"

"You better preach, Pastor," someone yelled. The congregation cheered and showed their approval while I brought the service to an end.

"Now we will have morning announcements. Please stay for the benediction. After all: God is watching."

I scanned the crowd from my pastoral throne as the projector screens lowered for our video bulletin. All I could think was what a long way All Praise, Glory & Honor Baptist Church had come from our humble beginnings on Alabama Avenue. Back then, video announcements were a dream as our church news was read to all 100 or so of us by 80-year old Sister Felton with a microphone and a handwritten sheet.

After Dad stepped down and I stepped in, we became more active in the community with ministries, fellowship, retreats, and drama productions. Our congregation grew so large and so fast that we were forced to move to a bigger location. I could have signed off on that property on the nice side of Prince George's County, Maryland, but our home was in the southeast quadrant of Washington, D.C., no matter how rough it was. My trustees thought I was crazy to not grab hold of the opportunity to relocate, but as I looked over my flock of almost 1,000 members in our beautifully designed new building with the exterior made entirely of large glass windows, I had proven that faith in God was stronger than any doubt from man. In four long years, I had actualized my father's vision and we had blossomed into a family; a big church family. Still, every family has its secrets.

Once the morning announcements ended, I motioned for the congregation to stand and began my benediction. "Father God, I pray that each person under my voice has heard the Word and will apply it to their lives. Protect them as they travel home, and grant each person a prosperous week. In Your name, Amen."

The crowd surged towards the sanctuary exits while I waited in the pulpit for anyone that might have wanted to chat briefly with the pastor. A young man approached me wearing a pair of baggy blue jeans and an oversized white tee that fit his small frame like a thick winter coat on a wire hanger. "What can I do for you brother?"

"I've been tryna do right for so long Pastor Brooks," he explained, "but I couldn't let the streets go. But your sermon really hit me."

"That's one thing about the Word," I began, "it may not hit everyone at the same time, but when it jumps on you, you can't shake it off."

"Yeah, so for real for real I'm tryna be saved and get in them new member classes."

"Amen!" I shouted excitedly. I reached out to shake the young man's hand and reeled him in for a hug. "Dear Lord, thank you for using me to bring another soul closer to You. I pray that You keep this young man close to Your heart, and that the streets will no longer have a hold to him. In Jesus' name, Amen."

Every Sunday was the same thing: some young hood would walk up to the front seeking salvation, I'd bring him in for prayer, and while others in line were applauding this brave soul, he would discreetly transfer a nickel bag of weed from his hand to mine. Oh yes, Pastor Brooks was a saint, but Stephen Brooks was the devil himself.

With the exception of a few stragglers, the church had completely evacuated. I stopped in the bathroom to check myself in the mirror, fixing the collar on my navy blue blazer and straightening the striped tie around my white shirt. Later, I joined the rest of the staff in the business office to see if the tithes and offerings were locked away.

"Pastor Brooks," called Travis, a young man who I had been mentoring. He had been studying religion in college and since First Lady Victoria and I hadn't had any children yet, I felt he would take over when it was my time to step down. "That was a great message, sir."

"Thank you, Travis, but I told you it's alright to call me Stephen. How did the collection look for this week?"

"Not bad," he said. "We made almost $12,000."

"Praise God," I said excitedly. "We'll be able to do a lot of good programs if our members continue to be so generous. I'm sure the First Lady Vicky will be happy to hear that good news when she gets back." My wife had taken a group of women to the Massanutten resort for a spiritual retreat. She enjoyed bonding with our members, raising them so they would become strong disciples of Christ. And if she was happy, so was I. And when the cat was away . . .

I had gotten so aroused thinking about the fun I had while she was gone that I forgot Travis was speaking with me. "Soon you'll be the one delivering the life-changing messages."

"I don't know if I'm there yet," he nervously chuckled.

"Everybody's gotta start somewhere. In fact, two Sundays from now, how would you like to preach your first sermon here for our ten o'clock service?" Travis was speechless. "Don't worry, if you have any questions, you know my door is always open and my phone is always on."

"Thank you, sir. I mean, Stephen." I could tell he was nervous, but at the same time overwhelmed with appreciation. He scurried away with a jovial bounce in his step and I dismissed the rest of the administrative staff as well, letting them know

I would lock up. Once the room was cleared, I pulled out the small baggy of weed, held it up to my nostrils, and inhaled its familiar aroma through the plastic. I could sense its potency from that deep sniff and could only imagine the high I'd reach once it was rolled and smoked.

It was just after four thirty and I was heading to the parking lot to join Sister Campbell at her home on Evarts Street for Sunday dinner. Sister Campbell—Maxine as I called her—was a very active woman in our church. She served on the usher board for our early service, taught Sunday school during the noon service, and kept me to screwing just her while my wife was away instead of giving into every fast ho wanting to put their moves on the pastor. But, of course there were a few that slipped through the cracks. When I couldn't wait for the next retreat, I'd just make up a lie, like visiting an elderly member in the hospital, all the while I'm rolling in the sheets with Maxine.

It was just something about her that I couldn't put my finger on, but whatever it was had me coming back for more. With her unkept hair, top lip whiskers, and a body like a chemistry beaker, Lord knows I didn't think she was more attractive than my wife. But pussy ain't gotta face, and dick ain't gotta conscience.

Just as the thoughts of what Maxine had possibly cooked up for dinner (and what she would "serve" for dessert) had entered my mind, I noticed two bodies standing near my black Acura TL. My first thought was that it was a couple of street punks trying to jack the car, but once I got closer I saw it was just Sister Wilkins and her eight-year old son, Donté. Damn, I almost wish it were car thieves.

"Good evening, Sister Wilkins," I said with a smile. "How are you and Donté doing tonight?"

"Skip all the pleasantries, Reverend! I would think by now we're past that," she sassed.

"You're right. What do you need, Rochelle?"

"I need to know why you told me you would mentor my boy, but when we came last Tuesday for the youth mentoring ministry they said you weren't there? Don't you care for today's youth?" Rochelle was no more than 5'4" and 120 pounds, but her attitude was 7-feet tall. She was in her mid 30's, tawny complexion, and was wearing emerald green contact lenses as if they were an accessory to her green choir robe she had worn for service earlier today.

"I'm a very busy man," I joshed, "and an even busier pastor. Why don't you bring little Donté down next Tuesday and I'll be sure to have another mentor work with him."

"I'm not leaving my son with some church man I've never met. I've heard the stories!" She covered her son's ears and began to whisper with an obvious angry tone. "Besides, I think you agree that what Donté really needs is a 'father figure'?" I chuckled nervously in front of the boy, and leaned in to whisper in her ear.

"What are you doing?" I sang through my teeth. "We agreed not to talk about this on church grounds."

"No, YOU agreed not to talk about this on church grounds," she corrected. "I agreed to play along as long as you paid me $700 a month every third Sunday, and you take time out to be his mentor until you're man enough to be what you really are."

"It was $500."

"Yeah, well these are recession rates," she bucked back. Donté sat there, obliviously eating a pack of peanut butter crackers Rochelle had packed to nibble on through church service. "Look Stephen, I don't care how much contact you have with me or what secrets you want kept, but for Donté I need you to be there. I don't want him getting into all the wrong shit around here. You know Ms. Bernadine's fifteen year-old grandson was killed two nights ago."

"OK, I promise I'll be there for next week's meeting. I'll look out for him myself. You hear that, man?" I asked Donté, pretending to box him around. He laughed and tried to fight back, but I picked him up and tickled him. Rochelle smiled a little as if our brief play period had backed up my word. She scooted from in front of the driver's door and I brushed my erection across her thigh as I got in. She rolled her eyes as if she was insulted, but she liked it.

Rochelle held the door while I pulled my trench coat inside and then sorrowfully uttered, "You've already disappointed your wife. Don't disappoint this child," before closing the door. I swatted my hand at her, dusted off my shoulder, and drove on to the warm piece of ass I had waiting for me.

I parallel parked in front of Maxine's row house. She lived in one of the older developments that someone's Granny and Pop-Pop probably called home back in the day. I followed the sidewalk up to the three cracked cement steps that led to Maxine's squeaky wire gate that closed off a small square of land she had decorated with perennials and garden gnomes. I knocked on her door and patiently waited for her to let me inside.

"Stephen?" she asked.

"It's me." I walked inside and was immediately confronted by the smell of garlic, citrus, and herbs. This wasn't the usual soul food Sunday dinner. There were two plates on the kitchen table filled with hearty portions of shrimp scampi over a bed of white rice, with two garlic bread sticks on the side. In the middle sat a bottle of Cabernet Sauvignon and two glasses of sweet tea. "I see you've been watching the cooking channel again." She smiled.

The dinner was amazing! I had eaten myself into a high cholesterol coma. Maybe it was that Maxine was such a homebody that knew how to keep a man happy, from the kitchen to the bedroom. Whereas my wife was always working, making a difference in this community or that women's shelter. I admired her commitment, but at the same time, I couldn't eat another hot dog or pack of chicken-flavored noodles.

As I pondered the differences between the two women in my life, Maxine walked into the living room with a dessert plate holding a piece of iced lemon pound cake with the thin line of margarine just like I liked and homemade lemon icing with a hint of rum. She placed it in my hands along with a fork and I went to work. And so did she.

Maxine rested her head on my lap and began to toy with the bronze zipper on my slacks. She pulled it down and carefully sifted through my briefs until she found what she was looking for. She teased the hairs around my dick with her freshly manicured fingernails before devouring me like a piranha, no teeth.

I didn't even have to let her know when it was cumming. Maxine had learned my body so well that she instinctively reached for a paper towel when the pitch of my moaning elevated involuntarily. After I caught my breath, I searched my suit jacket for my pack of rolling papers, and the bag of weed I had received earlier that day. I strategically spread the herbs around, rolled the blunt, and excitedly sparked the lighter.

"I wish you wouldn't do that," Maxine interrupted, wiping the corners of her mouth.

"I'm grown," I said, puffing on the joint while I spoke.

"You know that stuff makes you impotent. Hmph, probably why First Lady can't get pregnant now. That, or you sowing your seeds elsewhere around town."

"What the hell are you talking about?" I asked without emotion.

"Oh please," she said, "everybody in church is talkin' about the resemblance between you and that Wilkins boy. You didn't think you could keep that infamous Brooks' family big head a secret, did you?" I did my best to keep cool, but my armpits began to sweat, my face was making guilty expressions, and I was hittin' the joint hard. Were they really passing gossip around my church? And if so, what role did Maxine play in all this?

I hung my blazer over my right arm, inhaled the weed deep, and blew the smoke in her face. She squinted and turned away, but when she turned back I slapped her down. "You know I don't like hitting you!" I said.

"I know, baby," she coughed, still squirming from the pain. "Sometimes I do step outta line. I need to remember my place." I could hear the sincerity in Maxine's voice as I helped her off the ground.

"Let me see your eye. It doesn't look too bad. Make sure you put some ice on it right away, OK? We want you ready for Bible study."

"Amen," she whispered in tears. She leaned in to kiss my lips but met my cheek.

"Sorry, baby. I'm off to pick Vicky up from the church parking lot. I'm not gonna disrespect her like that."

Maxine walked me to the front door and I headed to my parked car. "Can't wait for next week's sermon," said an old woman sitting on the patio next door.

"Beg your pardon, ma'am?"

"Your sermon. Maxine's such a fine woman. She says that sometimes you come over and she helps with your message when you get stuck. You must've been working hard in there all this time. That message is gonna be some kinda dynamic!"

"One of my best," I agreed. My mind may have been playing tricks on me, but as I turned around I swear I heard the old woman let out an "Umm hmmm," under her breath. The church knew something, but I didn't have time to track down where it was all coming from. I had to pick Vicky up from the retreat buses.

I sat in the church parking lot in silence, wondering who could have aired the pastor's dirty laundry. Was it Maxine? Nah, she had too much love and lust for me to turn me in. Anything she had figured out, she would have kept to herself, or refute any rumors she heard circling through the sanctuary.

Maybe it was Rochelle. She definitely had the chip on her shoulder to do it, but if she wanted those monthly checks she knew it was better to shut the hell up and ride this thing out. It ain't "hush money" without the hush. Whomever it was, I took it as a sign from God that I've had my fun, but it's time to let it die down for a couple of months, even a year or two. And when it's out of everyone's head, I could roam again.

Suddenly, the coach bus pulled up and a sea of church hats poured from the glass doors. Vicky liked to do the High Tea luncheons on the last day, which explained the flying saucers and fruit bowls on the ladies' heads. Once everyone unloaded, there stood my Vicky in her cream skirt suit, pearl blouse the tone of her blazer buttons, and a matching hat with two pearl ribbons hanging from the back. She was beautiful, elegant, and a dear to everyone at that church. I couldn't believe how I had been stringing her along these past eight years.

"There's my God-fearing woman," I greeted.

"Heeeey, my God-fearing man," she joked back. Vicky blessed me with a little peck on the lips in front of the congregation. That quick mouth-to-mouth moment we shared sent me back in time, reflecting on our young adult dating years at the skating rink, the different church retreats we had gone on, and more. She transcended any piece of pussy that would ever throw itself at me. We were ordained by the heavens to be together, and what God hath joined together, let no man tear apart!

* * *

It was Tuesday night and like I promised I showed up for the mentoring ministry. To my surprise the ministry had outgrown the conference room and was moved to the sanctuary. I looked over the crowd and saw Travis with a group of Ballou Senior High students he had been working with. Donte was sitting quietly with Rochelle in the third row on the right. Meanwhile, Vicky and Maxine were in the back of the church conversing. The two suddenly exited the sanctuary together and Rochelle gave me that sinister crooked smile of hers. According to Vicky there was going to be a similar program for young women launching tonight. I figured it was best to play it cool, start the program, and ask Maxine what that was about later on.

"Praise the Lord!" I said from the pulpit. "Only God would have known how quickly this program would take off. Our children are in need, saints. They're in need of strong role models to lead them. And when Mommy and Daddy are working hard to keep food on the tables, it's good to know that the church is there to help out." There were Amens, Hallelujahs, shouts and applause from my energetic introduction. "Let me stop before I turn this into tomorrow night's Bible study."

"That's alright, Pastor Brooks!" a seasoned member yelled. "Take your time."

"My, my, my! Whew Lawd!" I calmed down. "What we're gonna do is start with the short mentoring video for all of our new mentors, and then I'll have Travis come up and do the prayer." I could see the eagerness on Travis's face as he noticed his responsibilities in the church growing. Even his students were shouting, "Yeah Big Trav," as he approached the mic. "Once he finishes, I'll let the mentors break off and find a child in need. Amen?"

"Amen," the church said in agreement.

The sanctuary lights dimmed, the projector screen lowered, and once again I took my seat in the pulpit. Unexpectedly, an instrumental hip-hop beat dropped, and the initials S.A.P. encased in flames were displayed on the screen in bold red letters. I was as lost as everyone else until the words Sorry Ass Pastor faded in.

Instead of the How-To video on mentoring, there were clips of me buying weed from kids on the basketball courts near Benning Road, rolling and smoking j's, and me taking money out of the safe for Rochelle and I was dumb enough to put it in an envelope labeled "R W's Money". You could hear the mumbles through the crowd and I grew more and more uneasy. I looked down and saw Travis staring up with disappointment, like a child who had been told Santa Claus wasn't real. He disgustedly walked back to his seat, but it wasn't over yet.

Perhaps the worst image was of me climbing on top of Maxine, audio included. Her screams and my grunts filled the open air of the sanctuary until the church began to boo. Thankfully, it covered up our passion noises.

The video stopped and the lights returned to their normal brightness. "You can learn a lot on these women's retreats, Stephen," a voice said. I looked around, but couldn't find a person to pin it to. "After all these years you still don't know my voice? Up here." I looked in the A/V room and saw Vicky and Maxine side-by-side. "I've known for some time now that something wasn't right. I knew you were creeping but I didn't know with whom. I'm grateful for Maxine and Rochelle's honesty. Does it make us friends? Heeeeell no! But this video was what I needed to see."

"Victoria, I am a pastor but I am also human," I explained. "It's not fair to put me on a pedestal. I'm sorry. What else do you want from me?"

"A husband that doesn't cheat on his wife!" she continued. "Man of God? Hmph, I'm just glad the all faithful pastor didn't believe in a pre-nup. See you in court. And if I were the rest of you folks, I'd find a new place of worship. The sheep are only as good as the shepherd that keeps them."

The congregation began to evacuate at break neck speed. How would I pay off this building and support myself with no one to attend service. "Don't listen to that bitch!" I said in panic. "It's lies! The video is fake. They're just tryna get me by getting to her." Travis unzipped his Bible from the engraved case I had given him, dropped it on the floor, and drove his shoe into it as he and his students headed for the door.

Rochelle mouthed "I didn't tell her nothing," while raising her hands up innocently before grabbing Donte's hand. As they turned for the door, he broke free of his mother's grip and ran towards me. "Donte, get back here!" she called out. He ran on stage, and wrapped his short arms around my waist.

"Dear God, please take care of Mr. Brooks. Amen." I bent down to hug him back, fighting back the tears that his genuine prayer had provoked. We stood that at the alter, the same alter where I had married so many couples, and also invited souls to know Christ. My only thought now was who saves the pastor?

Donte ran up the aisle and grabbed onto Rochelle's hand as she yanked him along. "He still loves you Daddy," he said. "And so do I."

T is for Tierra (Part III of III)

As I swept up the broken glass, flipped the tables back over, and cleaned up the remaining evidence from today's heavyweight throw down I realized the events that unfolded today were nothing like I had ever experienced with O. He took no-good niggas to a whole 'nother level. I had just gotten off the phone with him giving him permission to come back home, and not even ten minutes later I'm already having doubts. I left his key under the mat so I could finish preparing for his bittersweet return. O hated coming home to a dirty living room, but then again, what didn't he hate these days? Especially if it had to do with me.

I cleaned in darkness and the voices from the TV provided me with a false sense of company. It was dark; not just the room, but the pain that was covering my heart for the last two years. Nothing to show for the torment but the scars, physically and emotionally. And all I had to hold onto is the dream that one day, he'll change. But after today, I'm beginning to think that day may never come . . .

I had stayed home during mid-terms week to make a little extra money doing hair. Omar had spent some of our savings on tinting his windows, so it was up to me to see that we made rent . . . again. I was rinsing the perm out of old Mrs. Washington's hair over the kitchen sink early this morning while we watched another talk show episode. Today's topic was stone cold husbands and the wives who love them.

"I couldn't see me letting some old joker tell me to shut up on national TV," said Ms. Washington. She was a feeble woman, probably eighty-five or so, with thin gray hair, and a feisty personality paired with her sour facial expression. Everyone thought of her as the grouch of the neighborhood, but she was always cool to me.

"Oh yeah?" I laughed and asked.

"I'm serious," she answered. "These so-called men can't just disrespect us when they get good and doggone ready. And what kills me is the young girls that date these little pussies that think it's OK to hit a woman." Mrs. Washington was no fool. She lived directly under us and had a good idea of all the stuff that was going on over her head. I never talked to her about it, but I had a feeling she knew.

"Well, unless you're one of those girls I guess we'll never know why they stay."

"Yeah, well if Mr. Washington tried to hit me you'd know the next morning," she said. "See, what I'd do is let him win the first round cus nine times outta ten you can't beat a man when he's ready for you. But once he's all nestled in that bed after the dinner you've made for him, got him all comatose thinking about your smothered pork chops with the gravy dripping down to the rice . . . crack that wine bottle over his head!" As we fell out in laughter, I heard the door slam from someone walking in. I was curious as to who it could be. I didn't have an appointment scheduled for another hour or so.

I heard a few steps on the tile near the front door, and then felt the steps moving closer to the kitchen. Turning the corner was a woman and a little girl that was probably her daughter. "Hi, please tell me you have time to squeeze my little girl in this morning. I was referred to you and need someone to do a good job on my baby's hair." Referral or not, I needed as many appointments as I could get.

"Sure, not a problem," I answered excitedly. "Mrs. Washington your perm is all washed out, so we'll condition and have you sit under the dryer for about half an hour, OK?" She agreed, unhooked her cane from the kitchen counter, and limped over to the set of dryers on the dinner table.

"Oh, thank you," the woman said. "I'm Shannon, by the way."

"Nice to meet you," I responded. "And who is this?" I asked to my newest little client.

"Ciara," she said with a shy smile as she held onto her mother's leg.

"Well climb up in the chair Miss Ciara so I can take your braids out. What are you getting this time?"

"Mommy said I need a perm cus my naps hurt like shit."

"CiCi!" Shannon snapped. I tried to keep my laugh on the inside, but that sounded just like something a mother would say. "A perm and some first grader curls is all she needs." Ciara was the poster child for cute little girls of the ghetto. Shannon had Ciara's cheeks and forehead vaselined down 'til you could see your reflection in her brown skin. She was probably intelligent since she was wearing a navy blue jumper with a sky blue blouse; the same uniform the kids at the talented and gifted school down the street wore. Her hair was split into four sections with a braid and neon-colored barrette hanging from each one. And the icing on the cake: her bright smile with a tooth missing right in front.

"Not a problem," I assured her. "You can have a seat in the living room if you'd like."

"Oh, thanks girl. I've been running all day and haven't even had a chance to use the restroom. Do you mind?"

"No," I hesitated, "not at all." Normally, there wasn't a problem with someone using my bathroom, but this was a first time referred client, and her comfortableness around me kept me more alert than usual. Even Mrs. Washington raised the dryer as Shannon goofily crept past her. Shannon seemed alright, but there was something that made me think she wasn't all there. She seemed to take in everything she passed while tip-toeing to the bathroom, almost as if she were snooping for something. I sat the jar of perm on the counter and began to follow her to make sure she didn't have trouble finding the right door, when suddenly the phone rang. As usual, it was O doing his every hour on the hour check-in.

"Hey," I answered without emotion. I hated how he felt the need to keep tabs on me. There were kids home for spring break that got fewer calls home from their working parents than I did. And it was always the same questions every time.

"What you doing?"

"Hair. Mrs. Johnson's got a few more minutes and I'm starting on a new girl now. Why you call me from your mom's? She cooked lunch again?"

"Yeah, I took the whole hour and came over here." He wasn't fooling me. I knew he had lost his job almost two months ago, but to save myself from an unwanted fight, I wouldn't pressure him until times really got hard. He continued with his routine questions. "Terrell told me a dude in a gray car pulled up in front of our building a few minutes ago. You know anything about that?"

"No, I haven't looked out front all day."

"Oh. Anybody call today?" I knew what O. was getting at.

"I haven't talked to Kerry today," I answered.

"I didn't say anything about him," he responded. I could picture that dumb, jealous look through the phone. "You paranoid? Got him on the brain?"

"No. Look, I need to concentrate on puttin' this little girl's perm in. So just call me later."

He got quiet for a second before finally answering, "Ok. I get off early today, so just giving you a heads up to start dinner." I was exhausted from all the useless hours of studying I put in the night before, my fingers were cramping from nonstop washing and styling, and I still had to cook this grown ass man's dinner. Even this far into our relationship, his insensitivity still surprised me. It was me, me, me all the time, and the one time I would think of myself, I was the selfish one. I damn near cried in that kitchen, but instead I sniffed and threw my head back to catch any tears that tried to fall.

"It'll be ready by the time you get here," I agreed. I sat a pot of water on the stove and turned it on high. It looked like we were having spaghetti tonight. It was quick, filling, lasted a couple of days, and I could concentrate on Ciara's hair while I waited for the water to boil.

A few minutes into Ciara's treatment, Shannon came back into the kitchen holding a picture of O. and me in her hands. "This your husband?" she asked.

"Boyfriend," I said with a half smile before I mumbled "Nosey ass." She stared hard at the picture and rubbed around the frame's edges.

"How old is he?"

"He'll be twenty-five in a few months."

"Ohhh," she said. She sat the picture on the dinner table, which wasn't where she got it from, and stood beside me at the sink. "He looks so mature. Probably a good man, too. I know you probably think I'm crazy: asking about your pictures and everything. Ciara and I recently lost the man in our lives."

"I'm sorry to hear that," I said. "How did he pass?"

"He's not dead, just dead to me." Mrs. Washington swirled her finger around her ear, confirming that I wasn't the only person thinking this was one crazy bitch.

"Ooooooook," I said trying to change the subject, "well Ciara's perm is almost washed out. She shouldn't be under the dryer too long." I heard the door open once again as I wrung out Ciara's hair. I peeked around the corner and saw Omar wiping his feet on the welcome mat. "Shoot, I forgot to put the noodles in. I hope he doesn't show off in front of you all." I should've known he would pull one of his numbers. O. had a thing for saying he would be "a little early" when he was sitting right outside, hoping to catch me in some new lie he had conjured up in his head.

"Girl, I can throw those in for you," Shannon offered.

"Thanks," I said. "You're a life saver." Literally. With his "swing first, talk later" temper, there was no telling where this could lead.

"Hey Mrs. Washington," I heard him say, but I didn't hear anything back. She never cared too much for him and was always one to keep it real. I guess she was too old to start faking now. "Babe," he called out.

"I'm in the kitchen. I'm a little late with dinner. I thought you would be home a little later," I said, trying to turn his surprise arrival back on him.

"Traffic was really light." He is such a fuckin' liar, and he lied for no reason. I already knew the deal, and the more he lied for no reason just made my frustration with him grow even more. I guess I'll be sleeping on the couch again tonight. It may be backwards, but I knew damn well he wasn't givin' up the bed without a fight. A real fight. But really, how much worse could this soap opera starring me and featuring Omar get?

O. turned with a smile on his face that instantly dropped when he saw Shannon over our stove. "What the-"

"Daddy! Daddy! Daddy!" an excited Ciara interrupted.

"What?" I yelled in shock.

"Yeah, you didn't think I'd find you, did you?" Shannon asked with anger. "You stopped paying child support two months ago." Mrs. Washington pulled the dryer from over her head to get the full scoop. With all the neck rolling, finger pointing and yelling, she knew a good show was in store.

"Yo, I don't fuckin' know you," O. said. Shannon was rather odd, and I wanted to believe she had the wrong man so bad.

"Miss, I'm gonna have to ask you to leave," I warned. "I dunno what your problem is, but you need to leave. We got enough shit goin' on in this house and don't need you adding to it."

"Little girl you need to wake up!" she yelled. "This baby, this grown ass man-baby, has a daughter. Ciara is his daughter. And just to let you know, she's not his only one." My eyes bulged from Shannon's revelation, followed by my stomach twisting combined with intense nausea. My mouth dried up and the room began to sway like I had spun around one too many times. "Nigga you told her you're twenty-four?" She looked in my direction. "More like closer to thirty-four."

"Shannon, you need to get the fuck outta here!" O. argued.

"I thought you didn't know her," I cried. "You called her Shannon but I never introduced you." The sick feeling began to pass and was quickly replaced with wrath. I was on the verge of snapping. "Oh my God, how many lies can one nigga tell?!?!"

"How you gon' take her side over me?" he explained. "You don't even know this bitch." But I knew had I been in her shoes, I'd pull a stunt just like this.

"Oh, now I'm a bitch?" Shannon sarcastically questioned. "I was a bitch when I flattened your tires. I was a bitch when I keyed your car. This here, un un, this is just a tip of the bitchberg. But I gotta bitch for you." She lunged across the kitchen with her face scrunched and teeth clenched, flailing her fists at O. Ciara stood in awe and I stood right with her. I was glad to see someone whip his ass for a change. He was such a punk. When I was quiet and tried to reason with him, he would try to

121

hurt me, but when he got confronted by someone who wouldn't back down, it was a whole new outcome. I shoulda jumped in and helped her for the stuff he's done, and what I'm sure he's gonna do.

The two continued to battle throughout the house, knocking over the unused hair dryers and Mrs. Washington's glass of water. O. finally got Shannon's nail out of his shoulders and forcefully tossed her into a chair, causing it to flip over. "Babe, you not even gon' help?" he asked still breathing heavily. It was time to take some advice.

I picked up a glass jar of spaghetti sauced and slowly walked over to Omar without any expression. It was like I had been possessed. I stood by his side and without hesitation, cracked the glass jar across his back. Sauce painted the room as if a murder had taken place. O. yelled and cursed as he fell to his knees. I wanted it to hurt, but not as bad as if I had done it across his head. I wasn't sure of our future at this point, but if I decided to take him back, he wouldn't do me any good paralyzed. Not that he's doing all that much good for me now . . .

"Thank you," Shannon said as she stumbled to her feet.

"I didn't do this for you."

"I know," she said. "I'm just warning you because the last one didn't warn me. He doesn't have a job, can't hold one, and you're probably not his only girl. You can do better."

I appreciated her looking out for me, but the truth was that when she left, it would be me and O. squaring off and I wouldn't have her strength. "I don't need your advice. You're just jealous cus of all I got. Maybe Ciara is his, but we'll be aight. Now like I said, you need to leave." Shannon looked at me like I had gone crazy, but she grabbed Ciara's hand and jumped through clumps of spaghetti sauce until she found her way out the door.

"Can I get a towel to wipe off?" O. asked with an attitude. I brought him a dish towel and rat-tailed his ear with it. "Gotdamn, what you trippin' off of?"

"What am I 'trippin' off of'?" I repeated. "How you gonna act like that didn't just happen. You're a triflin' liar. Fuck you, fuck the womb you came out of, and fuck this relationship. You need to get the hell out of here." I was furious. I had never cussed so much in my life, but the situation called for it. He stood up like he was ready to take his anger out on me. That's when I had a "Snapped" moment.

I ran into the kitchen and grabbed the boiling noodle water and ran back into the living room. The pot was on the stove so long that the handles had become scalding, but I was so mad I couldn't even feel the pain. "Like I said, the best thing for you to do is leave." He could see in my eyes that I wasn't playing. "LEAVE!" O. bolted out of the door, and I threw the pot onto the carpet. Teary-eyed, I looked around the room as the mess staring back at me reflected my life: stained, worn down, and no one to clean it up but me.

My shoulders trembled as tears began to form in my eyes. "Uh uh now. You not gon' cry over that boy," Mrs. Washington said in her mother voice. "That's what cha won't do."

"This is not what I pictured for myself," I yelled. "I was supposed to be the first of my family to go to college, the veterinarian, the role model for my sister. Now I'm

122

cooped up in some apartment, paying bills in the order of which one they'll cut off first." Mrs. Washington stood firm, looking like my story was nothing new.

"I'm gonna put this tea on, and we're gonna sit down, watch these paternity tests results, and just talk." I really felt like being alone, but once the tea hit the boiler, you didn't tell Mrs. Washington "No." If she could spare the time, I could use the company.

For two hours she shared her wisdom with me about both serious and light topics all while Omar constantly blew my phone up. Mrs. Washington finally admitted to hearing the violent arguments flowing through her vents, and then asked me whether I had considered leaving. "But I can't do anything," I whined. "He's in my life too deep. I can't just up and leave. I've invested so much time into making this work. I wouldn't even know how to start over again."

"You sound like some old married woman with kids and real decisions to make," she laughed. "You're only as trapped as you wanna be. If I was twenty again I'd do what the hell I wanted!" She sat her mug on the edge of the coffee table and picked up her cane to leave. She leaned down as the cordless caller ID read his name. "I can only tell you what I know, but when you get tired enough of it, you'll get out of here."

I hadn't moved from that same spot on the couch once she left. The phone was ringing off the hook back-to-back, but I didn't even care. I just sat there, thinking of all the advice she had given me. "I really am too young for this," I thought out loud, "but I love him even despite his no good ways. He would fall apart if I left him. O. needs me, but I'm not gonna lose myself to help him find his way, especially for some twenty-seven year old man!"

Eventually, the calls stopped, and I had a chance to breathe. It had gotten to be late in the evening and I was worried. He was probably out getting drunk, smacked, or both, all because of me. I took a long shower and let my problems flow out with the steam. Once out, I walked to check the caller ID: still no calls. "He's been gone all day," I said to myself, "he's learned his lesson." Now here we are again.

The worst thing I could have done was feel sorry for O. I shoulda held my ground. I shoulda never gave him the chance to come back just to do it again next week. I damn sure shoulda never let him think I needed him. Once he knew I depended on his ass, he acted like it. He was probably nothing more than a couple miles away. It was a matter of minutes before he came in asking to "make up". A couple of minutes were all I needed.

Immediately, I dropped the broom and ran straight for the bedroom, grabbing the suitcase beside the dresser. I shoulda left a long time ago, but better late than never. I emptied out my drawers like a mad woman, spilling socks, panties, and shirts everywhere. I ran into the closet and pulled down three pairs of jeans that could mix and match with most of the tops in my suitcase. My hands were shaking. I could feel an eerie tingling in my palms as blood raced through my veins. I was breathing like I had just run a marathon, but had to force myself to calm down. I needed to think clearly and the more excited I became, the more likely I was to slip up.

I lugged the poorly packed suitcase out to the living room and took a light jacket out of the closet. I was almost out of here, but I had one more thing to take care of.

I ran into the kitchen and reached under the sink for bleach, ammonia, and dish detergent. I unscrewed the 40s he had in the fridge, poured a little out to make room, and threw in a cleaning product of choice. Next, I mixed the dish detergent with the instant coffee. I don't know if I expected him to die, or just slow him down, but I wanted to make the message clear: DON'T come looking for me!

I picked up the suitcase and smiled as I walked to the door. This was it. I had finally done it. Suddenly there was a noise on the other side of the door as if someone stuck a key in the hole. I threw my suitcase and jacket in the closet and swan dived onto the couch. He opened the door and I immediately saw his dumb face, eyes devil red from blunt smoke.

"Hey," he said in a low tone. "You sleep?"

"Just nodding off," I answered in a groggy voice. I stretched, yawned, and slowly sat up. I had to play this thing perfect or it would be my ass. He walked over to me and bent down to kiss my lips. I could smell the alcohol and weed floating through his pores and breath. I turned just in time to let him kiss my cheek. "We need to talk." I tried to speak loud enough for Ms. Washington to hear me through the ceiling.

"I know," he said. "TiTi I'm sorry."

"That's all you have to say for yourself? I just did your daughter's hair and didn't even know who was in my chair, and all you have to say is sorry? Nigga you need to do better than that. The cheating, the lying, the fighting, it all stops tonight."

"I'm sorry," he repeated, this time rubbing my neck. I shook him off, but his hands came back, this time attacking my spot on my left collar bone. I was moistening up, trying to stay strong. "I'm sorry."

"Not til we talk," I said while running my hands down his chest. He leaned in slowly and kissed my spot with his tongue. "Oh, God!" I bit my lip and gripped the couch. I was no longer in control.

"I'm sorry," he said once again. "I love you, girl. Don't make me beg, but I will if I have to to keep you." I could see his sincerity through his bloodshot eyes. Things were tough, but you don't just run away. This was my home, and it was on its way to being a happy one. The pain was in the past. The man I fell in love with at Fill Up On Soul had returned.

"Don't you wanna go to the bedroom," he said between kisses, "so I can show you how sorry I am?"

"OK," I blew out. We got up and slowly walked to the bedroom with his hands around my waist. I felt his grip loosen once we got near the kitchen. "Where you goin'?"

"I'll meet you there," he answered, "just need to get something cold to drink. Thirsty as hell!" I shoulda ran in and knocked the soda bottle out his hand. I shoulda, but I didn't.

"OK. I'll be there waiting," I said with a smirk. What? Just cus I took him back doesn't mean he can't learn a lesson. Good thing my bag was already packed cus I had a long night in the emergency room ahead of me.

U is for Uriah

The blizzard of 2010 would be one for the books. It was the first time in more than ten years that the District of Columbia metropolitan area was buried in snow. It was also when my older brother, Marcus, convinced me to drive down from sunny Philly into the heart of the severe snowstorm in Laurel, Maryland to meet his fiancée, Leah. I tried to put off the awkward visit, but after Ma caught wind of me not coming down for the umpteenth time, she called me up talking about how heartbroken she was I had moved away and never looked back, and how she and Dad had done all they could to give me the best life possible, etcetera, etcetera. So, I grudgingly packed a week's worth of clothes and headed easily down I-495 South before running into the slick, treacherous, and black ice covered Baltimore/Washington Parkway.

It was as if Maryland had become Alaska overnight. Cars were buried up to their door handles, parking lots were completely deserted, and the streets looked like the snow plows just said "Fuck it." What made it worse were the blustery winds whipping my Honda Pilot on the overpasses. This storm was giving my four-wheel drive a run for its money, taking my two hour drive to four, but eventually I made it to a single family home community off Contee Road. "*Figures*," I thought as I turned into the development.

From the outside, the house looked fully loaded: two-car garage with a four car driveway, patio that spanned the entire backside of the house, and a stained wooden door that sat between two white columns. I could only imagine what the inside looked like, and when I thought about it, I got sick. Marcus and I had been competing with each other for years, and this house was just another show-offy move to one up me again. I parked in the driveway, lugged my suitcase from the backseat, and fought the icy winds up the walkway to the front door.

I knocked and knocked for what seemed like forever. My fingertips were becoming numb from the wind chill and whiteout conditions. I almost froze to death until I remembered that ever since he lived in an apartment—luxury, of course—Marcus used to hide a spare key under his welcome mat. I pried the mat from the frozen concrete step and there lay my ticket into the "palace".

I could feel the toasty heat from an out of sight fireplace inviting me inside as soon as I flung the door open. I thawed out on the hardwood flooring near the entrance while taking in the laid out pad. To the left was a roomy study containing a tall bookshelf, black steel office desk, and a desktop computer. To the right was the dining room accessorized with a golden chandelier, glass dinette table, and

China cabinet. My envy was rising with every feature of the house I was exposed to. I explored the ground floor layout a bit more, making sure to leave snow tracks on the dining room carpet.

From the dining room I entered into the kitchen fit for a celebrity chef. The appliances were all black with silver handles. In the middle was a marble island with four gas stovetop burners. I was so stunned by the extravagance of the home I hadn't noticed the note on the fridge marked Uriah.

"Wassup Brah,

If you're reading this, then you remembered I always leave a spare under the mat. Lol. Hittin' the grocery store to restock while it isn't too, too bad. In the meantime, make yourself comfortable, help yourself to anything, and can't wait for you to meet Leah.

-Marcus

P.S.—Nice place, huh?"
Arrogant prick!

I met my bags at the front door and escorted them upstairs to an empty guest room as big as my apartment's master bedroom. There was a queen size bed covered with a striped teal and brown comforter set that complemented the mahogany bedroom furniture. Clearly Leah must have picked this out, and this nigga was sprung outta his mind to let her fix his house up like this. Aside from all the hating, Marcus did have a pretty nice crib. I tossed my bags in a closet and pulled out a pair of red-plaid, flannel lounge pants and an undershirt to change into.

I walked down the hallway and found the guest bathroom across from another guest room. As I stood and peed, I started thinking about the reasons for the tension between Marcus and me. How long would I let that sibling rivalry from way back when get to me? Yeah, he had the nice house, nice cars, bangin' fiancée, and everything else I wanted in life, but my turn would come sooner or later. Maybe it was time for us (mostly me) to act like brothers.

As I shook out the last few drops, I heard a noise coming from the kitchen. It was faint, like someone trying to silently close a cabinet door. It was probably just the refrigerator cutting on. Suddenly, I heard something like two glasses bumping each other. Damn, even in a blizzard niggas is out to get you! Whoever it was was in for a surprise; Marcus might be short and stocky, but I was 6'2, 200 pounds, and ready for whatever.

The toilet hissed, anticipating a full flush when I took my fingers off the handle. Hopefully, the bastard in the house would assume it was just a plumbing problem. I crept down the steps which seemed to creak every floorboard my size 14's touched, but the crook never showed fear. In fact, the sounds got louder and more confident. I sneaked through the hardwood hallway praying that it wouldn't be as difficult as the stairs.

I peeked around the kitchen doorway and saw a hand emptying chips onto a paper towel. This son of a bitch was stealing food, too? He must've been big, huge, to come in here alone and eat like he lived here. I reached for a nearby flower stand and charged into the kitchen.

"Ahhhh!!!" I yelled.

"Ahhhh!!!" a high-pitched squeal came back. The club bouncer I was expecting to battle was a short, Asian woman in a long t-shirt and wrapped hair, probably weighing a measly buck twenty. Scared to death, she had thrown her chips across the room and lost control of the juice in her hand.

"Who are you?" she screamed. "What are you doing here?" She began searching through kitchen drawers and cabinets, probably for a knife. It was funny watching her panic in her oversized radio station shirt, pulling out coupons, condiments, everything but a weapon.

"Relax, I'm Marcus's brother, Uriah." She laughed uneasily in relief.

"Boy you had me in here about to-"

"Bout to what?" I interrupted while grabbing some of the scattered coupons off the floor. "Save a dollar on Minute Maid?" She scrunched up her face, but I could tell she was trying not to laugh. "So, you must be Leah."

"No, Lele," she answered. I guess we're on nickname basis. After all, she was marrying my brother.

"Nice to meet you," I said, extending my hand and admiring my brother's taste. I couldn't help but notice her thin calves under her sleep shirt leading up to her meaty thighs like life-size chicken drumsticks. "It's really coming down out there. What time did Marcus leave out?"

"About an hour ago. And in this mess, it will probably be another two hours at least before he gets back." Lele laid a new napkin out on the kitchen counter and poured out another serving of barbeque potato chips. She shook the bag towards me as an offer.

"Nah, I'm good." She walked around the counter and headed over to the family room to cut on a talk show, but I walked to the pantry to see what Marcus had to drink. "So, you're who I've been hearing about?"

"I doubt that," she said with a laugh.

"Aww, don't be shy," I joked. I assumed Lele had some "sista" in her as her gently tinted complexion reminded me of the old saying: You want any coffee with that cream? She spoke without an accent, like maybe she was born here, but her parents were from "over there". She had dark brown naturally straight hair with a widow's peak that probably came from her Asian roots. Her eyes were a rare sea green and over top of them sat two thin and sexy ass arched brows that everyone was trying, but only a few could actually pull it off. She was one of them. Most importantly, she was flat in the gut, and phat in the butt. Her breasts were far from my normal standards, but I, I mean Marcus, could live with that.

"What are you over there fixing up?" she asked. "Didn't even offer me anything."

"Gin and Ginger Ale," I answered. "I woulda asked you, but I didn't see any fuzzy navels or strawberry daiquiri mix in here."

"Oh, you got jokes?" she said while walking into the kitchen. "I'll have what you're having," she said with a raised brow and neck cocked to the side, "but I take my gin straight up." She scooted over to me while I poured her a shot. Without thinking twice, she knocked it back, slammed the glass on the counter, and smiled a cocky smile before sliding her glass over for a second shot. "So you gonna babysit that all night?"

I chugged mine adding, "Ain't nothin' but a thang, baby. You sure you're ready for another one?" I poured us both a second round and we headed to the couch to get to know each other better.

She grabbed the bottle off the counter and brought it with us. "Just to save trips," she explained. I just hoped Marcus made it back soon. I didn't know how much longer I could resist that arched eyebrow look she kept givin' me.

* * *

"Wait, wait, wait," Lele laughed, "you moved all the way to Philly just to get away from your brother?"

"Hey, that sibling rivalry is a bitch," I joked. "I mean he did everything I did, but he did it better. I played football, he played basketball and gets MVP. I got him a job over summer break, he gets promoted before me." Lele was trying to hold her laughter in as I slurred through my explanation. We were both tipsy from taking at least three more shots of gin each. "But when he kissed this girl I wanted to ask to prom, I knew once I got the chance to move away I was taking it. Lisa Nichols. Damn, I'll never forget that name."

"Poor baby," she joked and rubbed my arms. "OK, I feel some cut on that arm. You're one of those gym fanatics?"

"Nah girl that's all natural right there. I can do fifty push-ups and a hundred sit-ups and have a beach bod." Part of me wanted to lift my shirt up and expose my pack, but I left it alone. That gin had me hot in more ways than one. I tried to shift the focus back on Marcus to remind us both that whatever I thought we were feeling between us was a bad move. "So when did you and my brother start talking?"

"Oh, well actu . . ." Suddenly the lights went out, the TV went dark and silent, and the heat shut down causing an instant drop in temperature. "Shit! The snow's been knocking the power in and out all week."

"What do yal normally do when this happens?" I asked. "Does he have a flashlight or candles or something?"

"Usually I just go to sleep," she started, "but today I have a big, strong man here to protect me in the dark."

"I don't think Marcus would like that too much," I said with a struggle.

"He'll be fine. We're just having some fun." Lele scooted closer to me, rubbing her hand across my lounge pants.

"You know if you're cold, you might wanna go grab some pants or something." I was trying hard to resist the bait she was throwing out.

"How about I grab some you instead?" Lele jumped into my lap and began to rub my chest through my fitted shirt. "Oooh, I can feel the 'natural' muscles." I was wondering how long I would let her do this. When she started going lower, I knew it was long enough. I grabbed her hands and put them behind her back like a cop, but she leaned in and kissed my neck. I tried to stay straight faced, but eventually my grip loosened and my hands were feeling on the small of her back.

"What about Marcus?" I asked between returned kisses to her neck. She kissed my lips, sliding in just a taste of her tongue.

"You talk too much," she replied.

I fell into a trance as she stroked my cheek with her Victoria's Secret Ember scented fingers. "*Snap out of it, Rye,*" I thought. "*This is your brother's girl. His fiancée. It's like screwin' with your sister.*" Just as I had finally convinced myself to stay loyal to my blood, Lele threw her oversized shirt off to the side and revealed her glistening abs and baby blue thong. On second thought, Marcus had outshined me in every way possible. After this, I would be able to say all was forgiven and mean it.

I was sportin' big wood by this time. I opened up the flap to my pants and let it poke out into the chilly air and motioned for her to come have a seat. Lele stood to drop her thong. "Just slide it to the side," I said. I was horny, but smart. If Marcus showed up without warning, she could easily jump into her shirt while I tucked back inside my clothes.

"It's OK," said Lele. She inched out of her sexy slingshot, floated over my lap, and delicately cradled her soft, warm ass over me until she slid down. I was in, and I was in raw! Every pump felt something like therapy. BAM! That one's for always being a show off. BAM! That's for that one Mother's Day where you made my cereal in bed idea look like shit compared to your homemade card. BAM! That's for little Lisa Nichols. And finally, a smack on the ass just for the hell of it.

Lele moaned and groaned as I rocked her like a sailboat in a monsoon. It was good to me, too. So warm, tight and wet just how ya boy likes. Before I even hit the five minute mark, I was pushing her off of me so I could release. She caught most of it with her snack napkins, but the runoff oozed down my pants leg. We both sat there wheezing and gasping like a fat kid stuck between two elevator doors. She pulled up her blanket, smiled, and rested her head on my pecs while the guilt rushed through my conscience.

I felt terrible once it was all over. It didn't even last five minutes but I would have to deal with this my whole life. And poor Ma. If her heart was broken beforehand, what would she think now? I was in deep shit. Then something happened that dropped my heart into my stomach and my stomach to the floor.

"Wassup, Rye," yelled Marcus. "Where you at bro?" Damn, Marcus must have come in while I was deep in thought.

"Is that your brother?" Lele groggily asked. Without even a second thought, I ejected Lele off the couch and onto the carpet, throwing her t-shirt at her. "Ow, Rye! What the hell? Calm down."

"I can't calm down," I whispered. "Shit, shit, shit! Go get dressed in the bathroom and I'll try to stall. Damn, and I still gotta semi. Uh, funerals, old people, little babies."

"What are you doing?" she questioned.

"Tryna think of anything that might turn me off so this will go down." I could hear Marcus's footsteps getting closer and our time was up. "Just stay down," I whispered. "He can't see over the couch." Suddenly, he entered.

"Little Rye. I haven't seen you in years man." He came over to shake hands and hug, but I met him at the kitchen before he came into the room.

"I know, Marcus," I said. As cool and collected as I tried to be, I know he could see something was up. I was speaking fast and sweating bullets.

"You gotta lil somethin' on your pants homey," he said. "I know you ain't been jackin' off on my suede couch." I just took the L on that one.

"You know how it is sometimes, bruh," I said with a laugh full of embarrassment. He scanned the room with a disgusted look for anything else peculiar.

"Is that a thong?" he asked. "Tell me that's not yours, too." I was gonna have to take the rap for a lotta this stuff if I wanted it to just blow over.

"This is ridiculous," Lele popped up. "That's mine, Marcus." She was embarrassed, but not as embarrassed as I would've been if I had to own up to that piece of string she called underwear. She hurriedly threw her shirt on as if him seeing her naked created an even more awkward moment. "I'm going to change into some regular clothes."

"What the hell is goin' on?" Marcus asked with intensity. His face twisted with confusion as he clenched his fists.

"I know you're upset man," I started, "but it just happened. I mean, we were drinking, telling stories and it just went down." As I pleaded my case, the front door opened and in came an unknown woman with both hands full of grocery bags.

"Thanks for holding the door, Marcus," she said sarcastically.

"My bad. Uriah and I were talking and I forgot all about the groceries." Marcus turned to me holding her left hand and engagement ring up for an introduction. "Rye, this is Leah. Leah, Rye."

"Nice to meet you," she answered. She was more his type: tall, brown skin, brown eyes and hair down to her shoulders. "I hope my girl Liang was a good host."

"Liang?" I responded.

"Well, she goes by Lele 'cus most people pronounce it wrong," she explained while unpacking the bags. "We went to school together and have been friends ever since. I told her I was getting snowed in with my babe and that his available brother was coming down." Safe!

"Oh, yeah. She was a great host."

"Better than what we'd thought," added Marcus. "I kinda walked in on her 'hospitality'."

"Wow," Leah said. "See baby I told you they'd hit it off. Well we're having a good dinner tonight, Rye. Dungeness crab legs. I bet you haven't had any good seafood since you left Maryland."

"Yeah bro, just make yourself at home and we'll call you and Lele in a few." I felt like a walking zombie leaving the kitchen as out of it as I was. I was thankful, but in the same sense remorseful that I still went through with it. I headed up to the other guest room and knocked on the door, hoping to try and talk to Lele about our little situation.

"Come in," she called out. I had walked in on her styling her hair in the mirror. She was wearing a pair of jeans and a plain black v-neck shirt. She wouldn't even look me in the eyes and played as if nothing had happened.

"So, why didn't you tell me that you weren't Leah?" I asked.

"I tried to, but I think the power went out." She forcefully sat the comb on the dresser and went straight for the balls with her interrogation. "The real question is why did you keep letting me hit on you and go as far as having sex if you thought I was your brother's fiancée? Pretty sick, don't you think?"

"You're right. It was sick, wrong, and messed up. But the good thing is you're not who I thought you were. I think we really had something earlier, and I'd want to spend the rest of the blizzard figuring out what it was. But, I'd understand if it was too weird for you."

"I guess I can't blame only you," she said. She walked over to me and laid her forehead on my chest. "Why don't we just take it slow, get to know each other's full names, and go from there?"

"That's an idea I can work with," I agreed. "We've already gotten the hardest part out of the way," I said pointing at the stain on my pants. She laughed and kissed me one last time before running back downstairs. It was too coincidental to be true, but I was thankful no matter what the explanation was. I wiped the imaginary sweat from my forehead, laughed a little in the mirror, and joined the rest of the crew in the kitchen, thinking that Jesus really looked out this time!

V is for Veronica

"Mom, the baby is crying!" I yelled out from my bedroom. I couldn't believe that baby had just fallen asleep at midnight and he was up before the sun was even up good. Sucking my teeth and grunting was all I could do as baby Jaymar hollered for his mom. I rolled over and made a sour face after the clock showed me it was just 6:27 in the morning. His crying had turned into a deafening squeal as no one had come to the rescue fast enough. "Mom, please I just got to sleep. Can you get him? MOM!!!" I could hear her stomping into his room before busting through my door like the police.

"Veronica, I can help you learn," she started, "but I'm not here to do it for you. You weren't thinking about sleeping when you were making this child, now you have to raise him. Get up and feed this boy." I took the pillow off my face and she handed Jaymar to me. I pulled open my once cute, now vomit stained pajama top and nursed my baby boy. Every position I found comfortable would cause him to cry, and every position that kept him quiet was a pain in my back. "I'll go make you some breakfast before I head to work," my mom said. "It looks like you'll be up for awhile."

As I tiredly sat up on the bed and rocked Jay in my arms, I thought to myself, *"Fifteen with a one month old: who woulda thought?"* I met Mom downstairs in a robe, slippers, morning breath, and who gives a damn ponytail. She was standing over the eggs on the stove in her nursing uniform while the bacon finished heating in the microwave.

"Good morning," she said all perky. I guess she would be seeing how she hasn't been the one getting only three good hours of sleep before having to wake up at the ass crack of dawn just to do it all over again. "I see you got your baby quiet. Did you schedule his one month check-up?"

"No, not yet," I answered. "I've been too busy feeding him, or holding him, or tryna get him to sleep. It's just always something I need to do. When do I get a day to myself? I haven't slept, I've forgotten what the mall looks like, the step team hasn't been looking as sharp since I left school, and I haven't spent any time with the girls since the first week I came home." My mother's face balled up in disappointment.

"Sleep? Mall? Step team? Listen Ronnie, all that is out the door so you may as well stop that crying. You don't get to be the baby anymore. That's his job," she said pointing to Jay. "Motherhood isn't a walk in the park, especially at fifteen, and even more when you have a jackass as his father."

"Christian is a good father," I argued back, "he just has a lot going on with basketball right now."

"Well did he bring those diapers last night like he said he would?" she asked, "Cus you only have two left. And only one case of wipes at that."

"He will, Mom. Why are you always coming down on him?" Just as our conversation was on the brink of an argument, my father came running downstairs in a hurry. "Hey Daddy."

"Whoo, no time to talk," he said. "You all have a good day." He kissed Mom and ran out the door without even taking a look in my direction.

"This isn't easy for him," Mom explained. "Don't worry. He'll come around sooner or later." She sat the plate in front of me with a side of toast. I buttered up the bread, stacked the cheese eggs on top, and piled on the crispy bacon. As I got ready to take a bite, the baby monitor went berserk from Jay's attention seeking cry. "Sounds like you're back on duty." She kissed my forehead and ran out of the door saying, "See you tonight when I get home. And no Christian until I get back, unless he's bringing over those diapers." She shut the front door and once again I was stuck at home alone all day. Well, he can wait til I at least get one bite of this sandwich and a swig of apple juice.

I was a rising sophomore at Beverly High School. I was on the Dean's list, co-captain of the school step team, and a peer tutor. When I wasn't in school, I buried myself in a good book just for the fun of it. I was a perfectly well-rounded student. So what made this good girl go bad?

While I was performing at halftime for a JV basketball game, my best friend, Tinese, and I were picking out all the players we thought were cute. When I went to the vending machines, she slid my number into Christian's—the star varsity point guard—sideline bag without me even knowing. By the time I got home, he called to speak to me. It was so random, but it didn't bother me because he was one of the cute ones I had picked. He was tall, solid arms, and a cut over his right eye from hitting the rim trying to show off and dunk at a preseason game.

With him having study hall and me having practice, it was hard finding time to hang out, but we made it work. We would walk the halls until afterschool activities started, holding hands and kissing in the stairwells and stuff. On his weight training days, I'd buy him a sports drink and slip it in his bag with a short little love note.

After I walked him to the gym one day, I headed up to the school cafeteria to start step practice. We were getting ready for a competition so I needed to make sure we were extra tight. Them Washington High bitches used to come in first place every time we were up against them, and I wasn't having that this year. We had glow-in-the-dark gloves, stunts, and an arsenal of new steps to knock them back. In the middle of the routine, Christian came to the side door and whistled for me. "You all keep going over the show," I said. "I'll be right back." I was surprised to see him before practice was over. The coaches normally kept a close eye on all the players. "What you doin' outta practice?" I asked.

"Ten minute break," he said. "Come with me." We walked through the dark school hallways, passing janitors and trash cans full of garbage from the day. After turning the corner, we stopped at a pitch black classroom. "My boys on the team said they usually leave this room open," he said while placing his hand on the knob. He walked in and I nervously followed.

He started to kiss me and I placed my hands on the back of his neck. I tensed up as I felt him poking through his jersey shorts. Afraid of what could possibly happen next, I pulled back. "It's ok," he assured. "Who gets pregnant on their first time?"

The answer: me. One month later after that exciting and emotional romp over the kitchen counter in a Home Ec. classroom, I tested positive for pregnancy . . . and syphilis. Turns out I wasn't the only girl he had taken there. I was depressed, disappointed, angry and scared. How could I have been so stupid? I should've known better than to ever trust an athlete. He argued he didn't know we were "official", so he kept talkin' to other girls at the same time, but with the baby on the way he would cut everybody else off. As far as I knew, he stayed true to that.

Eight months and thirteen hours of labor later, Jaymar was born. No matter how frustrated and borderline suicidal I was about the way life had turned out, Jaymar was my love, my heart, my little man. Even if I was pissed, exhausted, and missing the best years of my life as Mom called it, I had to remember that he didn't ask to be here. Whenever I was down, I would kiss his light brown skin and nibble on his little fingers and toes, run my fingers through his soft, silky hair, and just hold him close and breathe in a whiff of his new baby soy smell.

I had just gotten him settled when my cell phone went off. Luckily, the phone vibrating on the wood dresser didn't disturb his nap. I rolled my eyes as the phone flashed the last name I needed to see: Christian.

"Whaddup," I said with no emotion.

"Damn, that's all I get?" he asked.

He was trying to flirt, but that wasn't where my head was at the moment. "What do you want, Christian? I'm working on four hours sleep, two bites of breakfast, this baby needs diapers that you promised to bring LAST night, and-"

"Ronnie, Ronnie, damn," he said, "calm down! The diapers are in my trunk, plus I got fifty dollars for you. I can come over after our game today. I promise." His promises were as thin as a staple.

"He misses you," I said.

"I know. I miss lil' Jay, too. Tell him I love 'em." As much as I love that nigga I knew if anybody was gonna get my baby some diapers, it would be me.

Once we got off the phone, I slipped into a pair of sweat pants, threw on a hoodie, and picked out a hat and booties to keep him warm. Jay was too little for a stroller, but too heavy for me to lug around in a carrier, so I wrapped him in a blanket before strapping him into an infant shoulder harness. I don't see how people carry babies like this cus he was smashing the hell outta my sensitive post-partum titties.

The bus stop was normally a quick walk away, but with the baby dangling from my chest and a book bag full of cloths, a bottle, and the last of the wipes and diapers, it had become an uphill hike with ankle weights. I had broken out in a light sweat by the time we finally made it to the stop. This old Black lady was sitting there like she just was waiting for me to peel the blanket back for a glimpse of Jay. "Oh, he is adorable," she said. "I could just eat those big bwown eyes and wittle fingers up."

"And change his shitty wittle diapers, too?" I asked with a sarcastic baby voice and matching smile. I usually respected my elders, but I was running on fumes; the sooner I let her know I wasn't up for all of that, the quicker she'd keep to herself. When the bus came, the woman sat in the front and I trekked straight to the peaceful, lonely backseat.

I looked out the window for a second and then looked down at Jay, nestled in his cocoon of blankets and warm clothes. How cute? How cute Hell! I'm draggin' his ass around while he gets to sleep. I was beginning to understand why Dad would complain about Mom sleeping in the passenger seat on the way down to Atlanta every Christmas while he fought to keep himself awake for the long drive back to Virginia.

Once I finally made it to the pharmacy, I picked up the diapers and wipes as planned, and a pack of pumpkin seeds and a soda for me. I stood in line with Jay practically weighing me down now. It was so many people and only one register open. It ain't make no damn sense.

"Next in line," the cashier called. I approached the counter with my baby's needs and my wants. "Cute kid," she said unenthused as she scanned the items. I didn't even respond cus I knew she was just tryna fuck with me; the baby's face was covered and she never even glanced up from the items on the counter, so how would she know? "OK, your total is $17.94."

I reached in my book bag for my wallet and found a ten and a five. I thought I had a twenty here! Looks like once again the baby gets his way. I reluctantly put the seeds and soda to the side as the cashier sucked her teeth and groaned, "Manager to the front for a void." I dunno what she complaining for. I'm the snackless one.

Foodless, energyless, and grumpy, I began my journey back to the bus stop when suddenly this green Ford Taurus came barreling through parking spaces like it was gonna run me down. "Ronnie!!!!!" a high-pitched shriek called out. I didn't need to see the short bob, light brown skin with slight acne or the braces with red and white bands cus I knew that squeal anywhere.

"Hey Tinese!" I was so thankful to see one of my girls. "What you been up to?"

"Girl, just pickin' up some stuff for my mova before I head home. What you doin' out in this wevva?"

"Christian was on some ova stuff so I had to come get Jay some things."

"Ohyougotlil'JayJaywitchu?" she asked excitedly. "LilJayJay," she said pointing at the baby. She must've seen how confused I was.

"Oh yeah. He's hanging with his mommy today."

"Girl, when I fount out you was pregnant I was like, 'whuuut?'" she said with a dramatic reenactment. Tinese was my bestie and was always around when I needed a laugh. Even though we hadn't had much time to talk lately, it felt like we never missed a beat. "Well, I can give yal a ride. I just need to stop past the mall real quick."

"Thanks," I started, "but I should just take the bus. I shouldn't have him out too long." My clothes were stained, my hair wasn't done, and the last thing I wanted was Tinese's big mouth spreading how busted I looked.

"Aw, come on. Let 'Auntie' help out." I was pretty tired and her car was a lot safer than riding the bus with them nosy and pissy bus folks. Only thing was I didn't have a car seat for Jay. Oh well, he should be fine with me long as I buckle up.

"So, did you drop out of school?" she questioned as we headed to the mall.

"No, Christian brings my homework from my classes and my mom drops it off in the morning. How's school?"

"Ronnie it's the same shit, different day. And you know Rayliqua is jy blown cus you got Christian before she did."

"Well if I knew what I know now, she coulda been had him."

"Girl, say it again!" Tinese confirmed.

We pulled into the mall lot and parked in the expecting mother's section. I mean, no I wasn't anymore, but this was too much to be carrying back and forth. As soon as we entered the mall, Jay woke up from his nap and began to whimper. I knew it was too good to be true that he slept this long. I started thinking, "*If only I had stayed home. I could've had me some good sleep.*" In an instant, Jay put his cry in full effect.

"You go ahead, Tinese," I said. "He's probably just hungry. I'll be here on the bench when you're ready." As Tinese enjoyed her carefree window shopping spree, I sat in that mall publicly embarrassed while Jay nursed. I should have never started breastfeeding him. It felt like all eyes were on me: parents were judging me and the high school boys were hoping to catch a free glimpse.

While I sat there trying to pretend I was invisible, I could faintly hear girls sniggling and giggling behind me. I just drowned them out and continued to do what I had to do until one of them called out, "There go dat ho bitch right there." I didn't even turn around cus I wasn't anybody's ho or bitch.

"I know you heard me talkin' to you," said one of the girls. She yanked the cloth from over Jay's face, exposing my breast for all to see. Everyone around me was laughing hysterically. I was humiliated and steaming mad.

"What the hell is your problem?" I jumped, turned around, and saw that my opponent was none other than the reckless Rayliqua.

"You think you somethin' cus a basketball player paid your geek ass some attention?" she questioned. "You ain't no better than the rest of us, and that lil mistake you got hangin' from yo titty proves it."

"Aww, girl," said T'Onna. "You ain't have to do her like dat."

"Shut your sidekick ass up," I replied. "You ain't nothin' but a hop on. Stop ridin' her dick all ya life." They stood there shocked. "Yeah I know nobody talks to yal like that but I don't give a shit. You want Christian? Too mothafuckin' bad. Maybe if you stopped dressin' so damn hard you could get a man too." I should have known Rayliqua was not having that.

"Put . . . the muhfuckin' . . . baby down, Ronnie," she commanded. I propped him up against the nearest cell phone kiosk, tucked myself back in, and got ready for war.

We circled each other as T'Onna let everyone in the area know a fight was goin' down. I locked my fingers in her hair and pulled while she was swinging me around and punching my sides. I let her hair go and began violently slamming the sides of her head with my fist. A crowd had appeared out of nowhere to watch the first person stand up to Rayliqua. I was so caught up in the moment, I didn't notice she released me. She forcefully pushed me into the kiosk and I slid down knocking phones off the display. She came charging at me but I was only down, not out.

Without warning, I sprang up on one foot and lunged at her with a boot to the gut. The ooh's and ahh's from the crowd only fueled the fire. I wanted to seriously whip her ass! Suddenly, through the loud shouting I heard Tinese screaming for me with Jaymar in her hands. "Ronnie, Jay is burning up! And he's not lookin' good, either. Ronnie!" I lost my focus and gave Rayliqua the chance to open palm slap me down. She and T'Onna started stomping me out mercilessly. I just tried to protect my face and hoped that someone would eventually break this up. Boy, the bus ride home sounded so good right about now.

Finally, Tinese got through the crowd and pushed the two off of me. "Break it up," she said. "Something's wrong with her baby." Luckily, the mall cops came cus Rayliqua did not give a damn about Jay. They scattered with the rest of the crowd as me and Tinese rushed for the exit.

"Oh no his temperature is up," I said while pressing on his forehead. "I shoulda never kept him out this long."

"What are you supposed to do?" Tinese asked.

"I don't know," I responded. The more I tried to rock Jay, the louder his cries grew. I was desperate for a cure. I began to blow cool air on his face, hoping that would drop his fever, but it only annoyed him more. A quick errand had turned into the worst outing ever and I didn't need this crying right now. "Shut the hell up!" I screamed.

Just when I got ready to join him for a good cry in the passenger seat, my cell phone rang with my mother's ringtone. I wiped the tears forming out of my eyes, attempted to take the panicky tremble out of my voice, and turned Tinese's radio down. "Hi Mom."

"Hey, just checking up on you and Jaymar. I called the house, but didn't get an answer. You two OK?"

"No," I answered. "Mom he's hot. He won't eat, he won't stop crying, he's just miserable. I'm so tired of this baby."

"Stop all that whining," she said firmly. "Like I told you this morning you're not the baby anymore. You wanted to play big girl games now deal with the repercussions." Mom had never been so strict to me.

"What am I supposed to do?"

"When you get home give him a lukewarm bath," she instructed. "And I'll bring home some electrolyte formula from the hospital. And you call and schedule that appointment like I told you."

"Yes ma'am." Mom was good at building me up when I was weak I was so fortunate and thankful that unlike my dad, she was there to push me in the right direction. "Thanks Mom. I love you."

"Love you too, Ronnie."

Tinese dropped me off around quarter to five and I jumped out without even saying goodbye. Immediately, I took off Jay's clothes and stuck him in the sink. The volume of his cry began to go down as the water air dried off his skin. I was so sore from the mall scuffle that I could still feel the tension every time I showered the water over his head. I wish someone was here to draw me a bath.

Once I got him settled and into a onesy, I tried breastfeeding him again; he took this time. I rocked him in the old wooden rocking chair Mom used with me and we slowly drifted off together. Today was a trying day, but it was at that moment where we comforted each other that I felt I was somebody's mother.

The peaceful mood was unexpectedly interrupted when the doorbell rang. Jay squirmed around, but he didn't wake up. I placed him gently on the sofa and walked to the foyer. I peeked through the peephole and immediately felt my anger stirring all over again. I snapped off the chain, turned the deadbolt, and pulled the door open to reveal Christian.

"Hey," he said with that stupid smile that at one point in time was cute. While he stood silently thinking of the right thing to say, I stood in silence waiting for him to come up with it. "We won." That wasn't it.

"You're lucky I just got Jay to sleep," I whispered angrily. "What took you so long?"

"My bad," he started, "but after the game we went out for pizza. This was a big game baby. We haven't beaten them in two seasons."

"Well why don't you ask how my day went? While you were out living it up, I'm trying not to overfeed this baby so he doesn't shit in his last two diapers. I had to take him out before his check-up, drag him around on the dirty bus, kick Rayliqua's ass and let her kick mine back all before finally checking that Jay has a fever. And you're wasting my time because it's only about another four hours before he decides to wake me up in the middle of the night when nothing's on but paid programming. So unless you have a bag of diapers and fifty dollars like you 'promised' then all this talkin' can wait until tomorrow."

"First of all," he said holding up a value pack of diapers. "Second, here's the money, minus ten dollars. I had to put in for the pizza, but I'll get it to you ASAP." I rolled me eyes to show my disapproval, but it really didn't matter. I was just glad to see he kept his word for once. "Is your mom home?"

"No," I said with attitude. "But I guess you can come in. Just don't stay too long." We walked over to the couch and hovered over Jaymar. Christian stood and watched with the same amazement as when Jay was first born. It was so sweet to watch him looking over his spitting image. I know it was hard for him to be an athlete and a daddy and he was new at this just like me.

We stood over our child like a happy little family, but the truth was we knew we were in over our heads. Nine minutes of pleasure ended in something that would last us a lifetime. And although this situation was an accident, I would never refer to Jaymar that way. He was beautiful, but he would have been just as beautiful if he were here ten years later. Now I'm forced to travel this road for at least the next eighteen years. I guess it does pay to wait.

W is for Walter

I had been waiting for this day since last year and finally it was here: August 28, 2010. Olivia and I had sworn to each other that no matter how long we were married, we'd never lose our spark. Our annual weekend getaways were just one of the ways we kept the passion alive. We had been married going on fourteen wonderful years, so obviously, we were doing something right.

I drove around the block until I thought she was ready, and then called her when I stopped in front of the house. Ever since we'd met, she liked to take her time getting ready for me, and now at 38, nothing had changed. But I didn't mind. In fact, it had given me a chance to run wild with our little dating game. I created a fantasy of sorts out of our getaways. I would pretend as if we were young and dating all over again. To make it even more believable, I placed my wedding ring in the glove compartment to really get the feel of courtship.

"Hello?" she answered with that soft, melodic tone of hers.

"Is this Olivia?" I jokingly asked. "Would you tell her I'm downstairs?" Her giggle lifted my spirits, and she hung up without saying goodbye.

Within a few minutes, the front door swung open, and Olivia appeared dressed in a hippie inspired white sundress and bronze sandals. Her beauty was paralyzing, as if I was witnessing it for the first time. The afternoon rays bounced off of Olivia's "blacker the berry" skin tone. Her mahogany eyes were hidden behind a pair of sunshades, perfect for a day as bright as today. Her shoulder-length hair was tucked away in a neat ponytail held by a black scrunchy. I imagined myself resting my hands on her slim face, grabbing her prominent cheekbones and planting a romantic kiss on her full lips. She gracefully tip-toed down the walkway as her sundress blew in the airy, end-of-summer breeze like a music video.

"Hi," she said, fastening her seatbelt with a smile. She reached over and laid her hand on my knee. As she rubbed my thigh, I noticed the deep tan line where her 3-karat diamond ring usually sat. She had taken hers off as well. I could see she was into the fantasy this time just as much as I was. This weekend we weren't going away as husband and wife, but as two good friends looking forward to falling in love all over again.

We talked the entire ride, but Olivia never asked where I was taking her. In the past, we had gone to wine festivals, all-day jazz concerts, and would spend the night in a hotel for the night-cap. But this time, I tried to think of something out of the routine. After all, that was the purpose of these adventures in the first place. Wherever we were headed, she knew that I wouldn't let her down.

After an hour and a half of driving, talking, and groovin' in our seats to a mix of Chuck Brown and the early go-go bands, we arrived in Solomon's Island, Maryland: a quiet little beach town off the Chesapeake Bay. Right away, we could see jet skiers speeding across the water, and crabbers casting nets from the pier. Children flew their colorful kites high above the dock with one hand, while eating ice cream bars with the other. "What are you up to?" Olivia asked while grabbing my hand and smiling that smile of hers I lived for.

"Just wait and see, Libby," I said. I parked, helped her out of the passenger seat, and we prepared for the fun-filled day ahead.

We walked a couple blocks until we came across a seafood restaurant on the waterfront, nothing too fancy, but from the beach house theme and the smell of salt water and Old Bay seasoning in the air, we knew we had found the spot for good eatin'. We grabbed a booth on the patio and held hands across the table just smiling. She took off her sunglasses and I was in a trance. My heart warmed as I thought of the last decade and a half well spent with my Libby. The good, the bad, the unforeseen, I wouldn't have traded it for anything.

"Hello, and welcome to Pride of the Pier," our waiter interrupted. She was a young girl, about twenty or so, probably waiting tables while school was out. "Would you like to hear our specials?"

"No, thank you," I said. "We'll start with your raw oysters appetizer. I hear they're aphrodisiacs."

"Is that right, Wally?" Olivia sarcastically questioned. The server was uninterested in our flirty remarks.

"Did you need a few minutes to look over the menu?"

"No, we're good," Olivia answered. "He will have your 8-ouce crab cake lunch with steak fries, and a mug of whatever's on tap." I don't know why I was impressed as if she were a complete stranger.

"And she will have the jumbo stuffed shrimp, Caesar salad, and a piña colada topped with strawberry puree. And make sure it's thick, or she'll send it back." Olivia looked at the waitress in a way that let her know she had no problem asking for the manager.

"Well, great. I'll go ahead and put these orders in. You should have those oysters out in a few."

As soon as the appetizer arrived, we both dug in and enjoyed each other's company a little longer. I began telling Libby about the downside of being a high school English teacher. "And now the boys are walking around with jeans tighter than the girls. And have the nerve to sag 'em!" I explained. "Terrible." Libby just laughed.

"It can't be all bad," she said. "I'm sure you have some that cling to your every word. You're a great speaker, Walter. I'm sure you reach the good ones. The bad ones, too."

"Yeah, that's true." I loved how she could put a positive spin on any of the crap I threw out at her. In her mind, nothing was ever as bad as it seemed. "How are things on your end?"

Libby sighed a little. "They're good. Home's OK, but work keeps me busy."

"Just OK? Everything OK with you and your husband?" I joked. She opened her mouth and lifted her hands like she were about to say something, but nothing came out. She hesitated again before finally speaking.

"Everything is good, but I wish there were upgrades, you know? In the bedroom department?" My face twisted at the revelation. "Oh, I hope I didn't make this uncomfortable. I knew I shouldn't have said anything."

"No, you haven't done anything wrong," I assured her. "It's good we're talking. What's wrong with the sex?"

"It's not wrong, just needs some improvements," she sugar-coated. "For example, I like mine for at least fifteen minutes. But if I spend a lotta time massaging you and giving you oral, then you're halfway there and I usually come up short."

"That's reasonable," I commented.

"And the whole head thing: I really don't like it, so it should be an every now-and-then thing, but you want it like your vitamins: One A Day." I laughed at that one cus I knew there was no way that was changing, but I made it sound good for her.

"I'm sure he would've worked on it if you told him," I said, continuing our little game. "No one should have to put up with unfulfilling sex."

"You know I don't. I have my ways," she said with a grin.

After a very satisfying lunch, I led Libby to the dock. The next part of our date was a trip out on the bay with a rented motorized sailboat. I drove us far into the bay, then cut the engine off once we met up with the windy current of the Patuxent River. I took off my blue and white striped polo, and began to raise the sails. I glanced down and saw Libby staring at my sweaty arms and muscle gut. "See something you like?" I yelled down sarcastically.

"I'm just wondering when did you get into boating?"

"What? I've been doing this since waaaay back." The vessel took off with a sudden jerk as I tied the last sail down.

"Whoooo!" Libby screamed. "I see you caught some wind."

"Come up here and I'll show you how to steer." Olivia unloosened her ponytail and threw her hair as she seductively walked up the steps. I knew what she was doing, and that she was doing it intentionally. "Just hold the wheel, and I'll guide you."

"You mean like this?" she asked, poking her butt out.

"Yeah, just like that." I stood behind her and grabbed her waist. We raunchily sailed the river, not giving a damn who happened to pass by. I started getting hard just fantasizing about lifting up that sundress and taking her out in the open.

"Is that your . . ." she questioned.

"You say it like you don't want it there." She leaned back and our faces inched closer and closer together for a kiss. She turned around, looked me in the eyes and in a dramatic fashion, we kissed.

"I think I've had enough sailing for today," she said between deep breaths. "I'm ready for bed now. Can we check-in?" She wasn't as subtle with her approach as I was, but I liked her taking all the guesswork out of it.

I dropped the sails and eagerly started the ignition. It stalled. I turned it again, but still nothing.

"Is this another part of your game?" Libby joked. "Oh no, now we're stuck out at sea," she said in a southern cartoon voice with one hand over her forehead. "I declare, who will come and save us."

"I'm not joking. We really are stuck."

"Well, can you fix it fast? It's starting to look like rain."

"Girl, I know the seas," I said. "It's just a few clouds. We won't get more than a drizzle, light rain at most." Suddenly, the skies opened up and rain heavily poured like a Caribbean tropical shower. The water was coming so fast, I could hardly see right in front of me. Even worse, lightning began to strike and we were surrounded by nothing but metal.

"Walt! Walt!" she cried out. "I'm scared."

"Stay near me," I shouted. "I'll drop the anchor and we can go downstairs. Just keep your head low and watch for the sails."

Olivia and I ran downstairs completely drenched from head-to-toe. She flicked the light switch, but as luck would have it, no power. I searched around and found a walkie-talkie in the corner on the charger. "Hello, hello. This is boat fourteen. We're stalled out in the middle of the river and can't get back."

"Boat fourteen, we read you," a voice answered back. "The water's too choppy for a rescue mission. We'll make the trip out as soon as the storm dies down. Radio us on your status."

"How long do you think they'll leave us out here?" asked Libby.

"Just until the worst part passes," I said calmly.

"I'm soaked and I'm freezing."

"It's those wet clothes. You should probably get out of those. I'm sure they have a blanket around here somewhere. I went on another search for a blanket but came up with nothing.

"It's ok," said a shivering, naked Olivia. "I could really use some body heat anyway. Bad!"

I rushed over to her and picked up where we had left off on the deck. I ran my fingers down the small of her back and grabbed a handful of cheeks. She unbuckled my belt and then placed her hands on my shoulder.

"I thought you didn't like it?" I asked.

"Not all the time," she began, "but I want to this time." She lowered herself to knee level and untucked the flap of my briefs. In an instant, the warmth of her mouth caused me to forget the arctic feelings I felt less than a minute ago. I braced myself holding a ceiling rail, while the boat violently rocked from the waves. Remembering our dinner conversation, I forced myself to stop.

"That's enough," I whispered. "Now it's your turn." I placed Olivia's cold hands on the warm spot of the bar where I rested mine. I kneeled down and threw her legs around my neck. I stood up, and tasted her while she remained in pull-up position. I could tell by the way she moaned and shook that this was the type of loving she was seeking. When she began beating me in the back of my bald head, I knew she couldn't take anymore.

I lowered her legs around my waist, and slowly stuck the tip of me inside of her. Without warning, I forcefully thrust the rest of my shaft in. "I love you," she breathed out. I stumbled the two of us over to the desk where I'd found the walkie talkie, and we made love to the rhythm of the waves. The thunder and lightning continued, but it only added to the natural feeling of it all. I watched the look of pain cross her eyes during the hard bangs, but knew from past experience that she liked it rough.

The ship tossed us onto the floor, and Olivia landed on top of me. We laughed it off, and continued screwing. She planted her palms into my chest, and gently rocked her hips until she found a fast pace that did the trick for us both. She grinded harder and moaned louder. I grabbed her abs to steady her as I came. We lay there chest to chest, breathing like we had one lung to share between the two of us.

Just then, the door opened and a man in an orange vest entered. We had forgotten all about the rain, and that I had radioed for help earlier. Libby scrambled to find something to cover up with, and I cupped my package with both hands.

"Happens more than you can imagine," the shoreman laughed. "I'll just turn around until you get dressed so everyone won't know what's going on down here. Need a blanket?"

After we found our clothes, we hopped into the speedboat with the rescue crew and headed back to shore.

"Still wanna check-in?" I asked Libby.

"I think I've had enough adventure for one getaway," she laughed. I couldn't have agreed more. We bought some dry clothes from a nearby souvenir shop and made our way back home. This was a getaway for the books!

The sun had just set as I dropped Olivia off. I double parked in front of the driveway, and leaned in for one last vacation kiss.

"So, same time next year?" I asked.

"No question about it," she confirmed. She opened the door and began up the walkway.

"Libby," I yelled out of the window. "Don't forget your ring. Your 'husband' would be mad if you came home without it, don't ya think?" She walked back over and smiled, grabbing the ring from my fingers and placing it back on hers.

"You better put yours on, too. I hear that wife of yours has some temper." We laughed a little and I watched her in, just like a real first date. Once she waved she was in, I drove off. We had this game down, pact.

I drove home thinking of how much of a success the day had been. I almost wish it could be twice a year, but that would take away the fun.

Once I had finally reached the house, I grabbed my bag and did one last check to make sure my tan line was completely covered by my wedding band. I walked through the front door, and saw my baby pretending to be sleep.

"Walter, is that you?"

"Hey, Amanda. I'm home early." I walked over to the sofa and kissed her forehead.

"What happened to the teacher's convention?"

"They just went ahead and canceled it due to the rain. I think they're gonna just wait until school starts next week."

"Well, I didn't cook anything."

"It's Ok. I'm not hungry," I said running upstairs. "I'm just gonna grab a quick shower and get in the bed. Is Walt, Jr. sleep?"

"I just put him down. So, you should be able to sleep for a few hours," she yelled up.

I made it! Another year masked by the "teacher's convention". Hopefully, Olivia had gotten past her husband as easily as I just did with my wife. It's not that I don't love Amanda, but there was something about Olivia that day at the grocery store that I couldn't let slip away. We knew if we wanted this to work, we'd contact each other as little as possible, and around the time when we would meet for the year. Now, fourteen years later, both of us married with children, our tradition lives on without the slightest detection.

Well, until next year, Libby.

X is for Xzotic

"Didn't Mama tell you she was gonna put it on you?"

"Whew! Damn Crystal, what's gotten into you?"

"Just you, boo." I leaned forward, aligning my lips with James's. We shared a deep, intimate kiss until his hard-on went flaccid inside of me. I rolled onto my side of the bed and wrapped his arm tightly around my hips.

I was a virgin when James and I first met, but he didn't hold that against me. Unlike the others I dated, he respected my decision to protect my body and stay true to the Lord. Although he was already experienced in that department, he remained celibate with me the entire time we dated. Three years later, he asked me to marry him. I remember spending the whole wedding day thinking, "*Oh boy, I hope it doesn't hurt.*"

I must admit, those first couple months as newlyweds were hell. Most nights I would lay stiff as a board, bracing for impact. We joked around, calling it the "Teaching Year". Lucky for me, James was a patient teacher. When I screwed up, he laughed with me, not at me. If I threw my hands on his chest, he knew to slow down. Eventually, the tension eased, I calmed down, and the pain turned into pleasure. I had even learned to swing my hips into his thrusts and throw it back at him. With only a year and a half of experience under my belt, I had learned the ins and outs of pleasing my man. Or so I thought.

"How was it, Jay?" I asked for his validation, but I really didn't need him to evaluate my performance.

"It was your usual good job, Crys," he said. With a big smile on his face, he closed his eyes and began to drift off. Maybe it was the oncoming period that got me riled up, but something about that comment didn't set well with me.

"Wake up, James," I said angrily. "What does that mean?"

"What does what mean?"

"You called me boring." He scrunched his face up as he tried to figure out where this was coming from.

"I said it was good, babe."

"No, you called it 'usual', sweetie," I quipped back. "If you don't think it's a problem then forget it." I fluffed my pillow, threw the sheet over my head and sprawled across the bed.

"Baby, come on," James said. "I can't sleep with you spread like that."

"What's wrong? This is my 'usual' way of sleeping."

"I don't need this," he mumbled to himself. Peeking through the sheets, I could see him furiously grabbing a blanket out of the closet, and heading for the couch.

I got dressed for work in silence the next morning. It wasn't because I was mad, I was worried. I guess we did kind of have a routine going on: James on top, then me on top, and then the grand finale of gettin' it from the back. What else was there to do? We hadn't even been married two years yet and he was already bored with me. Well, I was familiar with the old saying about a man who wasn't sexually satisfied at home and James would not have to look beyond these four walls to find what he was missing. I was willing to do whatever to satisfy my man.

I pulled into my office's parking garage at 7:53am. Good. Being a few minutes early meant I had time to call my sister, the doctor, for advice. And if there wasn't any scientific advice, I knew she would just keep it real. Young or old, Vivian never had a problem in the pleasure department.

"Hello," she answered.

"Hey Viv. What have you been up to?"

"Busy. Getting ready for the next semester. I'm actually meeting with a student right now."

"Oh, but I called you at home." Silence. "Anyway, I was calling for some help. Last night, James said I did the usual."

"Uh huh."

"I was hoping you could use your expertise and give me some suggestions." I could hear my sister's nails tapping the table on the other end of the phone as she mentally flipped through her inventory of tricks. Finally, she responded with a novel idea.

"Suck his dick."

"That's it?" I asked shockingly. "No secret position? No special technique to make him erupt like a volcano?"

"Hey, I know what works," she stated. "If you want all that creative shit, you need to do some research." I was floored that was the best she had to offer.

"Let me find out I stumped the sexpert."

"Crystal," she called with aggravation, "I told you I was busy. Now I gotta get back to grading this extra credit."

"Uh huh," I began, "just make sure you keep a warm bottle and blanket near the bed when you're done, cradle-robber." Suddenly, I heard a click on the line, followed by dead air. I know she didn't go crazy and hang up on me. I checked my cell and laughed as *Call Ended* flashed across the screen. "At least I got the last word," I said to myself.

I was so unfocused all day at work. "*Usual*," I thought out loud. "*Common. Predictable. Ordinary. Unspecial.*" I shed silent tears at my desk as I conjured up more synonyms to describe my now mediocre love-making. Then, I remembered Viv's advice: do some research. I did a quick search, and came up with 738,759 results for "Better Sex."

After weeding out the porn sites, I was able to find some new positions, like the reverse cowgirl so James could see my ass bounce while I rode him, or maybe a freaky public sex excursion would keep it fresh and filthy like he likes it. Next,

I shopped for some interesting sex toys for couples. James loved those cherry flavored oils and edible panties, but they reminded me of cough syrup.

"Oh, well. It's not about me this time. Hmmm, what about this prostate massager? Yeah right! My boo ain't wit those booty games. Well what about . . . or maybe this . . . or how about . . ."

As I searched and searched, I began to realize this was all in vain. If James didn't ask for any of this, what's the use? I could buy a million toys and he'd still just think of me as a usual bitch with a bag o' tricks.

I was no less distraught on the way home than I was all day. I kept picturing my happy home crumbling down after just a few short years. What if James was no longer attracted to me? What if he'd no longer be able to stay awake during sex? On my worry-filled ride home a sign presented itself as I turned off the highway. "Sucksexful Gentleman's Club: Now offering striptease lessons every Wednesday at 6:30pm!" The idea of me stripping was so out of character. I was classy and sophisticated, and a kinky new idea such as stripping would surely be enough to release me from my "usual" description. I raced home, slipped into my velour pink sweats (you know, the ones that make us look more phat in the back), a pink head band, and a black baby tee. Oh yes, Miss Crys was ready!

I made it back to Sucksexful just in time and was surprised at the mixed crowd. Black, White, Latin, Asian, young, old, thin, not-so-thin, and more. Regardless of what we looked like, we were all there for the same purpose. The practice room had several circular tables and fold out chairs pushed against the wall. To my right was a slightly raised stage with a polished, gold pole sticking from the floor.

"Well hello my beautiful sisters," a voice called from behind the curtain, "and welcome to Sucksexful strip lessons." The lights dimmed, and music with heavy bass flew from the speakers. At that moment, a middle-aged, brown skin woman wearing a silk red robe with a lace lingerie set took center stage. She grabbed the pole close to the floor, and then used her arms to slowly maneuver herself upside-down. She then stretched her legs in a perfect line, spreading all her business. Some laughed, and others were mesmerized.

After the stranger's brief introduction, the DJ cut the music, and we all applauded. "Good evening, ladies," she said. "My name is Oooh Nasty, and I will be your instructor for the next 6 weeks. Before we start, I want everyone to tell me one thing they hope to learn in this class."

"How to make him feel like it was the first time," one senior citizen said.

"I'll definitely teach you that," Oooh Nasty assured. "Don't sleep on the older ladies. I'm 52 myself." Not that 52 was old, but her body and dance moves were not synonymous with her age. You could hear everyone gasp, and then applaud after revealing her age. She looked good and was FLEX-i-BLE! "What else?"

"I want to learn to pole dance," a younger, Asian lady stated.

"That's week 5, but we'll cover it."

Finally, I raised my hand and added, "I wanna learn how to make your buttocks ripple." She laughed at my innocence.

"Oh, you mean the ass clap?" she said with a demonstration. "Baby if you can't say it, how do expect to do it? Men want their lady in the street, not in the sheets. In here, proper is out the door. We gets nasty, OK!!!"

In just six shorts weeks, Oooh Nasty showed the class how to master the pole, belly dance, bend like a rubber band, and yes, make our asses clap. She had turned us into professional novices. At the end of the sixth class she made one final announcement.

"This Friday we will be having our Amateur Night showcase. It's a great way to test your skills in front of a controlled audience, and see if the $200 fee was worth it. So, I'll pass the list around for those who are interested."

"You should do it, Crystal," Gladys, an older woman urged. "You've been talking about being bold and unpredictable. I bet this would change his mind." While holding the sign-up sheet I thought about it long and hard.

"Hmmmm. Ok, I'll do it." The class applauded as I signed away my clean image.

*   *   *

Thursday and Friday afternoon had come and gone. James agreed to meet me at Sucksexful after work for drinks. Little did he know, I had all the right moves to make this an extra happy hour. I left home a little early to snap on my extra long ponytail, get made up, and do a stage run-through.

"OK ladies," said Oooh Nasty, "we have a pretty good crowd out there. Crystal? Has anyone seen Crystal?" I raised my hand excitedly. "Go on Crystal!" she said complimenting my pink glitter eyelids. "We have you up first, Miss . . . what's your stage name by the way?"

"Xzotic," I said. "So what do you think of my outfit?" I untied the robe so that she could see my black and white naughty maid outfit. My taupe legs were shimmering from the airbrushed glitter tan. I thought it was hot, but Oooh Nasty stood there speechless.

"That might work," she began, "if this were 1960 and you were dancing to 'Hey Big Spender'. Get with the times." I felt like no matter how hard I tried to be sexy, it was always a fail. She could easily tell her comment had upset me. "Here, we keep some costumes in the back for our newbies. You'll be a hit."

The show began while I changed into my new clothes. "Wassup everybody! I'm your host, comedian Eric Jones." Great; a comedian at an amateur strip show spelled disaster. "We've gotta lotta good-looking women about to hit the stage so show 'em some love. So, if they do something you like, make it rain. But, if they're whack, boo these bitches! Don't take it easy just cus they're amateurs. Hell, they gotta learn."

The audience's laughter made me panic. I peeked through the curtain in search of a familiar face and a confidence boost. My eyes caught James sitting two rows back. I thought it would help, but I was even more nervous. Then, I remembered why I was doing this. This was for my marriage, for James, but most of all, for me.

"Our first dancer for the evening is a 27 year-old sales rep from DC. I see you Chocolate City! She's easy on the eyes and thick in the thighs. Give it up for Xzotic."

The music played as I slowly approached center stage. Immediately, the room filled with excitement and the fellas went crazy, howling, whistling, and toasting to my debut. I looked over and saw James stunned as hell. I couldn't quite tell if he was stunned good, or stunned embarrassed. Either way, I was so overwhelmed that I had forgotten to take off my robe before going out. I tried to play it off as part of the routine, swinging on the pole like a child on the monkey bars.

Maybe it was the slow music, or maybe it was the robe, but the intensity from before had died down. They began to boo in the middle of my routine. Even James hunched down to laugh. Once I saw his shoulders jump from laughter, I cast the nervousness aside and snatched off my tear-away robe. The naughty maid outfit was replaced with candy cane patterned lace boy shorts and matching peppermint nipple pasties. At my signal, the DJ switched the slow song to something I could really freak to: "Bring it Back" by Travis Porter.

I squatted low, lifted my arms over my head, and oscillated my ass left-to-right while clapping my cheeks to the beat. James damn near choked on his water. Next, I pulled my leg straight up, letting the crowd see more than my flexibility. With my leg up, I came crashing down into a split. You could hear the men in the room losing their minds. As I bounced up and down on the cold stage, I flung my neck to add some ponytail action. "You sure this is your first time?" said the comedian. Hmph, I was just getting started.

I rolled onto my back and used a can of spray-on hair mousse to draw an X on my belly. I then grabbed a cigar out of some old man's mouth in the front row. Once the tip came in contact with the mousse, it created a blue flame. Without warning, I smacked the fire and sent flaming cream all over the audience. Dollars went flying! "Now that's some new shit!" Eric added. "What else you got girl?" James was in awe. I had completely changed on him, and he looked to be enjoying himself with that Kool-Aid smile on his face.

I swung my legs around to seductively stand to my feet, but lost the sex appeal when my heel kicked some old guy in the front row. "Damn Helen Keller. Can you see?" I was losing points with Eric, and didn't want to hear the audience booing again. I ran my breasts across the man's face as a symbol of my apology.

"I'm so sorry, sir," I quickly said before jumping back into the groove. No matter how angry and bloody he was, Oooh Nasty said don't stop dancing.

Next was the pole tease. I clutched the pole with both hands, spread eagle, dropped my ass and then looked back while I picked it up. As I danced in a circle, I built up enough speed to get airborne and spiral downward around the pole. Nobody told me that the first dancer up has to deal with an extra waxed pole. "Shit!" I yelled out as my fingers slipped in mid-air, flinging me across the room and into the lap of an unknown stranger. Somehow, the accident must have looked planned because the audience continued throwing dollars. I bounced in his crotch before jumping back on stage for the grand finale.

On all fours, I crawled back to center stage, jiggling my booty with every inch closer. I slithered around the cold, gold steel like a python around its prey. Once on my feet, I positioned the pole between my cheeks to perform the Oooh Nasty exclusive move known as "the butt floss". I felt sorry for the chick that went after me, because I didn't have a chance to shower when I got off work.

My last trick was the one that we had seen on our first day of class. I grabbed the pole down low, and used my newfound arm strength to raise my legs over my head.

The audience loved it! I had gotten so caught up in their screaming and hollering and the dollars being thrown that I didn't notice the spider climbing down the pole. Its legs tickled my hands. I looked up (or down depending on your angle), and freaked out. "AHHHHHH!" I released the pole, and crashed head first into the stage. My legs came down shortly after, twitchin' and all.

It was blurry, but I think I could see James running to the stage. He wrapped me in his leather jacket and yelled, "She's OK," to the audience before taking me backstage. They applauded my effort as they got ready for the next act.

He handed me a bottled water and some tissue to wipe away my tears of embarrassment. "What were you doing out there?" he asked.

"I don't know."

"Well, do you at least know why you did what you did?" I couldn't even look him in the face.

"I just wanted to be different and sexy." He sucked his teeth.

"Don't tell me you're still tripping about that comment I made almost two months ago." I shook my head yes. "Baby, I already told you I wasn't complaining. You know your sex is unquestionably good. I just wanted something a little extra."

"Like what, James?" I asked angrily. "I did anything you wanted. I tried all those positions, shower sex, and even dining room sex. We eat there, James!" He looked away as if my embarrassment had jumped onto him.

"What do you think about oral?"

"Oral?" I spent $400 on classes, make-up, and clothes, had a concussion, and all of this only to learn that Vivian was right after all? "Bitch got me again."

"If you feel that strongly we don't have to."

"No, no," I laughed. "I guess everything is worth trying once." His eyes lit up at my willingness to experiment.

"Come on, let's get out of here." James helped me up and we headed for the dressing room door. As we approached the exit, I locked the deadbolt, unzipped his pants, and pulled out his goods for an impromptu blowjob, cupping his scrotum and teasing his head with my tongue. Once I got it wet enough, I grabbed him with both fists, twisting in opposite directions like a peppercorn crusher. James moved my hands, curled my ponytail around his knuckles, and once again assumed his role of my patient teacher as he guided me through another lesson in love. Sometimes you have to do something out of the ordinary. Sometimes you have to do something unusual. Sometimes you just have to be . . . Xzotic.

Y is for Yusef

Sudden flashbacks in mid-August of Pops' homemade BBQ sauce on everything from chicken wings to baby back ribs, kids running in and out of the house while Mama yelled, "Stop lettin' that air out!", the hum of the snow cone and cotton candy machines, and the air filled with the speakers blasting Marvin Gaye's famous lyrics "I used to go out to paaaaartaaaays" could only mean one thing: the Wests' Family Reunion was about to go down!

I hadn't had much time to visit Atlanta since I started my new job in Raleigh, North Carolina, but this was a seven hour drive I was excitedly looking forward to. My mouth watered in the driver's seat just thinking about Mama's grilled shrimp and pineapple kabobs. Keeping me company in the passenger's seat was my babe, Shawniece. I met her not too long after moving up north, but from our first date we hit it off strong. A few months in, I took her down to meet my parents and they loved her, probably more than any of my exes. So, when I told Mama I would make it to this year's reunion, she told me not without Shawniece.

"Do you think your family's gonna like me?" she asked.

"Babe, you already got my parents on your side," I assured her, "the rest of them are easy."

"I just hope they like my attempt at bread pudding. I studied your mom's recipe all week making sure it was just right."

"I'm sure it looks and tastes as good as you." Shawniece was the type of girl that even I wondered how I pulled someone so gorgeous. She was beautiful: flawless almond brown skin, honey eyes, full lips, shoulder length jet black hair, and glistening long legs sticking out of her white, cookout short shorts. Most would call them too short for meeting the fam, but they were perfect for the relentless Georgia heat wave.

I parallel parked my Acura MDX SUV on the cul de sac where my parents' house sat. Childhood memories flowed through my mind every time I pulled up front. As soon as I cut the car off I could hear the Electric Slide instrumental filling the neighborhood. Shawniece looked at me as if nervousness instantly took over. "You'll be fine, Shawnie," I told her, "and I'll be there with you." As confident as I sounded, I was just as nervous. Mama by herself was one thing, but Mama with my two aunties was a whole new battle.

I grabbed Shawniece's hand and walked her through the metal front gate. The herd of kids ignored us as they continued their boys against girls water balloon war.

151

Blue, my parents' bulldog, occupied himself by cleaning the sidewalk of someone's dropped cookies n' cream ice cream cone.

We entered the screen door to the all-brick row house and made our way through the living room. I dunno why my mother insisted on keeping that wool, floral patterned living room furniture. It was probably as old as I was, but I guess it had so many memories built into it that she couldn't just let it go.

We passed the antique sofa and could hear the roaring laughter coming from the kitchen, followed by the intense change of heat from all the frying and baking. My mouth watered at the smell of homemade macaroni and cheese with the crusty edges, and collard greens and neckbones boiling in salt, pepper, vinegar, and seasoned salt. I walked in first as Shawniece followed behind, still holding my hand.

"Awww, Little Earl!" Mama shouted, "you made it." I hated when she called me by my father's name, which was also my nickname.

"Mama, *Earl* is so country," I said between her hugs and kisses.

"And you think Yusef is any better?" said my sarcastic Aunt Feather while snacking on a watermelon slice. Her real name was Faye, but from all the stories about "back in the day", Mama and the rest of the neighborhood kids used to tease her 'cus she was so skinny. I guess the name just unfittingly stuck with her all these years seeing how now she was a chicken wing away from morbid obesity. And she always tried to stuff her big fifty-something year old tail into those khaki-colored capris every year since it "matched perfectly with our navy blue reunion shirts," as she would say. "So when you gonna stop standing there smiling and introduce your lil' girlfriend?"

"Oh, everyone this is Shawniece. Shawniece, you remember my mother and these are her two sisters, Faye and Rhonda."

"You ain't got to be so formal, baby. Don't pay Little Earl no mind, girl. We family now," welcomed Aunt Feather. "So you call me Feather and that's Aunt Rhonda, but you ain't gotta pay her too much mind."

"Aw, bitch ain't nobody paying YOU no mind," Aunt Rhonda playfully jumped back. Aunt Rhonda was fifty-seven, the oldest of the three. She wore her hair straight back with an upward spiral bun sitting on top. She cussed, drank, and gambled on every hand of Bid Whist. She was also one of the ministers at the church down the street from her house. I could only imagine the sermons she was giving that congregation.

"Hi," Shawniece shyly waved. "Nice to meet you all."

"Well take her down to see your father and some of your cousins," Mama rushed. "Yal are just takin' up all my standin' space in my kitchen, now! I haven't even mixed up the bread puddin' yet."

"Mrs. West I actually made up a batch. I saw your recipe in one of Yusef's cabinets." While Shawniece proudly held up the glass baking pan, Aunt Feather and Aunt Rhonda gave each other a short side eye, then quickly focused in for how this would play out.

"That's so sweet of you," Mama began, "but did you bring the praline sauce? Cus you can't have mama's bread puddin' dry." My two aunts nodded in support of Mama.

"Well, actually I made a rum sauce instead," Shawniece answered holding a plastic jar filled with a syrupy topping. "That recipe looked loaded in sugar, so I found a quick recipe online. It's still sweet, but a little healthier."

"Hell, you can never go wrong with rum," Aunt Rhonda interrupted. "Let me get a spoonful of dat dere." Aunt Rhonda stuck her spoon in, paused to let the flavor sink in, and did a two-step dance to express her approval. "Dayum that's good!" Mama was pissed.

"Well, it's always good to have a selection," Mama added. "So we'll put yours over here, and I'll get started on mine once I get a stove burner free. Why don't yal go out back and see if your father and Thereeis needs any help with the grill."

"Who's Thereeis?" asked Shawniece.

"Oh, that's just little Earl's cousin. My son," explained Aunt Feather, this time between chomps of baked beans. "Yeah, me and his Uncle Kelvin didn't wanna know the sex of the baby until it was born, but we both prayed for a boy. So when I went into labor, I pushed and pushed until I saw that little 'Peter' come out. And I yelled, 'There he is', aka Thereeis." I always tensed up when Aunt Feather told that story. It was a hot, country, ghetto mess that should've been buried and never told again, but Shawniece cracked up. "Yeah, so if it wasn't for him I would still have my slim girly figure."

"Girl, you ain't had a baby in twenty-two years," joked Aunt Rhonda, "I think that excuse bout had it."

"Lovely seeing you again, Niecy," rushed Mama again.

"You too, Mrs. West." As I walked her out back to meet the rest of the family, I could feel Mama staring a hole into the back of Shawniece's head while my two aunties snickered us out the back door.

"Be nice," I mouthed back at them.

We walked down the patio steps into the enormous open field that my parents claimed as their backyard. The music was on blast, the smell of charcoal floated in the air, and the kids had moved on from the water fight to a game of freeze tag. "Yusef!" a high-pitched voice called out as we neared the grill. As the person got closer, I grew excited.

"Wassup, now!" I yelled.

"You better stop playing and gimme a hug," he joked.

"No, you better stop playing and shake my hand," I laughed back. Shawnie laughed and took it upon herself to do the introductions.

"Hi, I'm Yusef's friend Shawniece. Are you Aunt Rhonda's daughter?"

"Ooop, no you di-int! No. You. Di. Int!" Our playful reuniting had just turned sour. "I ain't no damn girl. I'm Faye's son, Thereeis. Do I look like a girl to you?" With his saggin' red skintight jeans, crisp white V-neck shirt, long locks, and heavily glossed lips, he did. To put it nicely, Thereeis was one of those family understandings where nobody asked questions, but everybody knew everything.

"Chill, cuz. She didn't mean any disrespect," I calmed him. "She was just tryna feel welcomed. Southern hospitality, remember?" Arms folded, he rolled his eyes and stared at the sky until he thought it over and then began to smile.

"Guurrrrl, you lucky he was here," we laughed, Shawniece a bit more uncomfortable than the rest of us.

"Is he giving you a hard time?" Pops walked up with a barbeque stained undershirt and a beer bottle in hand, leaving Uncle Kelvin in charge of the grill. Even as a fifty-five year-old army retiree, he kept his 5'11" two hundred something athletic build, with the exception of his belly.

"What's goin' on sir?" I greeted him with a handshake, and Shawnie did the same. "What time is the food gonna be ready?"

"About another half hour on the ribs and the rest of the chicken, but I told your mother it's plenty of hot dogs and hamburgers to start with. Go tell her we're ready." As soon as I turned to run back in and get the ladies from the kitchen, Pops hollered out, "CHERYL! CHERYL! Lil Earl say he ready to eat!"

"We're coming, we're coming," Mama shouted on her way down the steps with an aluminum pan of greens. Several of the younger kids followed her with other dishes, while Aunts Feather and Rhonda brought up the rear in a heated debate.

"I'm not saying give all your money, but you are supposed to tithe Rhonda."

"Feather, some people can't afford ten percent. So, here you are giving all your money away to God and living on a prayer all the while you singing the theme song from Good Times."

"Hmph, well that's what us Christians call faith," debated Aunt Feather.

"Well that's what I call dumb."

"Whatever, 'Minister'." Aunt Rhonda was furious.

"And what the hell is that supposed to mean Faye?"

"Just drop it Rhonda," Mama pleaded. "Just bless the food."

"Now wait a minute, Cheryl, cus she tryna talk slick, but I'm time enough for her fat ass today!" Aunt Rhonda slammed the potato salad down, rolled her neck and eyes, and then calmly asked, "Will everyone please grab a hand, and bow your head as we turn to the Lord?" Mama shook her head, and Shawniece's eyes looked as if she wanted to ask if this was the exception or the rule. Unfortunately, it was the latter.

"Hoh Lawd!" Aunt Rhonda shouted, "we come to you to say thank you," in which the elder family members all replied "Thank you". "Thank you for this food, and the hands that prepared it. Some families don't get the chance to see each other, but we thank you for bringing the fifty sumthin' souls here today." At this point Aunt Rhonda began her signature dramatic cry. "Isn't He WORTHY?!?!?" The family began to fan her as she shouted, stomped, and squeezed my hand tightly. "Thank ya Lawd! In JESUS name, I pray. Amen." She wiped her eyes with a paper towel and blew her nose as if her little display had not even occurred.

"OK, the line starts this way," she directed. "It's sodas and waters in the plastic trash can. And if anyone wants beer they're in the cooler over there."

After a crazy afternoon, dinner had finally begun. Fried chicken wings, fried whiting, spicy barbeque ribs, potato salad, shrimp pasta salad, firecracker string beans, collard and kale greens, grilled hot dogs, hamburgers, melon trays, and Aunt Rhonda's famous maple syrup cake-like cornbread were just a few of the options on this year's menu.

"I don't see my bread pudding," Shawniece whispered. We scoured the card tables covered in appetizing main dishes and desserts, but hers was nowhere to be found.

"They probably just didn't have enough hands," I reasoned, but Shawniece looked back like she wasn't buying it. "It's cool. I'll check it out."

Through the long lines of distant relatives and friends, I found Mama and Aunt Rhonda already with their plates, sitting at a table under one of the trees, gossiping about some of the others at the reunion. "Mama can I talk to you?"

"Shhh not right now boy," she hushed. "Don't you see me and your aunt talking about something?" Using me as a shield, they peeked around me and stared and Aunt Feather making her plate. "Look at Feather trying to psych us out with that salad. That heffa knows she wants more than that." Next, she made her way to the grill for some of Pop's acclaimed barbeque. "Ribs AND chicken? She knows she shouldn't be eatin' all of that." It was a lose-lose situation for poor Aunt Feather. You would've thought Mama and Aunt Rhonda would've stopped talking as she walked over to join her sisters under the shade, but instead they just whispered until she was close enough to hear.

"I bet her pressure is through the roof," Aunt Rhonda said, rolling her eyes in disgust. "She called me talking about she lost eight pounds, but when a bitch is a biscuit away from fo' hunnid pounds, can you really tell?"

"What yal over here laughin' about?" Aunt Feather inquired.

"Just your relatives," Mama answered. "There goes cousin Andre, Yvette and the kids."

"You mean all them kids," Aunt Rhonda emphasized. "Five kids and all they sent was a damn fifty dollar deposit for the food?"

"We did put 'per household' on the invitation," argued Aunt Feather. "It's not our fault we got some triflin' relatives. And you know his oldest moved up there by Yusef for school."

"Deja?" Mama asked.

"Mmmhmm," Aunt Feather confirmed, "but you know Aunt Maxine said she ain't studying nothing but them boys. Ha! Called her 'the Harlot of Charlotte'."

"Oooh, no she didn't," Aunt Rhonda jumped in.

"Girl, yes!" I shook my head as I approached my mother's seat. When I thought I had found an opening in their gossip, I slid into the conversation.

"Mama, where's Shawniece's bread pudding? We didn't see it with the rest of the desserts."

"Really? You didn't?" Mama asked half-heartedly. I knew that she had done it intentionally, but she continued to play it off. "Everyone's hands were so full, we probably just overlooked it. But I'm sure we have enough desserts that no one will even know it's missing."

"But Shawniece will," I said. "She really wanted to bring something to get in good with the rest of us. It would mean a lot if you set it out with the rest of the food." She looked away for a second to watch the family enjoying their plates, and then back at my long face.

"Oh, alright," she huffed. "It's upstairs on the kitchen counter."

"Thanks, Mama," I said with a kiss.

"Whatever. And hurry back before your cousins try to steal Shawniece from you. Thereeis has been eyeballing her all day," she joked, knowing Thereeis wasn't interested in my girl in the least. Shawniece looked over at me as I climbed the patio steps to the kitchen, and I gave her a wink to let her know everything was cool.

*   *   *

A couple hours later, dinner had begun to wrap up and no one could move an inch. No one except for Aunt Rhonda and a couple of old school Bid Whist players, that is. Mama suddenly sprung up as people began to make their way to the dessert tables.

"Ok yal we gotta new entry for desserts this year!" Mama shouted. "Well, not really a new recipe, but a new baker." Shawniece poked me as Mama was not letting this thing go. She was stuck on the belief that Shawniece had intentionally stolen that recipe from us. "Anyway, be sure to try the bread puddin'. I didn't make it this time, so I'm not sure what it tastes like. BUT, I know this sweet potato pie, peach cobbler, and sour cream pound cake are just whatcha lookin' for."

The crowd gathered around the tables, grabbing paper plates and plastic ware to take on their dessert of choice. Mama stood nearby like an eagle, overseeing and making sure her desserts were tasted first. And whenever anyone headed back to their seat with just bread pudding and ice cream, she would say, "Don't see any pie on your plate," paired with a soft laugh that instantly let you know that her words were more than a gentle reminder.

I was next in line and thought that I would play it safe and try some of everything. "Now Little Earl, I know you can't resist Mama's peach cobbler," she baited. "Here let me cut you a piece with the crust like you like." Mama scooped a heaping helping on my plate, with the purpose of blocking any unwanted desserts from sneaking their way there.

"Don't forget to try mine, 'Lil Earl'," Shawniece sarcastically said back, handing me a big chunk of bread pudding covered in her rum sauce. Damn, all this over dessert?

"I'm sure everything's good," I said, trying to mediate. Mama put her hand on her hip while Shawniece rolled the black out of her eyes. I held up Mama's cobbler and dug in. "Mmm, Ma you know this is good, right? And you can tell these peaches are home grown. No cans over here." Mama smiled and patted me on my back, but her smile quickly faded as I sat her plate down and picked up Shawnie's.

I brought the plate to my face and took in the smell of sweet liquor and cinnamon rolled into the warm, spongy dessert. "Dayum Shawnie. You keep cooking like this and I might have to marry you, girl."

"Lemme try," said Thereeis switching over to the dessert table. "Guurrrl this is thebomb.com!" Everyone knew how much Thereeis loved my Mama's recipe, but when he gave his review over Shawnie's, everyone circled her pan for a square.

"Well you all go ahead," Mama shouted. "I'm having pie!" Her pitiful attempt to gain fans fell on deaf ears. Even Pops crowded around for bread pudding.

"Watch this," Aunt Rhonda whispered with a devilish grin. "Oooh Shaw-NIECE! This is so good. You gotta give me your recipe, OK?"

"That is MY recipe!" Aunt Rhonda and Aunt Feather fell out laughing at Mama gettin' salty. She watched as the family stole the tub of vanilla ice cream away from the cobbler section and scooped it onto their bread pudding plates. The 90-degree weather didn't compare to Mama's heat right now.

"Just try a little piece, Mama. For me? It'll make me feel good you made Shawnie feel good." As angry as she was, Mama knew the dish was a hit when even the kids were enjoying it. She fought the idea for a second, but finally gave in.

"Oh, alright," she said with a smile. We walked over to the table where Shawnie was still serving out helpings for everyone to try. "Shawniece go ah ead and cut Mama a piece of that . . . WHOA!" As Mama neared the table, she lost her step and stumbled in a rehearsed, dramatic fashion, falling hands first into the bread pudding pan. Shawnie's face dropped.

"Ohhhhh nooooo. I am sooo sorry," Mama acted. "This is terrible. And everyone was in line for a piece too. Aww, shoot."

"Did you see what your mother did?" Shawnie yelled. "Mrs. West, you did that shit on purpose!"

"You watch your mouth young lady. You're not gonna talk smack in my house," Mama snapped. "Now I done told you it was an accident." Shawnie wasn't fooled.

"Ok," she said calmly. "No use getting bent outta shape. If it's gone it's gone. By the way, I really enjoyed your sour cream pound cake, Mrs. West. But I normally add a little 7-Up to the recipe." Shawnie grabbed a canned soda out of the trash can and walked over to the pound cake. She forcefully shook the can and popped the top, spraying soda all over the cake. When it was empty, she stuck the can in the soggiest spot and watched the cake crumble apart. Mama gasped in disblief.

"Now look here you little heffa . . ."

"Heffa?!?!" Shawnie jumped back. The two began to argue as me and Pops stepped in to try and control our women as best we could. As if the day could get any stranger, suddenly, a young, unfamiliar woman approached the scene.

"Excuse me, is this the West Family Reunion? I'm looking for Thereeis." We all stood there puzzled. "I'm Kiara, his girlfriend."

"His what?" we all shouted.

"Whew, oh praise God," shouted Aunt Feather. "Honey I don't care who you are, but you don't know how happy I am to finally see you here. You hungry? Let me make you a plate. Thereeis! Your girlfriend's here." Aunt Feather's reaction to Kiara was nothing different than the rest of the confused looks we all had on our faces. It even put a halt to the dessert duel.

"Thereeis, how come you never told me you had a girl, man?" I asked. "All this time, we thought . . ."

"Why, cus I'm studying fashion? Nigga puh-lease," he said with a deep masculine voice. "The girls up there love a guy that knows his fashion. I mean, it is a fashion institute, and you gotta look the part if you're tryna make it in the industry."

"But sometimes you go a lil' too far with the whole fashion thing, don't you think?"

He lowered his shades, swirled his wrist, and laughed, "To each his own," with a tongue pop before going to stop Aunt Feather from smothering Kiara any further.

Just then, the music for the Booty Call line dance began to play and everyone rushed to the open yard. Still upset, Shawniece stayed behind and cleaned up the mess from before. "Come on. Let's show 'em what you got," I joked.

"Nah, you go ahead," she said unenthused, "I don't think your mom really likes me."

"Aww, hush up there child. It was just a little friendly competition gone wrong," Mama kidded. "Outta all the girls Little Earl's brought home, you were the first to even offer to bring something. So, don't worry; you're still Mama's favorite." Shawniece smiled at Mama's mood-lightening words. "Now come on. With those little white shorts I KNOW you finna do the Booty Call."

The three of us made our way to the yard and joined in with the rest of the family. Every year these family reunions got more and more crazy, but that's what I always loved about the Wests. We could gossip about each other, fight and argue, but at the end of the day, we were family again.

Z is for Z-ya

"So, Ms. Hill and Mr. Campbell, what brings you here?" Reverend James asked with a smile, already knowing the answer.

"We want to get married!" I responded excitedly. Aaron was cool with his excitement. "February 16, 2008."

"Wow, that's less than a year away," the Reverend replied, "but if you two have really thought this through, then we'll proceed. First off, if I'm going to marry you, you'll need to sign up for my marriage counseling courses. And if you aren't saved yet . . ."

"No, we are," I interrupted. "We've been coming here together since we started dating. We took the new member's classes and everything." Reverend James stared at Aaron and me with a stern face, gauging our visual compatibility. When he finished, his joyful smile returned.

"OK, kids. Marriage counseling starts at 7:00pm every Wednesday for twelve weeks. We're not like most churches. We'll dig deep. You'll laugh, you'll cry, but by the end you'll know exactly who you are taking this big step with."

"Oh, we know everything about each other," I laughed, and so did the Reverend.

"So, joining us next week will be Mr. Aaron Campbell and Ms. Z-ya Hill. Now, is that Z-ya like Zion, or like 'See ya later', but with a Z?" I don't know what my parents were smoking when they named me. Oh well, here we go again.

"It's Z-ya, as in Zuh-Dash-E-Yuh. You have to pronounce the dash."

* * *

Who would've known that marriage appointment eight months ago would fly by that fast? It seems like just last week I was picking my bridesmaids, and now I'm only one night away from becoming Mrs. Z-ya Campbell! But first, there are some things that need to be taken care of, like this unorganized wedding rehearsal.

"OK people, take your places. We're not eating until this rehearsal looks like we halfway know what we're doing," I ordered. So much for my so-called wedding coordinator. She was supposed to be running this, but there were some things that had come up with a lot of my plans and needed immediate attention. My bouquet wasn't the one I ordered, they fried the shrimp when we asked for shrimp cocktail appetizers, and the bakery tried to sit a white couple on top of my cake! This is why your cousin should never coordinate your wedding, no matter how much she brags about taking event planning courses at community college.

"Ok, cue the wedding processional," Reverend James said to the pianist. The musician played a soft, lighthearted melody as Aaron and his best man, Eric, entered from the side door. He stood in place, dressed in a pair of navy windpants and a somewhat fitted half-sleeved red shirt. I got butterflies in my stomach, as if I were seeing him for the first time all over again.

Next up were Mr. and Mrs. Campbell with my mom escorted by an usher following five rows behind them. I wasn't really feeling Mrs. Campbell seeing how she had been trying to run this wedding since Day 1, talkin' bout I should wear her dress, nobody wants salmon at a reception, and blasé blah. I told Aaron to check her, but being the sweet Mama's Boy that he is, he didn't. If I would be wearing anyone's dress it would by my "real" mother's, and I'm not wearing hers either. Mr. Campbell was all smiles, but Mrs. Campbell maintained her sour face down the aisle. It's not too late to have her X'd outta the processional, so she better get it togeva!

Then came the maid of honor, my sister Bridget, whose face wasn't any less twisted than Mrs. Campbell's. Earlier in the week, we had gotten into an argument cus she decides that the week of my wedding is the date to confront her boyfriend's side piece, and loses the fight. And all the while she's telling me what had happened, I'm thinking of how bad my pictures are going to look from trying to cake on mascara to hide her puffy eye. And on top of that, she showed up to the rehearsal almost a whole half an hour late. When I asked her why, she said, "Cus yal started before I got here." Salty bitch! She was lucky I didn't black her other eye.

Bridget walked down the aisle, dancing to the pianist's tunes just to piss me off, but Aaron mouthed to me, "Just let it ride." He was such a gentleman. The type of man us sistahs dream about. And to think, I almost missed out on him.

I met Aaron while I was working at a sports clinic. He and his boys were regulars and would come in after their community center football games. I was dating the quarterback of his team, Reggie. Nothing serious, but nothing light either. Anyway, the other therapists must have been busy that day, and Reggie was flirting with the receptionist, as usual, when this thin-haired unfamiliar face walked up to me.

"Do you massage?" he asked with a pained look on his face. He was wearing a tight, black Under Armour suit that was still reeking of outdoor football practice, but it was something sexy about his athletic musk.

"Um, yes," I said with hesitation. "Hop up on the table." Aaron limped up and rested on the cold, foam-topped table and slowly took the pressure off his feet. "Sprained ankle?" I guessed.

"Rolled it making a catch," he strained to say. I rubbed his right ankle to see where exactly the pain was. He squirmed and crinkled up his face as I felt around. I remember wondering if he made those same faces in the bedroom and how tempted I was to hit his sore spot again just to hear him moan. Before I lost my job, I grabbed a hot pack from the supply closet and strapped it to his ankle.

"Better?" I smiled.

"Much," he said, smiling back. I quickly snapped back, remembering that I was in my unofficial boyfriend's view. "Let me guess, Reggie?" he asked after catching me staring at the receptionist's desk.

"Yes, but just still dating. No title, nothing serious."

"That's my boy and all, but trust me, if it's with Reggie, it's always 'nothing serious'. Let me take you somewhere nice. Just new friends hanging out." I looked at the receptionist and saw her laughing and playing in her hair while Reggie was just eating it all up. Then I glanced back at Aaron with every bicep, tricep, ab, and calf muscle bursting through that sport's suit, with a look on his face like anything other than yes would break his heart. My hands were tied.

"OK, OK. Just one date," I answered, pretending to be annoyed.

Aaron picked me up later that night, still hopping on that bum ankle. I must've really had him sprung at first sight. Regardless, he still showed me a good time. Instead of just honking the horn for me, he actually walked up to my apartment with a dozen roses. The entire night, my hands never touched a door's handle. It had been so long since I had been finessed, but he was the perfect gentleman. That night, he introduced me to chivalry and sushi, and at that rate he coulda got it on the first date. Instead, he dropped me off, walked me to the front door, and kissed the back of my hand and said, "Pick you up Saturday, seven o'clock."

We started dating more and more until I eventually forgot about Reggie. He rang whenever he got the urge to drain his pipe, but I ignored the calls. I was too into Aaron to put up with Reggie's mind games. As fast as he faded from my memory, Aaron moved into the picture. By the end of the month, I was at his games cheering like a groupie.

Exactly one year later, we made plans to meet at the same sushi restaurant from our first date. I had on jeans and a blouse, but he had shown up in a suit because he was "working late".

"Baby, what are you smiling so hard for?" I asked.

"I'm not smiling," he argued playfully. Something was up, but I hadn't figured it out just yet.

The hostess led us to our table and Aaron demanded that he be the one to seat me. I sat down and jumped up after immediately feeling a pain in my ass. "It's something in this chair!" I yelled. Aaron had placed a jewelry box in my seat when I wasn't looking. I turned around and saw him on bended knee.

"Z, this last year with you has been one of the greatest, happiest years of my life. And I hope you don't think it's too soon, but I can't see my future without you in it." He popped up the top of the ring box and exposed a glistening engagement ring. "Will you marry me?"

I was excited, embarrassed, and hesitant all at once. It wasn't like he was a bad guy, it's just it had only been a year. I felt like there was still more to learn. On second thought, with the number of unmarried, single, black women as high as it is, I thought it was best to snatch this good catch while he wanted me! "I do! Now get up off that floor." The restaurant exploded with applause as Aaron and I kissed to celebrate our engagement.

"Z," Bridget called, snapping me out of my romantic flashback, "this is the part where you and Daddy walk down." My stand-in hadn't arrived yet, so I quickly strutted down the aisle. You would've thought I had just committed a crime.

"The bride never walks down at the rehearsal," Mrs. Campbell grunted. "Everybody knows it's bad luck."

"Well, I'm not tryna be here all night," I sassed back, rolling my eyes.

Reverend James stepped in to continue leading the rehearsal, hoping to avoid the mother-in-law/daughter brawl that was about to go down. "Why don't we try the processional again? Then we'll go over the ceremony quickly and try to get done in the next half hour. I know we're all hungry and ready to make it to that rehearsal dinner, Amen?"

"Amen," we all laughed in unison.

As promised, Reverend James got us through several rounds of processing, recessing, and mock vows in thirty minutes. We made our way into the church multipurpose room where my mother and Mrs. Campbell had joined forces to fix up wingettes fried hard, homemade meatballs, string beans and potatoes, rolls, and crispy topped macaroni and cheese. We circled around the Reverend and prepared ourselves for him to bless the food.

"I'm not big on speeches or whatever, but before we pray, I just want to thank everyone here for participating in Z and me's special day," Aaron said while grabbing my hand. "We really appreciate you all being there, and helping out if, and when we needed it. We really love you all, and now I'll turn it over to the Reverend." I wrapped my arms around Aaron's waist, showing I backed his lil' speech.

"Bow your heads in prayer," the Reverend commanded. I could already tell he was gearing up for a long one. He prayed that we would have a blessed union; that there would be good weather for our wedding; that we would have a covering as we traveled the "highways and byways" to get home; that we'd all be in perfect health and well-rested for the long day ahead; for the hands that prepared the food; and finally that the meal would nourish our bodies, "In Your name we pray, Amen." That long grace damn near sweated out my perm!

I spent the rest of the dinner holding onto Aaron's hand, thinking about how hard it was going to be not calling or seeing him until tomorrow morning.

"You good?" asked Aaron.

"Yeah it's only for a few hours. You just better behave at that bachelor party," I jokingly warned.

"Huh? What? Who said I was having a party?"

"Play dumb if you want, but you better not have no bitches throwing their big asses in your face."

"Chill, Z," he laughed, "we still in church."

"I'm serious."

"Aight. I won't let anybody throw their butt in my face . . . that much." He laughed as Eric pulled him out the door to get him to the party. He yanked back and got one last kiss before the wedding. I was a little uncomfortable, especially after the stuff that went down at my bachelorette party last weekend. But I guess fair is fair. I guess . . .

Once we had finished cleaning up, I rode back to Bridget's place with the rest of the bridesmaids following behind. I quietly stared out the window for most of the ride. Finally, Bridget gave in and broke the silence. "So, you excited yet?" she asked. I knew that was as much of an apology as I was getting from her.

"It hasn't really hit me yet," I answered, showing her apology was accepted. "Prolly not until we wake up tomorrow. I always thought it would be you and Keith before me though."

"Girl, don't even get me started on him. You know he hasn't even called me since the fight?"

"Whaaat? Just an example of an ol' punk nigga." Suddenly, my phone played the ringtone for one of the numbers I had listed as Do Not Answer. "Oh my God. Do you know who this is?" I asked Bridget, pointing the screen in her face. She immediately broke out in gut-busting laughter.

"Answer it!" she laughed. "Put it on speaker phone."

"What?" I answered with irritation.

"Damn, that's how you talk to me now?" Bridget was in the driver's seat cracking up. I fanned her down, hoping I wouldn't join in laughing at this fool, too.

"What do you want, Reggie?"

"I had heard from my sources that you're gettin' murried damarrow," he said with his hood accent.

"Yeah," I replied with attitude. He laughed.

"Ol' Urron went behind my back like that though?"

"Look Reggie," Bridget interrupted, "my sustah is a vurry busy woman wit all this wet'in plannin'. She ain't eem tryna hear your 'shoulda, coulda, wouldas'." He laughed again.

"Hi, Bridget," he said. She rolled her eyes and neck as if he could see her. "Well, I just thought I'd call and tell you congratulations, and even though you prolly could do better, I'm happy for you."

"Thank you, I guess," I said while Bridget hummed "Here Comes the Bride" in the background to get to him even more. "Let me go cus Bridget's acting crazy. I'll talk to you lat—well actually, just have a good life." I hung the phone up before he even had a chance to say bye. Bridget and I laughed so hard we ran through a red light, making several oncoming drivers honk angrily.

"Fuck is yal honkin' at?" Bridget yelled out the window.

After an eventful day, we had finally made it to Bridget's apartment. To say I was exhausted would be an understatement. I was drained, physically and mentally. I spent all my energy fighting with family, soon-to-be family, the "wedding coordinator", the florist, and anyone else that tried to mess up my day. I was on a warpath, but my battles were catching up to me. I put my Vera Wang wedding dress up to my figure in the mirror one last time before I would actually wear it.

I stared into the mirror, hoping to catch a glimpse of how tomorrow would play out. I pictured the doors to the sanctuary opening and all the guests standing and admiring me as I did a pageant wave down the aisle. I imagined myself walking to a perfectly arranged version of Brian McKnight's wedding classic "Never Felt This Way" while cousin Tyrell sang every note perfectly. Once I reached the halfway mark, I could clearly see Aaron with one tear rolling down his left eye, watching me approach the altar with Daddy. Just when I had reached the front and grabbed Aaron's hands, my dream was suddenly interrupted by my phone vibrating. It better not be Reggie!

I was pleasantly surprised to see it was Aaron. He had taken time away from his partying to say "I love you. Get some rest, Mrs. Campbell." I hung my dress back in the closet, laid in the bed, and obeyed my baby's request. Goodbye forever, Ms. Hill.

*   *   *

I couldn't sleep at all last night. I was up and in the shower at 7:00am. I knew it was a good idea to get up before the other four heffas tried to rush in this bathroom all at once. As I dried off, I could hear the rest of the apartment waking up. "Come on yal. The limo will be here at ten o'clock and we need to leave outta here by 10:30," I yelled from inside the bathroom. "Bridget you heard from your cousin Keisha yet?"

"That's your coordinator," she joked back. "Keisha said she'll be at the church at nine. Bout time she finally acted like a real wedding coordinator, right? Ass couldn't have stepped up any sooner?"

"Hey I'm just happy she's doing something," I said. In mid-sentence, I felt a sharp pain in my stomach. The pre-wedding jitters were starting to take over. I walked out of the bathroom clenching my hips.

"You ok?" asked Bridget.

"Just nerves. Let's keep moving," I said. I had no time for nerves to get the best of me. I was getting married!

Yolanda—a bridesmaid—started on my make-up ten minutes to eight. I was paper bag brown, so she thought a good color for me would be walnut. Wrong! It looked good on paper, but on my face I looked like I was part of a blackface minstrel show. The pain in my stomach returned as my anxiety grew.

"Get that stuff off of her. I have some of my regular bronzer in the bathroom," Bridget said. "You don't need all that fancy expensive stuff anyway. We're goin' for natural beauty here. Step back. Can't learn this at beauty school, Yolanda."

With a couple of brushes and a few spot treatments of concealer, Bridget had saved the day, but I couldn't help but notice Bridget's dress was so snug.

"What's going on with your dress?" I asked.

"It ain't fittin' right," she said.

"Bridget, I thought you were gonna slim down a little bit for the wedding?"

"Bitch, I did!" she argued back. "I think the seamstress took my dress in too much." Yolanda and Shé tested theirs out and the fit was perfect. Bridget rolled her eyes. "Well, yal are smaller than me so you could fit it anyway."

"Maybe we can have a maid of honor bouquet to cover that bulge up."

"Girl I ain't worried. This is your day, not mines. I'ma rock this dress just like this and play the maid of honor role like I'm supposed to. You don't want somebody standing next to you that's gonna outshine the bride," she explained. She probably would outshine me, but not in a good way. I just hoped the photographer would be able to see around her huge hips.

I had slipped into my all-white gown with the help of my two bridesmaids that weren't busy, Tiffany and Shé. Bridget came in snapping pictures of the process. "Aww, I'ma cry," she said, fanning at her eyes. "You look so beautiful."

By ten o'clock, the four of us were ready and walking down to meet the driver and the photographer. Everybody was on time and things were running smoothly, but the day wasn't over yet. I'd watched enough of those wedding shows to know there would be some last minute drama before show time.

The ladies and I lined up in front of the limo while the photographer snapped and snapped. After we took our serious pictures, he told us to loosen up and have some fun. The five of us immediately went back to our old skating rink pose: one hand on the hip, knees bent, and booties in the air. Bridget hit the jail pose and squatted down with the peace sign, and suddenly we heard a rip.

"Shit!" she yelled. "Does anybody see the rip?" She did a spin, but there wasn't a hole to be found.

"Maybe it was just a warning," I said. "If I were you, I wouldn't do too much moving from now on though."

I got a call from cousin Keisha as we headed to the church. She was checking to make sure we were en route and on time. She had checked the church out and everything was beautifully decorated, the flowers were arranged as ordered, and the caterers had replaced the fried shrimp with shrimp cocktails as requested. Things were turning themselves around the more the day went by.

We turned into the church parking lot and instantly, I felt blood nervously rushing through my fingertips. My heart began to beat fast, and the pain in my stomach returned. I made a sour face and grabbed hold of the door to brace myself for the pain. Suddenly, I knew this was more than nerves.

"Yal, I think I'm crampin' up," I cried, "and I don't have a tampon. Why is it starting so early?"

"Don't cry, you're gonna mess up your make-up. Do you feel anything?" Shé asked while dabbing at the tears forming around my eyes. "Like is it on your dress?"

"Not yet, but if yal have a pad or something to spare I need it now." The girls dug through their purses and came up empty-handed, but Bridget handed me some Ibuprofen to stop the cramps. Once the driver opened the door, I raced to the restroom. "Take their pictures first," I yelled back to the photographer. In desperation, I rolled the toilet paper around my wrist several times and laid it in my panties. This quick fix would have to do for now.

I stepped out of the bathroom and ran into Eric, the best man, escorted by the other groomsmen, Damien, Anthony, and Rashard.

"Ohhh shit!" Eric shouted. "Z you look like you stepped out of a wedding magazine." Eric was stumbling, slurring, and his eyes were half closed.

"Thanks. Is he . . ."

"Twisted," Damien finished. I was beyond disgusted.

"What the hell, Eric? You partied that hard last night you're still drunk at almost eleven o'clock?"

"Ay Z I'm sorry," he mumbled. "But once I told them it was Aaron's bachelor party they just kept pourin' shots and poppin' bottles. You mad?"

"Am I mad?" I screamed. "Is Aaron drunk, too?" They shook their heads no. "I'm not dealing with this right now. Get him some coffee or something and make sure he can stand himself up by noon."

Damien and Rashard dragged him back to the holding area, and then I heard Eric yell, "Shit, where the rings at?" My eyes bulged at the thought of him trading my ring for free shots, but Anthony put my doubts to rest when he mouthed to me he had them.

"Z," called a voice from down the hall. It was Keisha, dressed in a traditional coordinator's black dress. "Looking good, girl," she said with a soft hug, trying not to touch my face. "How you feeling?"

"Not good," I said. "I 'came on' this morning, and the best man is drunk off his ass." Keisha looked down as if there were more bad news to add. "Just say it."

"Reverend James woke up with flu-like symptoms. His wife called the church this morning. He's not going to be able to perform the ceremony." In mid sigh, Keisha interrupted, "But don't worry. He's sending one of his ministers down in his place. No big deal, right?" I rolled my eyes before finally nodding my head that I was cool with the replacement pastor, although deep down, I knew this was some bullshit.

It was 11:30 and Keisha was busy lining everyone up. I peeked through the waiting room door and saw Aaron's parents at the front of the line with Mrs. Campbell in a white dress. Everyone knows you don't wear white to a wedding unless you're the bride. "That bitch just won't quit!" I said to my dad.

"Her tackiness isn't important now," Daddy comforted. "My little ZiZi is getting married, and that's all that matters." Daddy held my hands and smiled. He reached up on his toes and lowered my veil. The sanctuary doors had swung open and the procession had begun. It was time.

First, Mr. and Mrs. Campbell walked down the aisle with my mom escorted behind them, just like in rehearsal. Next came Damien and Shé, then Rashard and Yolanda, Anthony and Tiffany, and finally Bridget. Keisha ran back trying to hold in a laugh.

"Did you know your sister's dress was ripped?" she asked.

"We heard something earlier, but we couldn't find anything."

"Well, your guests found it. There's a big tear right along a crease under her stomach, and she's oozing out of it. And what's so bad is I don't even think she feels it."

"Maybe it's not that bad," I said.

"Put it like this: you and your dad will see it before you reach the altar," Keisha explained.

The last two in the procession were my co-worker Debbie's twins, Danielle and David, who were my flower girl and ring bearer. Danielle had thrown all of her flowers before she reached the end and cracked the attendees up by shrugging, asking her mom what to do. Debbie quickly pulled her to the side and once again the doors closed. Keisha waved the signal for Daddy and me to move to the main doors and we slowly walked out.

I stood there with goose bumps while I waited for the doors to open. I was so happy and excited, but so nervous at the same time. Everything that had angered me from the day suddenly no longer mattered. This was my moment!

Without further delay, the replacement pastor made the announcement. "P-p-p-please stand f-f-for the bride." I was too through when I'd heard Reverend James sent stuttering Pastor Fields as his back-up. We wouldn't be outta here til five o'clock tomorrow evening as long as it would take him to get through our vows. Daddy just shook his head and we made our way into the ceremony.

My walk was just like I had pictured it. The pianist had gotten the music right, and Tyrell was singing his heart out like he was chasing a record deal. It was hard not to do my pageant wave to the many childhood friends and distant relatives that I was happy to see in attendance. I glanced down at the wedding party, and as Keisha said, Bridget had a gaping hole in front of her dress like a C-section and the bottom half of her stomach was the baby. To the right was an even worse sight: Eric, still too drunk to stand, was seated in a fold out chair with his forehead buried in his palms. I don't know who thought that was better than just sitting him in the front row, but these photos would be of the wedding party from Hell.

"D-dearly beloved," Pastor Fields began, "we are ga-thered here t-t-oday to cel-cel-celebrate the joining of this man, Aaron, and-and-and this woman, Z...Z... Ms. Hill." I knew my name was gonna give him trouble. He continued, "Whoooooo gives this woman away?"

"I do," said Daddy proudly.

"If anyone has ANY reason why these two should not wed, t-t-too b-b-bad, so sssssad. Too late now." The guests laughed along with Aaron and I, while Pastor Fields thought we were laughing at his corny joke. We had all seen it as a good place to play off laughing at his stuttering.

"I do," a voice called from the main doors. We turned to face the back and there stood the last person I expected: Reggie.

"I can't let you do this, Z," he said as he walked down to the altar.

"You need to leave," Daddy yelled.

"It's Ok," said Aaron calmly. "This should be good."

Reggie met us all at the front while the guests looked on as if they had priority seating at a stage play.

"Baby, I can't let you go through with this. I was a fool to act like this didn't bother me, but it did. It still does. I should've given you the attention you deserved and I was wrong. I can apologize a million times and it still won't be enough, but I can't let you do this. Please. I love you." I was shocked. This was like something from the movies, not something in real life, let alone at MY wedding. Bridget snapped and motioned for me to say something to get him out of here.

"I'm glad you told me all of this, Reggie, I really am. But you don't know how insecure you made me feel throughout the time we were supposed to be dating. Just watching my man laugh and flirt with so many other women right in front of my face. It hurt. And you decide to show up on the day of my wedding to tell me you were wrong? What were you thinking?" I stepped down and gave him a friendly hug, which he did not return. "I'm sorry, but I'm marrying Aaron and I'm very happy with my life. And you need to leave." Reggie stood there stunned as if my words had dealt him the hardest hit he's ever faced in his football career.

"He's not speaking to you," said Aaron. I looked down my row of bridesmaids to see which one had been dipping into Reggie behind my back. Suddenly, I began to notice that Aaron's grip was becoming looser until he had let go of my hand completely. Aaron walked down to Reggie, hugged him, and then kissed him as the crowd gasped in disbelief. Just then, Eric woke up and leaned out of his chair to throw up some of the drinks from last night. My thoughts exactly.

"I'm so sorry Z-ya," Aaron said, "I tried to shake it off by getting serious with you, but I love him. I don't think there's anything I can do to change it."

"I knew you two weren't over," Mrs. Campbell added with a smile.

"Oh that's it!" Bridget yelled. "This old bitch knew the whole time her son was lickin' lollipops and never said anything? Z you can stand there lookin' dumb if you want, but I'm bout to whip some ass." Bridget leaped off the stairs and went charging at Mrs. Campbell. The attendees went into riot as my guests attacked anyone that was on Aaron's side. It was mayhem! There were fists and heels flying everywhere.

"I'm so sorry," Aaron yelled with an unconvincing smile as he and Reggie darted hand-in-hand out of a side door. I stood there like a figurine, holding my bouquet and smiling to hold back my tears as I watched the ordeal take place before finally blacking out. And just like that, my perfect wedding was ruined.

Four years later . . .

With a lot of time, a good counselor, and even better antidepressants, I had finally gotten myself mentally stable enough to start dating again. Shé had set me up with one of her closest friends from college and assured me there was nothing to worry about with this one. We dated for about a year and she keeps asking if I think he'll pop the question anytime soon. I can see it down the road, but I'm in no rush. I wanna get every little detail before I ever make that mistake again.

As for Aaron and Reggie, they're still together. The crazy thing is I'm still cool with the both of them. No beef over here, well not anymore. I'm glad I found out before I jumped the broom than to come home to my "manly athlete" gettin' it on with a man in my bed.

Even crazier, they recently adopted a little girl, made me the godmother, and I accepted as long as they named her after me. What's her name, you ask?—awn.